PRAISE FOR BRIANNA LABUSKES

What Can't Be Seen

"The book's well-constructed plot matches its three-dimensional characters. Psychological-thriller fans will be eager for more."

—*Publishers Weekly*

A Familiar Sight

"A horrific brew for readers willing to immerse themselves in it."

—*Kirkus Reviews*

"A strong plot and unforgettable characters make this a winner. Labuskes is on a roll."

—*Publishers Weekly*

"*A Familiar Sight* has everything I crave in a thriller: a shocking, addictive female lead; unexpected twists that snapped off the page; and an ending that made me gasp out loud. I never saw it coming, but it was perfectly in sync with the razor-sharp balance between creepy and compelling that Labuskes carries throughout the novel. This is a one-sitting read."

—Jess Lourey, Amazon Charts bestselling author

Her Final Words

"Labuskes skillfully ratchets up the suspense. Readers will eagerly await her next."

—*Publishers Weekly*

"Labuskes offers an intense mystery with an excellent character in Lucy, who methodically uncovers layers of deceit while trusting no one."

—*Library Journal*

Girls of Glass

"Excellent . . . Readers who enjoy having their expectations upset will be richly rewarded."

—*Publishers Weekly* (starred review)

It Ends with Her

"Once in a while a character comes along who gets under your skin and refuses to let go. This is the case with Brianna Labuskes's Clarke Sinclair—a cantankerous, rebellious, and somehow endearingly likable FBI agent with a troubled past. I was immediately pulled into Clarke's broken, shadow-filled world and her quest for justice and redemption. A stunning thriller, *It Ends with Her* is not to be missed."

—Heather Gudenkauf, *New York Times* bestselling author

"*It Ends with Her* is a gritty, riveting roller-coaster ride of a book. Brianna Labuskes has created a layered, gripping story around a cast of characters that readers will cheer for. Her crisp prose and quick plot kept me reading with my heart in my throat. Highly recommended for fans of smart thrillers with captivating heroines."

—Nicole Baart, author of *Little Broken Things*

"An engrossing psychological thriller filled with twists and turns. I couldn't put it down! The characters were filled with emotional depth. An impressive debut!"

—Elizabeth Blackwell, author of *In the Shadow of Lakecrest*

THE
TRUTH
YOU
TOLD

OTHER TITLES BY BRIANNA LABUSKES

THE
TRUTH
YOU
TOLD

BRIANNA
LABUSKES

THOMAS & MERCER

Published by Thomas & Mercer, Seattle

www.apub.com

Amazon, the Amazon logo, and Thomas & Mercer are trademarks of Amazon.com, Inc., or its affiliates.

ISBN-13: 9781662511387 (paperback)
ISBN-13: 9781662511370 (digital)

Cover design by Damon Freeman
Cover image: © Reilika Landen / Arcangel; © LambArtist, © Jamen Percy / Shutterstock

Printed in the United States of America

To my sister

CHAPTER ONE

Raisa

Now

Someone was watching her.

FBI forensic linguist Raisa Susanto didn't need her training to tell her that—she'd learned the weight of a predator's gaze long before she'd stepped foot in Quantico.

Raisa shifted over to the coffee shop's pickup counter, searching for reflective surfaces. She found one in the fancy espresso machine, but all she could get was the impression of dark hair, a blurred face.

She touched her shoulder, an instinctive gesture she'd been trying to fight for the past three months since a bullet tore into her flesh right at that spot.

The injury had made her paranoid, jumpy in crowds—she could admit that. But this was experience, not fear, talking now.

When the barista called her name, Raisa bit her lip, wishing she'd given a fake one instead. If whoever was watching her had any doubt about her identity, that had just been wiped away.

The mistake made Raisa long for the solid press of a gun against her rib cage. But she'd stopped at the little shop after a run, and had only the essentials with her.

She forced a smile for the barista, and then, instead of skirting around the gaggle of other patrons, she wormed her way directly into the middle of the group. They grumbled at her, but the move gave her some cover and let her scan the room.

The place was packed, as expected on an unseasonably pretty Saturday. She didn't catch anyone watching her, and for one moment she doubted herself in a way she hadn't before she'd been shot.

Crowds did make her more jittery than they ever had in the past, and her fight-or-flight mode was easily triggered by unexpected noises, by the brush of a stranger's arm against hers.

But the echo of the stare lingered on her skin.

Raisa had a few options here.

She could wait, see if the person came to her. The coffee shop was a relatively safe location, where she could easily call for help. The downside was that it carried a higher risk of a civilian getting hurt in the confrontation.

Or she could force their hand.

Raisa had never been one for the passive approach.

Murmuring her apologies, she exited the gaggle and headed for the door, deliberate and purposeful so she would be seen.

It didn't take long for the predator to follow, close enough for Raisa to hear the bell chime as the door shut behind them.

Bold.

Or inexperienced.

Raisa took the next left and then sprinted up to the alcove just ahead of her. She pressed her back to the stone wall and waited one beat, two.

A woman came into view.

She was short and curvy, her dark hair piled into a messy bun that showed off an undercut. She wore leggings paired with combat boots and an oversize flannel shirt open over a white tank. There was no sign of a weapon.

Not exactly threatening on first glance, but Raisa wasn't, either.

When the woman stuttered to a stop, Raisa wasted no time stepping out of the hiding spot, yanking the woman by the collar, and pushing her up against the wall. Raisa pressed a forearm against her throat, hard enough to show she meant it but with just the right amount of pressure that she could apologize if this was all a misunderstanding.

"You have about three seconds to tell me why you're following me," Raisa said.

The woman blinked at her in apparent confusion, her hands coming up to pull at Raisa's arm. At least Raisa could be reassured there was no hidden strength beneath that hipster wardrobe.

"One," Raisa said.

"I'm not following—"

"Two." Raisa didn't need to explicitly state what she'd do at three. If this woman was stalking her, she knew who Raisa was. It didn't hurt that Raisa also had her forearm shoved up against her windpipe and, between the two of them, was clearly in control of the situation.

"Lady, you are paranoid. I'm not—"

"Thr—"

"Okay. Okay, okay, okay. Fine, you're right. Christ, let me go," the woman said, slapping at Raisa's arm. Raisa released her, but didn't relax. "Isn't that police brutality?"

Raisa lifted her brows. "We both know I'm not the police."

"You're a glorified cop," the woman said, all piss and vinegar.

"Why are you following me?" Raisa demanded, uninterested in all her diversionary tactics. Giving her more time just to let her figure out ways to lie.

"Good lord, I'm just a student," the woman said, all huffy about it, still rubbing at her neck as if Raisa had actually caused any damage.

All her bluster seemed like too much, though. She wanted to convince both of them that Raisa was the unreasonable one in the situation, but it had been Raisa who'd been followed by a stranger while out on her morning run. "That doesn't answer my question."

"I'm trying to get into grad school," the woman said. "For forensic linguistics. It's a hard program to break into, so I thought if I could talk to you . . ."

She shrugged and trailed off.

That was plausible. Raisa was one of two forensic linguists employed on a full-time basis by the FBI. While there were certainly smarter, more experienced experts in her field, that type tended toward academia. They might have been called in to consult on bomb threats and kidnappings every once in a while, but Raisa was the one who dealt with those kinds of cases on a daily basis, along with murderers, rapists, and run-of-the-mill white-collar criminals. She had a range of experience someone sitting in a classroom wouldn't be able to impart.

But this was Tacoma, it wasn't the right time of year for grad school applications, and Raisa had contact information on her website.

A student looking to get into a graduate program—unless independently wealthy—wasn't flying out to Washington and then stalking Raisa just to get her advice on grad schools.

Even if she'd been looking for a recommendation, she probably would have tried email first.

"Okay," Raisa said. "Now the truth."

The woman's eyes flew to hers. She smothered the surprise in them quickly but didn't do as good a job at keeping the annoyance out of the twist of her lips.

"Yeah," Raisa drawled. "You can try another lie on for size, but I already started with about zero patience and it's only wearing thinner. In fact, I'm about to call in backup. So, if you'd like to do this here instead of at the police station, I'd suggest you start telling me what you really want." When that got nothing out of her, Raisa pushed on. "Isn't that why you're following me in the first place? To get something?"

The woman's eyes darted over Raisa's shoulder, but Raisa knew better than to fall for the basic ruse. She kept her attention on the woman's face even as she reached for her phone. At the movement, the woman lifted her chin, decision apparently made.

"Okay, fine," she said. "I'm Kate Tashibi."

"The documentarian?" Raisa asked.

A couple of weeks prior, she'd gotten an email from Kate, asking her to talk about the Alphabet Man, an infamous serial killer who'd tattooed ciphers onto his victims, using them to taunt law enforcement with coded messages. Raisa had deleted the message before she'd even gotten to the end of it, then informed the front desk of the FBI field office that any of Kate's calls should be held.

"You've been ignoring my requests," Kate said.

"Yeah, some people would take that as a hint." Raisa turned away, no longer worried or interested. Now she just wanted to put as much distance between them as possible. "Next time you follow me, I'm having you arrested."

"For sharing a sidewalk?" Kate called after her.

"You want to test me?" Raisa asked, shifting once more so she was walking backward. Kate needed to see that she was serious about this. "Because I'm pretty sure you don't just happen to frequent the same coffee shop as I do."

Kate's mouth worked until finally she spit out, "I'm telling an important story."

Raisa usually tried to take the high road. At work she was forced to do so, more often than not, and it wasn't just the criminals who tested her, either. There were plenty of fellow agents who made condescending remarks about her specialty, who looked at her like she was a novelty at best and a waste of resources at worst. Most of the time, she could rise above it.

But Kate Tashibi was a vulture.

She called herself an artist. A filmmaker. That email she'd sent had been a longer, less petulant version of *I'm telling an important story*. Kate had listed all the awards she'd won at some distinguished MFA program, and had even included early reviews of the Alphabet Man project, which was set to air on one of the more prestigious streaming services.

But the world didn't need another documentary memorializing a man who'd kidnapped, tortured, and killed twenty-seven women.

Anyone who thought that it did didn't deserve Raisa's time or respect.

"I promise you, you're not telling an important story," Raisa said, and meant it.

The serial killer Kate had picked to feature in her cash-grab documentary was a run-of-the-mill psychopath. There was nothing special about Nathaniel Conrad—a.k.a. the Alphabet Man—beyond what made any of those monsters gruesomely fascinating.

"Now, if you want to make a series on one of the Alphabet Man's twenty-seven victims, we can talk," Raisa continued. "Until then, stay the hell away from me."

Raisa turned again, this time tuning out anything else Kate Tashibi had to say for herself.

Once she was out of the other woman's sight, she tossed her coffee into a garbage can and ran the rest of the way back to her building.

The place was nothing fancy. Raisa spent most of her life shipped around the country to the task forces that needed her specific expertise, which tended to be any case involving some kind of written communication as a central component. Her apartment often served as a landing spot for a night or two a month instead of a home.

But it was hers.

Once inside, Raisa slid behind the small, uncluttered desk that overlooked the one window in her living room. Her laptop was the Bureau-issued dinosaur she barely used—preferring her tablet most of the time—so it protested when she asked it to turn on. Still, it had enough juice for a simple Google search on Kate Tashibi.

The latest news article on her project populated the top carousel of the results page.

Documentary maker Kate Tashibi promises bombshell revelations in new series on the Alphabet Man

Raisa rolled her eyes. She'd been loosely following Kate's press coverage ever since that first email. The headlines on the articles always promised jaw-dropping surprises, and yet the stories themselves were all just teasers, lacking anything of substance.

There had been so many of these pieces in recent weeks as the Alphabet Man's execution date neared that Raisa was starting to get a familiarity with the case even though it had happened long before her time.

Most of the details were fairly typical serial-killer stuff. Fifteen years ago, a woman's body had been dumped in a field outside Houston. She was young and pretty and clearly had been tortured before she was killed.

The twist with the Alphabet Man, and the reason he'd been given his moniker, was that he'd tattooed a cipher onto the woman's arm after she died. The code, called an Alberti Cipher, had been key to decrypting messages the killer had sent to law enforcement.

He had always included his victim's name in the letters he mailed to the FBI—in theory, giving them a chance to save the person—but the message could be decoded only once they found the body.

Raisa had always found this detail particularly sadistic.

Would the name of the victim matter in the bid to save her life? Maybe not. But how could the agents not feel extra guilt for knowing a clue was in their grasp if only they could understand it?

The Alphabet Man had terrorized Houston and the counties surrounding the city for five years, the pattern always the same. Kidnap someone, write a coded message to the task force, torture the victim for three days, send more taunting letters to law enforcement in the meantime, kill the victim, tattoo the Alberti Cipher on his or her skin, and then dump them somewhere in the open to be found easily.

His body count had climbed well into the double digits. Most of his victims were white women in their twenties, but not all of them had been. Two had been men—an anomaly Raisa had never seen a good explanation for—and five of the women had been middle-aged or older. Three of his victims had been Hispanic and one had been Black.

The fact that he hadn't seemed to have a type had made those years even more terrifying for Houston's residents.

He had been vicious and prolific. And he'd never made any mistakes. Until the last victim.

In that case, the letter the killer had sent the FBI had been encrypted with a code he'd used for a previous victim, a duplicate that had allowed the FBI team to quickly figure out the name of the woman he was planning on kidnapping.

Nathaniel Conrad, an unassuming social worker who had never appeared on any suspect list, had been found sitting outside the woman's apartment with a gun, a rope, and a tarp in his car. That had been enough to get all the warrants the FBI needed, and they'd found a bounty of evidence—everything from DNA to souvenirs and tattoo equipment—in Conrad's house, tying him to at least fourteen of the victims.

Conrad claimed innocence and misunderstanding, but at that point, the case was a home run and everyone knew what his fate would eventually be. Now, ten years after he had been caught and fifteen years after he'd started killing, Conrad was less than two weeks from his execution date.

Raisa closed out of the article about Kate Tashibi's documentary that had been a nothingburger, as expected, and navigated to one of Kate's social media pages. It was slick, a carefully curated layout that was fully dedicated to the upcoming series.

Are you ready for the truth? the caption on her latest post read, and Raisa rolled her eyes again. There was no *truth* here to uncover. There was no mystery to peel back when it came to the Alphabet Man. This was clickbait, pure and simple.

The rest of the page was more of the same, and Raisa made note of Kate's idiolect—her unique use of language, including but not limited to grammar, vocabulary, and writing errors.

Raisa didn't always read with an eye toward creating a linguistic profile, but as she scrolled, she couldn't help but pick up a sense of the woman behind the glossy marketing campaign. Of course, any social media analysis like this—where someone else might have been running this page besides Kate—had to come with caveats. There were a host of reasons that this particular writing wasn't actually a good representation of Kate's idiolect. She might have to run each post by the marketing department of the big streaming service and get input and corrections before posting, for example.

But Raisa was one of the leading forensic linguists in the country, and she had been paying attention to Kate for a few weeks now. She was starting to get a feel for the woman.

Kate Tashibi had a dramatic and brash tone that stood out, and a style that exuded confidence. If Raisa had been cataloging her authorial tics, she would note that Kate's sentences varied in length—a sign of a strong writer—and that she had a way of leading in with a complex one before dropping the mic with a short one right after.

> When we think of monsters, we think of the shadows where they lurk, the darkness from where they emerge, but Conrad hunted his prey during the day. He thrived in the light.

Her voice was distinctive and thus easy to build a profile around if Raisa had been doing so within the capacity of her job. Now, though, all she wanted to find were hints of the bombshells. Even if Raisa didn't believe they existed.

The only post that broke free of the rigid, sleek, and yet boring marketing campaign was a personal photo at the very bottom of the grid.

The first thing Kate had ever posted.

It was a close-up of two girls hugging, both grinning wildly at the camera. If they weren't sisters, they looked similar enough to be mistaken as such.

The caption was simple: For you, H.

Raisa stared at the girls and wondered whether Kate ever took into account that these victims, whose tragedy would become a feast for a voracious public, had been someone's sister, maybe. Or someone's friend, or someone's lover.

Or were they just names and numbers to her? Serving as nothing but narrative tools to get across just how truly villainous her documentary's Bad Guy was?

Maybe Raisa should give Kate the benefit of the doubt. Maybe that first picture was a message in and of itself—that every victim *was* someone's sister, lover, friend.

But Raisa wasn't feeling charitable.

Not when Kate had picked this particular serial killer.

Raisa's phone dinged, and she smiled when she saw the preview text.

If someone had told her four months ago that FBI forensic psychologist Callum Kilkenny would be texting her a ridiculous cat meme on a random Saturday, Raisa would have called bullshit so fast. But now it was a standard occurrence.

Most of the time that Raisa had known Kilkenny—about three years now—they had been cordial colleagues.

As a forensic psychologist, Kilkenny had been in a similar boat to Raisa. He was shipped out to task forces instead of working in one area. It was hard to make friends, or even just allies, that way, and so whenever they'd been assigned to the same case, they'd naturally teamed up.

They'd never been on a texting basis, though.

Of course, everything had changed three months ago. She'd been shot and he'd been there to save her life, and now, if she tried to scroll to the top of their thread, she would be going for a while.

She hearted the meme Kilkenny had sent and then tossed her phone back onto the desk.

Raisa once again stared at the picture of the two little girls.

Kate had clearly done her homework. There was no reason for her to contact Raisa otherwise. Raisa had been a teenager when the Alphabet Man had been active, and she'd never done any special research on the case.

Four months ago, Kate probably hadn't even known her name. She might pretend she was hounding Raisa for an interview about the linguistic shortcomings in the Alphabet Man case, but Raisa knew she had an ulterior motive.

Kate knew exactly what she was doing and exactly who she was hurting with this film.

And for that, Raisa would never forgive her.

Because for Kate Tashibi, Shay Kilkenny was probably just number twenty-three on a list of the Alphabet Man's victims.

For Callum Kilkenny, she'd been his whole world.

EXCERPT FROM *HOUSTON CHRONICLE*

WIFE OF FBI AGENT REPORTED MISSING

Shay Kilkenny, the wife of FBI forensic psychologist Callum Kilkenny, was reported missing this afternoon. Her car was found at the Willowbrook Mall parking lot, and the police were called after shoppers noticed that the front door of her sedan had been left open for several hours. There were no other signs of struggle.

For the past four years, Agent Kilkenny has been hunting the serial killer known as the Alphabet Man, who has murdered more than 20 people in the Houston metro area.

"It's a nightmare scenario," said one task force member on the condition of anonymity. "We've all been worried about our loved ones being targeted by this sicko; it's what you fear the most when you sign on to a job like this. Maybe it's not our guy who took Shay . . . but you have to think it is."

EXCERPT FROM *HOUSTON CHRONICLE*

CANDLELIGHT VIGIL HELD FOR WIFE OF FBI AGENT HUNTING THE ALPHABET MAN

Hundreds of friends, family and strangers gathered

Sunday evening for a candlelight vigil on the third day of Shay Kilkenny's disappearance as the task force hunting the serial killer works around the clock to find the wife of one of their own.

Throughout the evening it was clear there was one fact on everyone's mind: all the Alphabet Man's previous victims were killed after being held for 72 hours.

Agent Kilkenny, the forensic psychologist who has been engaged in a cat and mouse game with the killer, did not make an appearance at the event.

According to a source close to the investigation, cadaver dogs will be brought out Monday morning to search likely drop sites.

———

HOUSTON CHRONICLE DATABASE OF DECRYPTED LETTERS WRITTEN BY NATHANIEL CONRAD, MAY 2009–OCTOBER 2014

"This wasn't a decision we took lightly," FBI Special Agent in Charge Xander Pierce said of working in partnership with the Houston Chronicle to publish the 81 letters written by the serial killer known as the Alphabet Man to the FBI over a five-year time span.

(Read all 81 letters below.)

"We didn't want to give him what he wanted, which was more media attention," Pierce said. "But we left no stone unturned in every other part of the investigation. We couldn't miss out on the chance that someone in the public might be able to identify his writing."

Although no one came forward in the five years that the Alphabet Man wrote to the task force, the letters were ultimately responsible for his capture, as he made a crucial mistake in his last message to law enforcement, allowing the FBI to get a step ahead of him for the first time.

One of the lines in the message written to Special Agent Callum Kilkenny after his wife, Shay, was kidnapped and killed by Conrad became something of a rallying cry for the city in the months following her death.

"She never stopped fighting."

CHAPTER TWO

Shay

August 2009
Four and a half years before the kidnapping

Shay Baker sucked in her breath to get the button on her lucky Levi's to go through the hole, then tugged her white tank top down to reveal the lacy cup of her bra. She needed the extra tips tonight. Their electricity would be shut off in two days if she didn't somehow magic up the hundred bucks she owed.

Her choppy blonde hair was freshly washed, her blue eyes rimmed smoky black, and her mouth smeared red with the last of her cherry lipstick.

If she squinted, she almost looked hot. Not pretty, not like the girls who sometimes slummed it in the bar with their cardigans and tasteful makeup. Shay would never be the girl you took home to Mama, but she might be the girl you tipped a twenty because she made you feel like you were eighteen and sexy and suave.

That's all she cared about.

The CD player blared from the living room, and Shay shook her head as she grabbed her purse.

Max was rapping along to Eminem's lament about losing his spaghetti due to stage nerves, spitting beats and not missing a single note, when Shay yanked the snapback from her head. Her sister ratcheted up the performance, gesturing to their own dilapidated house and stagnant life.

Just because it had Shay rolling her eyes didn't mean she could resist the song that had become their anthem. She plopped the snapback on her own head and took over the rap, the fast part about normal lives being boring, about a father not knowing his own daughter. They were her verses, even though they were Max's verses as well.

They both hit the *da da dum dum dum* hard right before the last chorus. Max jumped, one hand in the air, as Shay hair-banged like the child of Nirvana she was.

Shay dropped the hat back on Max's head as the outro played and then went to make sure there was one more box of mac and cheese left. Max was probably sick of it, but it was better than nothing. It sucked that Max had experienced too much hunger in her short life.

"Beau said he'll be home around ten. Until then, Mrs. Marlow will be next door if you need anything," Shay said, even though Max already knew. Shay and Aida Marlow had long ago come to an agreement where Shay brought home a couple of cartons of Marlboros a month and Aida kept an eye out in case Max accidentally started a fire in the couple of hours that Shay's shift overlapped with their brother's. As Max's legal guardian, Shay felt compelled to add, "Read a book or something."

"Yeah, yeah, yeah." Max waved a hand at her. She'd had the attitude of a teenager since she'd come out of the womb, but she was really embracing the *I'm over it all* vibes as she stared down her twelfth birthday in a few weeks. Before Shay had even stepped out onto the dust-covered steps, Max was already rapping the next song.

Shay worked at a shithole bar where the bouncer, Craig, had to throw someone out more nights than not, and she was fairly certain the owner was deep into some laundering and/or drug scheme. But he had been the one to hire her nineteen-year-old ass six years prior, willingly pretending her fake ID was decent. There was some built-in loyalty there.

Also, the other bartender was a fifty-year-old man with an impressive beer belly. Shay got a lot of tips, even if they were off three-dollar beers.

Except she'd had a bad streak recently. She blamed the heat advisory. Everyone was too goddamn sweaty to heft themselves out of the trajectory of their fans and go to a place that didn't have AC. And Lonnie refused to invest that laundered and/or drug money in making the place slightly more bearable in the Texas summers.

But for some reason, the place was busy when Shay got there for her shift. She raised her brows at Lonnie, who just shrugged and scuttled like a cockroach back into his broom closet–size office. She wouldn't see him again until closing, and she was fine with that.

"Didya hear?"

The question buzzed like a mosquito through the crowd at the bar all night. For the first two hours, Shay was too busy to loiter and ask any of her customers what they had heard—she was just grateful for whatever it was. Big news brought people down to the watering hole to wag their jaws about it. She was going to be able to keep the lights on in their little house. A small accomplishment to most, a big one to someone who felt like a failure most hours of the day.

". . . a girl . . ."

"There were tattoos on her body . . ."

"They found her in a field."

When Shay finally had a minute to breathe, her brain started piecing together the tidbits. She sidled over to two regulars who had set up camp at the end of the bar, two Shiner Bocks in front of each of them.

"What are they saying about a girl?" Shay asked, wiping away a nonexistent spill.

Bobby Dole grimaced around his toothpick. "Dead girl found up at the Double X Ranch yesterday. The foreman all but tripped over her."

"Lost his lunch in the process," Tim Stuebens added with a snicker. He worked as a hand on the ranch right next to the Double X, which explained his newfound popularity tonight.

Shay swallowed hard. Dead girls meant cops. Or worse, feds. She'd never exactly been fond of law enforcement, but as of late, her general distaste had ramped up to paranoia. She'd even stopped speeding just so she wouldn't be pulled over.

An image of Max from a few hours earlier, rapping away to some ridiculous, misogynistic song, flashed into her mind. Then the memory shifted, and all she could see were Max's hands covered in blood, her eyes defiant.

Her sister—always one blink away from the worst version of herself.

"A suicide?" Shay asked now, daring to hope. Murder would be the worst option. Cops might start looking around. They might hear some of the rumors that swirled around Max, might wonder why she had to see a psychiatrist who specialized in violent children. They might even find the gun hidden beneath Shay's porch.

"Nah, that's the wild thing," Tim said. "It seems like one of those serial killers got her."

Shay tried to hide her relief but probably did a piss-poor job of it. Of course, that kind of murder was terrible in the grand scheme of things. But it meant she could relax.

"A serial killer?" Shay asked, giving up all pretense of work. Lonnie was in the back room anyway, and there were only two people trying to get her attention. It didn't get overwhelming until it hit five. "What are you talking about?"

"She had letters written all over her. Maybe it was some kind of satanic ritual instead."

A man a few seats over cleared his throat. It hadn't been to get their attention, though, because when Shay glanced over, he was staring down into his glass. Four Roses, neat. He'd looked like he needed a double pour, so she'd given him a splash more than she should have.

He could not have been more out of place if he'd tried. His suit was expensive and impeccably tailored; his haircut had probably cost more than what she owed for her electric bill for the entire summer; he spoke without an accent and said *Please* and *Thank you*. She couldn't remember the last time she'd gotten both.

"Something to add?" she asked as she finally moved toward the two—well, now four—people waving dollar bills in her direction.

The man just slid her a look, seeming to understand the question had been rhetorical.

Smart, then, too.

Shay had barely made note of him before, beyond hoping he tipped better than most of the rich boys who ended up in that seat slumming. But for the rest of the night, she felt his eyes on her.

It wasn't in a sleazy way, either. He wasn't ogling her ass or her chest like every other red-blooded male in the joint. He seemed to be studying the way she moved, her face, who she talked to.

When she lifted the Four Roses in his direction, brows lifted in question, he hesitated, eyes flicking down to his empty glass and then to the door. He knew he shouldn't stay.

But then his attention returned to her, and she could see the decision made behind his carefully controlled expression.

Shay had to admit she was glad he wasn't leaving. It had been a while since a man had lit a fire in her belly. She could admit he did, even though he wasn't her usual type. He was too polished, too professional looking. Not a hair out of place. But she couldn't deny that this made her want to get her hands on him, to muss him up and see if there was anything beneath that perfect facade.

She sashayed on over to him even before he nodded, and she poured him a real double this time. He inhaled like he was about to sink beneath some waves.

Then he handed over two fifties. "Keep the change."

Shay made the bills disappear. She didn't really want to be dealing with money and him right now, not with how she was already thinking about just how long it would take to get him out of that nice suit. "You don't think it was a Satan worshipper?"

His mouth tightened and he looked away. She knew immediately she'd misstepped. This time he stared at the door longer, as if he really might change his mind.

"Our Satanic Panic came, like, ten years after the rest of the country," she said quickly. "Like everything else here, we're late on the trends."

He was still hesitating, toying with his glass instead of drinking the pretty liquor inside it.

"Yeah, it came about when *Sabrina the Teenage Witch* debuted," Shay continued. "The moms all held a rally to burn stuffed black cats. Like Salem, on the show."

He laughed, then looked immediately surprised that he had.

Oh no. She could become addicted to that sound.

"Fictional teenage witches, not okay," he said. "Promoting animal abuse is fine, though."

He was joking, and she liked it.

"That's what I said." Shay grinned at him. "I wrote a letter to the editor of the local paper and everything."

"Did anything happen?"

"Someone threw holy water on my mama at church, and so she whooped my ass," Shay said, still amused. But she must have revealed too much, because his face softened with sympathy. She didn't want that—she wanted him thinking she was hot, not sad. "Don't worry. I was a brat. I held a little memorial for all the lost cat souls. It made the school paper. I never quite shook the witch allegations."

Someone a few stools over called, "Witch or b—"

"Oy," she cut them off. It was Jimmy Thatcher, who grinned at her, pleased with his own joke. He was playful and kindhearted, so she just rolled her eyes and flipped him off.

What mattered more was that she'd successfully wiped the pity from Four Roses's face. He was back to watching her with that careful expression that seemed to hide something fascinating beneath it.

He nursed that drink for the rest of her shift and was still sitting there as the last of her inebriated regulars staggered out.

"You don't have to go home," she said, as the other bartender, Harry, started closing down the place. He'd snark at her tomorrow about doing her share of the work, but for all his griping, he was a fairly solid wingman. She liked to think she'd returned the favor enough times that they were even.

"But I can't stay here," Four Roses said, and then nudged his long-empty tumbler in her direction. When she'd offered him a third pour earlier, he'd declined, but he hadn't left.

His eyes slid to Harry, then back to hers. "Well, have a good night."

Shay gaped at his retreating back, and stopped him only when he put a hand on the swinging door. "You put in all that time just to say good night?"

He turned back to her. "It beat an empty hotel room."

"Yeah, but so do a lot of things," Shay said, untying her apron strings. She glanced at Harry, who gave her a thumbs-up without even looking in her direction. "Like a not-empty hotel room."

She would never call it her smoothest line, but Shay was attractive. She didn't need to be smooth, she just needed to indicate that she was interested. The other party usually did the rest of the work. That was no different with Four Roses, who politely ushered her into a nice sedan that was more budget conscious than she'd been expecting.

"Rental," he murmured, the tips of his ears pink. And, again, she thought, *Oh no*. It was easier to know he was passing through, though. No need to get anything but her body involved here. Her heart could take the bench for tonight.

His hotel room was standard fare, but again on the budget-friendly side. She wondered what had brought him to the suburbs of Houston. Work, of course, considering that both the car and hotel were probably the level they were because the trip was being paid for by a tightfisted CEO.

But they didn't have much in these parts besides suburbs and ranches and trailer parks. They were caught in a weird limbo between three big cities, their outskirts creating a Bermuda Triangle that seemed to transport those in it back at least a decade in time.

Shay didn't bother to follow up on her curiosity. The less she knew the better.

And it was fun, so much fun. She liked laughing during sex, but he also had this uptight intensity that was kind of endearing. She half expected him to murmur *I love you*, but for once she didn't find it cheesy when a man told her they wanted to watch her face.

He fell asleep after, as most of the guys she'd ever been with did. But Shay wasn't about to be vulnerable with a stranger.

She went to the bathroom, collecting her clothes along the way. She shimmied back into her jeans and tank top, thinking about how she'd done so earlier only worrying about the tips the outfit would get her.

It had been a far more successful night than anticipated.

Shay smiled to herself as she crept through the darkened room. The curtain was open a sliver, and moonlight poured into the room. Something gold glinted on the dresser. His wallet.

But that didn't make sense.

She shook her head. It was probably his watch—or a wedding ring, even. At that thought, she couldn't help but take a step in that direction. Just out of curiosity, really.

Her head went light and the world tipped sideways as she realized what the gold actually was.

Not a watch. Not a ring.

Her heart pounded in her throat, in her wrists, in her teeth, as she reached out a shaky hand.

Before she could touch it, she snatched her fingers back, not wanting to leave prints behind.

Still, the thing was easy to see and understand.

Darkness crept in at the edges of her vision, but she concentrated on her breathing and it receded. The worst thing she could do was pass out right now.

Because the flash of gold? It was an FBI badge.

Oh no, she thought for the third time that night.

CHAPTER THREE

Raisa

Now

Raisa didn't tell Kilkenny about her encounter with Kate Tashibi.

She wondered if Kate had gotten through to him, but of course she hadn't. If Kate had been successful with Kilkenny, she wouldn't have had to come after Raisa.

Kate had framed her interest in Raisa through the lens of Raisa's expertise. She'd wanted a linguist to talk about the Alphabet Man's letters, about what might have been done differently had there been someone like her on staff at the FBI at the time.

But Raisa knew what Kate was really after.

An interview with Callum Kilkenny. The man whose name would forever be tied to Nathaniel Conrad's. The man who'd spent five years hunting the monster, only to lose his wife to the very killer he had been chasing.

What a coup that would be for Kate's miniseries.

She must have thought she could get Raisa to talk about Kilkenny. That wouldn't be nearly as powerful, but at some point, beggars couldn't be choosers.

Raisa just hoped Kilkenny had completely blocked out the fact that the documentary existed in the first place.

They had other things to think about, after all.

Her shoulder ached, but she ignored it as she headed to the courthouse. Kilkenny would be waiting for her there, on the steps, so she wouldn't have to go in alone.

She'd been dreading going in alone.

The last time she'd seen Isabel Parker was when the woman had put a bullet into Raisa's shoulder. Only luck and Isabel's poor aim had saved Raisa.

And even though Raisa had lodged her own bullet in Isabel, the woman had lived to die another day. Which meant now she was on trial instead of rotting six feet in the ground.

Raisa wouldn't typically call herself bloodthirsty—she was a linguist, after all—but she wasn't sure she would have been crying too many tears had Isabel died that night of their standoff.

Even though Isabel was technically her sister.

It wasn't as if Raisa had known that fact prior to that night. They had been separated when Raisa was only three, after Isabel killed their parents and their brother, Alex, whom she then framed for the deaths. The mini-massacre had kicked off a twenty-five-year-long killing spree that had culminated in Isabel returning to their hometown, Everly, to commemorate the anniversary with even more deaths.

That—and pulling Raisa into the mix—had been her downfall. Today, she would be answering for her crimes, and even if Raisa would prefer that her own bullet had been a few centimeters to the right, she was happy Isabel's victims were getting justice.

Including herself.

No one expects you to just shrug off a near-death experience, Kilkenny had told her plenty of times in the three months since her standoff with Isabel.

But it wasn't the bullet that had done the most damage. Instead, what had rocked the ground beneath her feet had been the string of revelations that came with it—that Raisa had an entire family she hadn't known about, that there was a darkness in her past that seemed to newly define who she was as a person. That she had been one of two sisters to have survived Isabel's massacre, and that the other, Delaney, had been somewhat complicit in Isabel's murder tour. That the parents she'd loved, the ones who'd taught her to be fair and just and *good*, hadn't really been hers.

For most of her life, she'd prided herself on being tough, on her thick skin and ability to roll with whatever came her way. After her adoptive parents—the ones who'd raised her—had died when she was only ten, she'd been bounced around the foster system, too old to land anywhere permanently. She wasn't soft; she hadn't had an easy go of it. And yet this, this, she couldn't shake off.

At some point in the past three months, Kilkenny had quietly sent her a list of FBI-vetted psychologists, but Raisa hit a brick wall every time she imagined explaining what was wrong with her. She didn't know how to put into words the way the bottom had dropped out of her world.

Kilkenny smiled at her now from the courthouse steps, his eyes dropping to her shoulder. He'd been the one to find them that night, the three Parker girls, both Isabel and Raisa bleeding out on the ground from each other's guns, Delaney crouched over Isabel, her loyalties cemented long ago.

Raisa had thought—had hoped—she'd taken Isabel out with her shot, but Kilkenny had brought paramedics with him when he'd tracked them down in the woods. He'd arrived only minutes after Isabel had taken her bullet to the chest and had probably saved her life.

A life she would now spend in prison.

Isabel wasn't exactly happy about that fate, and as people like her were wont to do, she blamed Kilkenny instead of herself for it.

"You okay?" Kilkenny asked, as they made their way into the courthouse. She probably had that look on her face, the one she knew she got when she thought too hard about the nest of vipers she'd been born into.

They both knew she was lying when she answered, "Yeah, sorry."

Neither of them said much as they found seats and settled in. It wasn't until Isabel was led into the courtroom that Kilkenny tensed beside Raisa.

"What?" Raisa asked.

"She seems . . ." Kilkenny trailed off. "Happy."

He was right. Of course he was.

Kilkenny ran his thumb over his wedding band, a habit that she wasn't even sure he was aware of. "She's watching me."

Again, he was right.

Throughout all the opening statements of the trial, Isabel kept glancing back at them, wearing that same obnoxious smirk from the woods, the one she'd worn when she taunted Raisa with plans for her imminent death.

Raisa wouldn't have been surprised if Isabel stared at her throughout the whole trial, but she had not once caught her sister's eyes across the room. Isabel's attention was locked on Kilkenny.

Like she was waiting for something to happen.

"I don't like this," Kilkenny said quietly.

Raisa didn't, either. The lawyers were talking, but Raisa couldn't concentrate on what they were saying, her mind working through the possibilities. Isabel was behind bars, had been since that night in the clearing. She had tried to kill an FBI agent. Even if there hadn't been evidence of her other crimes, she would have been held without bail for that.

Isabel was scary smart, though. Raisa wasn't sure of the exact number of people she'd killed, and she doubted that even the prosecutors were aware of the full tally. But it had been dozens over a twenty-five-year time span.

Isabel hadn't operated that long without having a few tricks up her sleeve, even while wearing orange.

She was a planner, she was experienced, and she hated when things didn't go her way.

And she blamed Kilkenny for her current predicament.

All that meant Raisa's entire body was tensed, waiting for some shoe to drop.

It didn't take long.

Kilkenny's phone pinged, loud enough for the judge to shoot a warning look in their direction. The hunger on Isabel's face was clear and terrifying.

Raisa couldn't help but glance at Kilkenny's screen.

On it was a headline.

SEVENTY-TWO HOURS BEFORE EXECUTION, SERIAL KILLER SAYS FBI AGENT'S WIFE WASN'T ONE OF HIS VICTIMS

Beneath it, the subheadline read:

> While giving an interview for an HBO documentary, the Alphabet Man admits that Shay Kilkenny, the wife of the FBI agent who eventually caught him, didn't die by his hand.

Rage burned bright and hot in Raisa's veins. It wasn't enough for Kate Tashibi to make sure that monster's name lived on long after he was put down. No, she had to upend Kilkenny's life in the process, and for what? A lie and some ratings.

"Kilkenny," Raisa said, though she wasn't sure if it was in warning or to comfort him.

It didn't matter, because Kilkenny pushed to his feet, the courtroom door banging behind him a moment later.

Raisa met Isabel's eyes across the distance that separated them.

Isabel smiled, a victorious thing that confirmed exactly what Raisa suspected. She wasn't sure how Isabel had managed to get Nathaniel Conrad to lie about Shay.

But she knew, without a doubt, that her sister'd had a hand in it.

There was no reason to stay around to watch her gloat. Raisa slipped out of the room in a slightly less dramatic fashion than Kilkenny had, but she knew there would be people noting her exit, just as they had his.

Kilkenny had been faster than she would have given him credit for, though. When she searched the area around the courthouse, she came up empty. She called in a favor to get his address, then checked at the FBI office as well. Three texts went unanswered, as did two phone calls.

She wondered if Kilkenny was hiding from the world, hiding from her, or a little bit of both. She wasn't arrogant enough to think she was front of mind for him right now. Kilkenny had been pulled into her family's mess on his own—or rather, through Delaney—but it was still *Raisa's* viper nest of a family that had played a role in this.

Or a suspected role, at least.

Raisa wouldn't blame him if he held her a little bit responsible, even if that wasn't a completely rational reaction.

She did recognize a brick wall when she ran headfirst into it for several hours in a row, though.

"Shit," she breathed out.

Because if she couldn't reach Kilkenny, there was only one other place to turn.

———

Prisons didn't make Raisa nervous.

The muffled clang of bars, the guards with guns, the shouts—none of that was what had Raisa's hands shaking.

It was knowing what she had to do, being terrified to do it, and then sucking it up anyway.

The Styrofoam pieces Raisa had picked off the rim of her coffee cup were tucked in her clenched hand as if she could hide her own nerves the same way.

Turned out, she would march into hell for a person who, three months ago, she had barely considered anything more than a distant colleague.

"Agent Susanto?"

Raisa glanced up to find a guard in front of her, the woman's face impatient, like that hadn't been the first time she'd called Raisa's name.

"Sorry." Raisa scrambled to her feet, shoving the remaining bits of Styrofoam in her pocket and dropping the cup discreetly in the trash before the woman could see the dents she'd made.

The guard directed Raisa to an interrogation room, and it took only another minute for the door to open again.

Once upon a time, Isabel Parker had reminded Raisa of a punk-rock superstar, her neon-pink hair accented by metal in every imaginable piece of skin. She'd been compelling, magnetic. Now, stripped of her punk-glam makeup and at least some of her hardware, she just looked unremarkable.

This was why Isabel would have rather taken a bullet than be locked up. She'd lived her life as the main character, not because she'd been beautiful but because she'd been interesting. Now Raisa couldn't imagine her turning a single head.

The guard made quick work of securing Isabel to the table and then left as swiftly as she'd come.

Raisa didn't wait for whatever clever remark Isabel had locked and loaded. "What did you do?"

Isabel laughed. "I killed our parents. I was somewhat responsible for the death of your adoptive ones. I planned on killing both you and Delaney and then framing her for your murder. You'll have to be more specific, darling."

The list had probably been meant to rattle Raisa. But all it did was make her realize how much she'd been building Isabel up into some sinister puppet master in her memory.

Here, under the harsh prison lights, she was just as ridiculous as any captured mastermind, declawed and defanged but too used to having all the power to realize that she no longer did.

For the first time in what felt like three months, Raisa exhaled and she remembered. She remembered not the press of the gun to her spine, but just how silly she'd found Isabel's posturing on the long walk to the clearing. There had been short bursts of time when it was clear Isabel was dangerous—she'd killed dozens of people and had the moral makings of a sociopath. But most of the time, she'd just come off as a kitten playing at a feral cat.

"You know what I'm talking about," Raisa said.

Isabel smirked. "Can I buy a vowel?"

"Cute." Raisa's eyes narrowed. "You just can't help yourself, though, can you? If you were going to pretend not to know what I was talking about, that just disproved it."

Isabel's mouth twisted like she couldn't decide if she wanted to retaliate, banter, or move to the portion of the conversation where she got to brag about all the ways she'd schemed and manipulated people to produce this outcome.

The impulse to do the latter won.

"The Alphabet Man," Isabel drawled. "Yes, well, let me think, what did we talk about? Oh, I remember."

Whatever was coming next would be provocative, that much was obvious. Raisa controlled her expression accordingly.

"We compared notes about that feeling we get when we're snuffing the light out of someone's eyes," Isabel said, her own eyes hungry on Raisa's face.

All of it was so predictable, though. Why had she been so scared to come here?

"Yes, yes, you're very big and bad."

Rage flashed into Isabel's expression. "Why don't you ask your beloved Kilkenny how he feels about me right now?"

At the reminder, anger flooded in, making everything sharper. The lights, the smell of sweat and bacteria on Isabel's skin. The color of her eyes and the distant hum of the heat kicking on in the room.

"You got Nathaniel Conrad to lie for you," Raisa said, done with playing around. "How?"

"Why do you think he's lying?" Isabel shot back.

"Because a serial killer with his record wouldn't claim someone else's victim as his own."

Kilkenny might be the psychologist between the two of them, but even Raisa could guess that.

"Yes, but Conrad has always been different," Isabel pointed out. "And he never took credit for her kill."

"Semantics," Raisa said. "He didn't take credit for any of the victims."

"Until today," Isabel pointed out.

That was news, as far as Raisa could tell. Conrad, like plenty of other killers, had proclaimed his innocence even in the face of overwhelming evidence. She'd thought he'd keep doing it right up until his last words. Perhaps she should have read that article further than the headline, but she'd been too angry to even see straight at that point.

"He's lying," Raisa said, still confident in that fact. So what if he'd claimed the other victims and not Shay. He was a psychopath, a pathological liar and a man who'd tortured and killed twenty-seven people. His word wasn't exactly gold. "But I want to know what part you played in it."

"How about this," Isabel started, examining her nails in a way that rattled the chains. "An answer for an answer."

Raisa thought about the way Kilkenny had stormed out of the courtroom, the way he'd lost all the color in his face when the alert came in. Making a deal with Isabel Parker was akin to shaking hands with the devil, but Raisa would still gladly do it if she could get information out of her.

"Fine," Raisa said. "What did you do to get him to lie about Shay Kilkenny?"

"I gave you a chance to ask an actually interesting question and that's what you went with?" Isabel tsk-tsked. "He's not lying. I already told you that. Conrad didn't kill her."

"You said an answer for an answer," Raisa said, nails digging into her thighs through the soft fabric of her pants. "A truthful answer for a truthful answer."

"No one is forcing you to believe me, but I am being truthful," Isabel said. "Are you in love with Kilkenny?"

Raisa wanted to throw the *and that's what you went with* back in her face. Instead, she looked away, pretending to be embarrassed.

"No." She let the word linger in her mouth as if she didn't want to let it go. Then she shifted her eyes back to Isabel, who was grinning as if she'd figured something out. *Good.*

"My turn," Raisa said. "Have you been in contact with Conrad?"

"Yes," Isabel said, and despite the circumstances, Raisa couldn't help but feel satisfaction at the confirmation. She barely knew Isabel, but she'd been able to read *that*, at least. "We exchanged letters once I guessed that he wasn't the one who killed Shay Kilkenny. I wasn't the one who convinced him to share that fact with the world, though, if that's what you're really asking." She paused, but only for a heartbeat. "Do you love Delaney now?"

Raisa blinked at her. That was a much more interesting question, she had to admit, especially considering the last time she'd seen Delaney had been that night Isabel had shot Raisa. And Delaney had been holding Raisa at gunpoint only moments before Isabel's bullet had torn through Raisa's shoulder.

That had been a fun family reunion all around.

Isabel was obsessed with both of their lives to an unhealthy extent, but she was most possessive of Delaney, who was much closer in age to her than Raisa.

"No," Raisa answered honestly. Knowing someone had been your sister at birth didn't automatically create a connection that could withstand everything Delaney had done. But—and Raisa would never admit this, certainly not to Isabel—she did *like* Delaney.

Before the night in the woods, Delaney had been a crucial part of the investigation into Isabel's latest murders. She had a day job as a content moderator for a social media site but had been something of a dark-web vigilante, outing rapists and other creeps when they posted on those terrible forums Raisa liked to pretend didn't exist. That was how Delaney had originally started working with Kilkenny—he'd been her contact at the FBI for years before Raisa had met her. When Delaney had flagged a video that Isabel had posted of her crime scene, they'd all just assumed she was helping catch another random bad guy.

Delaney was weird, with odd social graces and an intense mind that saw patterns and logic in a way that would have made her an excellent linguist. She was funny and smart, and for some reason, they clicked when they worked together.

Raisa didn't have to like that she liked her, though.

"Are you angry she's not in jail?" Isabel asked, seeming pleased with Raisa's answer.

"My turn," Raisa said, feeling like she had the upper hand for the first time since she'd walked into the room. She had to be smarter here. Asking who had convinced Conrad to "confess"—or lie, probably—was pointless. Likely, it had been Kate Tashibi, possibly supplied with information from Isabel, possibly with her own. Still, Raisa couldn't think of a way into this that would force Isabel to reveal anything of importance. Except . . . Isabel had always liked to think of herself as smart.

"What is the question I should be asking?"

Isabel lit up, as Raisa predicted. "Ohhh, finally a hint of intelligence."

"That's not an answer."

"I'm thinking," Isabel said, and it actually sounded like she was. She hadn't anticipated these lines in her script. "You clearly already know why I'm screwing with Kilkenny. He messed with my plans and needs to be punished."

Raisa did know that. She'd been braced for *something* ever since Kilkenny had saved Isabel's life three months earlier. For anyone else, they would feel nothing but extreme gratitude for Kilkenny, but Isabel hadn't wanted this. She'd wanted the sweet release of death.

"It also doesn't really matter when I figured all this out," Isabel continued. "That was five years ago, by the way. When Kilkenny started working with Delaney. So. What would I ask if I were you?"

After one more beat, Isabel smiled with realization. "Why did I first suspect Conrad hadn't killed the wife?"

The wife rankled, but Raisa let it go. There were battles to pick here, and that wasn't one of them. "What was it?"

"You already asked your question," Isabel said, smug. "My turn."

Raisa tilted her head in acknowledgment.

"Do you have nightmares about me?" Isabel asked.

Dark woods, a cold stream. The clearing. Pain and then black. Sweat-damp sheets and screams that died in her throat. A fervent hope that her neighbor was a deep sleeper.

She kept her expression neutral. "I don't think about you at all."

"Uh-uh," Isabel said, a scold in her voice. "If you lie, the deal's off."

Raisa looked away. That had been careless, the lie too obvious. She should have spun something more believable.

"Yes," she gritted out. Because it would make Isabel chatty, and Raisa had already admitted the worst of it, she tacked on, "Most nights."

"Delicious," Isabel purred. "The idiolect in the letters written to Kilkenny from 'Conrad' during the time Shay was supposedly being held don't match earlier letters Conrad sent." She gestured as best she could to Raisa. "Linguistically speaking."

"What?" Raisa asked, even though she'd heard.

"Someone else sent them," Isabel said, lifting one shoulder in a lazy shrug. "They were forged to make it look like Shay was a victim of the Alphabet Man."

"How did the linguist not notice that?" Raisa asked, mostly to herself.

"Another interesting question," Isabel said, signaling for the guard. "But I'm all out of answers."

CHAPTER FOUR

Shay

August 2009
Four and a half years before the kidnapping

Shay should have seen the signs that the guy—Callum Kilkenny, according to that badge—was FBI. Or at least law enforcement. The cops cruised through her neighborhood enough times a week that she should have been able to pick one out from twenty yards away.

Her hands shook as she jammed her keys in the ignition of her car. The hotel room he'd taken her to had been a short jog from the bar's parking lot, and she barely even remembered the trip, panic chasing her.

The rational part of her told her to calm the hell down. The G-man hadn't been at the bar to question her—he'd been there to get a drink after a long day.

Probably he was in town for that girl they'd found at the Double X Ranch.

That made sense.

Hadn't he made some disbelieving sound when one of the men had guessed she'd been killed in some satanic ritual?

Shay exhaled. Her brain was still a bit staticky from fear, but she was at least able to take in her surroundings now. Almost home. Almost, but not quite. She parked a street over from their sad little house, and kept to the deep shadows until she could see Beau's car.

He was home, though that didn't come as a surprise. Her half brother worked erratic shifts at the hospital, which left Max alone more than either Shay or Beau would like. But he was also the most reliable man she'd ever met when it came to getting back to their house after his shifts. He never stopped off at a bar to obliterate the memory of a hard day, even if Max would probably be fine if he'd wanted to do that a time or two.

That wasn't how Beau was built, though. While Shay had to consciously choose to be responsible every day, it came naturally to him. Sometimes his *goodness* made her irrationally annoyed, as did the fact that he never judged her on the days that she was unable to consciously choose to be responsible. But mostly, she was just glad he was in her life, that they had been able to figure out this coparenting-a-sibling thing together.

Max seemed happy enough with them, even when they made mistakes. They were still probably better than her taking her chances in an overcrowded system that seemed designed to send kids into a terrible pipeline for violence and crime.

And it wasn't like their mother, Hillary, was going to take her back in. She showed up about once every three months or so, asking for money and a place to stay while she passed through this part of Texas.

They'd learned long ago to hide anything valuable or hock-able when they heard her shot-to-shit muffler turning onto their street.

So, no, they weren't perfect. But they were family.

You killed for family. You hid the body for family.

Sometimes . . . sometimes you hid evidence for them.

A dog barked a few houses over, and Shay flinched, nerves frayed. It got her moving again, creeping around the corner of the house into the "backyard." She crouched when she got to the flimsy wooden stairs that led down from the kitchen door.

One of the slats was loose, and she carefully worked it free to create a space large enough to slip her arm in. Shay closed her eyes and prayed that no creature had made the stairs into their little den and began feeling around on the ground.

A couple of times she yanked her hand back as imaginary whiskers brushed her fingers, but finally her knuckles tapped against metal.

She grabbed the handle and pulled the gun free, only half wishing she'd pulled out a snake instead.

The weapon looked so innocuous.

Shay couldn't ever see it without seeing Max, too. There had been so much blood, but none on the handle, where her little knuckles had gone white with how hard she'd been gripping it.

I'm glad he's dead.

Shay shook her head and shoved the thing in her waistband, scuttling through the dark back to her car, hoping the fact that it was just past 3:00 a.m. would give her cover.

She wasted some of her precious tip money from the busy night on gas—the bored teenager working the till nearly having to pull the bills out of her hand. It was a place close to their house, deliberately picked so that if anyone went asking later, she could just tell them most of the truth: she'd hooked up with a dude and then realized she needed fuel when she was almost home.

No one would ask later. She was being paranoid.

But that's how the best criminals got away with things. They thought through everything that could go wrong, and when it did, they'd already taken steps to avert disaster. All it took was one gas receipt from a station near Galveston to have the police getting interested in her.

The drive passed in a blur, her thoughts pinging between *This is ridiculous* and *This is the smartest thing you have ever done.*

She didn't land on either for long.

Callum Kilkenny wasn't going to come after her. Logically, she knew that. He didn't even know her last name. But he was smart, clearly. If he found the articles somehow, if he linked Shay back to Max . . .

He was an FBI agent, not some local at an overworked sheriff's department willing to believe an easy explanation when it was given on a silver platter.

Callum Kilkenny was harmless, maybe. But he had the *potential* to ruin their entire lives.

What it all came down to was that Shay should have done all this earlier. It had been almost a year now—it was time to get rid of the damn thing.

Maybe then Shay would be able to stop picturing Max's cold eyes that night.

The creeping dawn light brushed over rusted hunks of metal up ahead, and Shay slowed as she neared the junkyard. A couple of years before, a boyfriend had taken her here to drop off some car parts, but Shay had no other ties to it. There was nothing that could be traced back to her.

Shay pulled to a stop at the back corner of the place, the little office just visible half a mile away. There wasn't a security fence, likely because nothing in the yard that was actually valuable was easy to steal. She didn't understand the business model, but she did know there were hundreds of cars here that would never be sold. Maybe they'd be stripped for parts if someone ever got around to it, but if she found the right one . . .

She tucked her hair underneath a ball cap that had been sitting in the well of the passenger seat. It would hide the length and color just enough that any description of her would come out bland. Then she wiped the gun, getting all the nooks and crannies. She wasn't about to go to jail because she missed a partial print.

It took her twenty minutes to find the right car—a battered old Ford with just enough of a glove compartment left to hold the weapon. The thing was parked in the farthest corner of the lot, mostly crushed beneath the weight of three other trucks, all in better condition. If the gun was ever discovered, it would likely be in years and not months. And it was more than probable that whoever found it wouldn't be the type of person to hand it over to the police.

Careful not to leave any prints, she managed to get the weapon hidden and get herself back to her car without unspooling into a panic attack.

The whole way home, her eyes kept flicking to the rearview mirror, sure there would be red and blue lights there. But she pulled into her neighborhood, unimpeded.

The whole thing had been rather uneventful, and she was beginning to feel incredibly stupid about it all.

Beau was in the kitchen, leaning back against the counter, coffee cup cradled in both hands, staring at nothing. He startled slightly when the door banged open.

"Sorry," Shay said, listening for Max. She was in the shower, still rapping. It was as if the past twelve hours hadn't happened.

"Morning," Beau said, his voice a sleepy rumble. Then he wrinkled his nose. "You stink like sex."

Shay thought it more likely she smelled like gasoline and rust and that Beau was just giving her a hard time since she'd obviously spent the night out.

"*You* do," Shay said, mostly to be a brat. But he flinched like she'd struck a nerve. Shay paused where she'd been reaching for her own battered mug, and whirled on him. "Beauregard Samuels. Are you dating someone?"

Everything about Beau had relaxed in the minute since she'd accused him, and he was back to looking loose and tired, slightly amused and slightly irritated. Pretty much his de facto mood.

"Are *you*?" he shot back, the implication clear. She wasn't exactly in a position to judge anyone for a one-night stand. Still, she was curious who it had been with for Beau. She couldn't remember the last time he'd hooked up with anyone, let alone dated. He didn't even try to pick anyone up when he came into the bar on his nights off.

"Touché," she murmured. "I heard Mrs. Jackson has a nice—"

"Nope," he cut her off. "I don't care what relative that old bat wants to fob off on me. I'm not looking. And now, it's time to move on from Beau's Personal Life and to the electric bill."

"You're no fun," Shay said as she reached into her pocket, where she'd stashed her tips. Beau's paycheck, while not insubstantial, went to his father's medical bills. Shay wasn't exactly unsympathetic—and Beau certainly paid his equal share around the house despite the fact that his bedroom was a glorified pantry—but sometimes she wished they had the cushion of his full check.

"Thanks," he said. "I'll send it in."

"Let there be light," Shay murmured, and then headed for the shower when she heard Max's door close behind her. "I'll get to the groceries today."

After so many years living together, and now sort of raising a kid together, they'd worked out a fairly equitable system that left little room for resentment to fester. What Shay selfishly worried about the most was Beau wanting real dressers and his own bathroom and personal space away from his two sisters.

Except Shay wouldn't be able to afford the expenses by herself. That wasn't a problem she had to worry about today, and she had made a habit of only worrying about ones she would have to deal with in the immediate future.

As she stood under the lukewarm spray, she let herself wonder if life was ever going to get easier. Max still had six years before she could legally be in charge of herself. That might as well be decades for how daunting it seemed right now.

Shay loved Max, had since Hillary brought her home, smelling of baby powder and innocence. Max hadn't cried, she'd simply stared with those baby-big eyes and wrapped her tiny little hand around Shay's finger. But Shay wished for all their sakes that Hillary had been even a slightly responsible parent. That she'd stuck around, that she'd contributed to taking care of her own daughter.

Hell, if she simply didn't steal all the petty cash they had when she did swing by, that would be an improvement.

All of them had been forced to grow up too quickly, because Hillary wasn't just a crap mother. She also knew how to pick the biggest losers out there to father her children. The only halfway decent guy was Beau's dad, and even he was only tolerable because he had wrung out the hundred-proof liquor from his barely functioning liver.

Back in the day, Beau would come home after a weekend with Billy covered in bruises. Shay suspected there'd been a couple of broken ribs that had never healed right, because Beau sometimes got more winded than he should.

Shay's own dad was a blank spot on a birth certificate. A musician passing through, Hillary had told her the first time she'd asked, which made Shay think it was the closest thing to the truth. It changed after that—a truck driver, a dictionary salesman, a fugitive on the run from the law.

Maybe it was depressing, but Shay felt pretty lucky. At least no one had put cigarettes out on her arm.

That was the bar Hillary's children were working with. And the less said about Max's father, the better.

She pushed those thoughts away, her mind sliding back into that warm hotel bed with the FBI agent, his long, competent fingers, his half smile. The way he always looked a little surprised when he laughed. Like it was a rare occurrence.

Shay probably wouldn't laugh much, either, if her job was staring at brutalized dead girls all day.

How long would he be in town if he was working a murder case? Days? Weeks?

Would he come to the bar again?

For a moment, she was back in the junkyard, dogs barking in the distance, the gun cold in her hand.

Her stupid heart hoped he would return.

Her head knew better.

There would be no repeat of last night, even if he sat on that dang stool for every minute of every shift she worked until he left town.

Shay might curse her life sometimes, but there was little she wouldn't do to protect it.

Even say no to Callum Kilkenny.

CHAPTER FIVE

Raisa

Now

Kilkenny had to come home eventually.

Raisa held on to that thought as she passed the third hour sitting outside his apartment in her car.

They were thirty minutes from midnight, which would make it forty-eight hours until Conrad was executed.

She had her tablet out, the one she liked to use to run her analysis on writing samples. She'd pulled three of Conrad's earliest letters. And she'd pulled the three that were sent to Kilkenny after Shay was taken.

As much as she hated to admit that Isabel had been right, they didn't match.

There were complicating factors, of course.

Conrad had written his letters using a cipher. While the FBI had been able to decode all of them eventually with the keys from the victims' arms, the process could have theoretically messed with Conrad's idiolect. He might have made deliberate choices because the word was easier to encrypt rather than because it came naturally to him. And on the FBI's end, Raisa was trusting that the agents hadn't made any mistakes. A typo from Conrad might have actually come from someone else.

He had also sent the messages in blocks without any spaces around the words so that anyone trying to decode them couldn't use inevitable patterns in language to help with the process. There were only so many one-letter words in English, only so many two-letter words. If he'd written out the message with proper spacing, it became like playing hangman with the highest stakes possible.

Conrad had even added extra letters in the beginning and throughout to mess with any attempts to predict the words. Once the message was decoded, it was easy to discard the extra stuff as so much gibberish, but it would have thoroughly screwed with the decrypting efforts in the seventy-two-hour window the victims had until they were killed.

Still, Raisa had worked with ciphers before and had taken an entire seminar on the Zodiac Killer's letters. Since then, she'd dealt with plenty of other criminals who'd written to law enforcement in some kind of rudimentary code.

Raisa was trained to see the bones of a writing sample, even with all those complicating factors.

No matter how many caveats she added to the early, confirmed Conrad letters and the ones after Shay had been taken, she couldn't deny that the truth was obvious.

There had been two separate writers.

Everything from their grammatical mistakes to the use of similes, ten-dollar words, and slang was different.

Just in the first two letters, Conrad used six similes, two of which centered on animals—*clever like a fox, as black as coal, as sharp as a razor, as gentle as a lamb, as bright as the moon, as silent as the grave*—to describe either himself, his victim, or what he was doing to his victim.

There was not a single simile in Shay's letters.

In the earlier letters, Conrad also frequently used double comparatives—a rhetorical device to amplify increasing or decreasing returns.

The more I take from the girls, the brighter their auras burn.

It was obvious he liked his own voice. Whereas the author of Shay's letters was just trying to get the job done. They didn't use any rhetorical devices to pretty up the writing.

They did, however, have a strange tendency to drop articles and vowels from long words that ended in -ly. Raisa had seen the same patterns in people who wrote frequently and quickly for a living—journalists, court reporters, medical techs, jobs of those natures.

None of that alone would make a foolproof case, but that's why she built analyses that accounted for every aspect of an author's idiolect. And in this instance, when she started adding up the patterns, a profile started to emerge.

Or, rather, two profiles.

That didn't automatically mean Conrad was completely innocent in Shay's murder. Maybe he had an accomplice. Maybe he'd drastically changed his voice, either because he had been trying to mislead any possible experts brought in by the FBI or because his writing really had evolved.

That wasn't unheard of, per se, especially since it would have happened over the course of four years while he was still young. She'd need to go through all the letters to see if there had been a gradual shift throughout—which would take time she didn't have.

In the quiet of her car, with just herself as the audience, she could admit that she was starting to doubt that Nathaniel Conrad had been the one to kill Shay.

And yet, she had never before wanted to be so wrong.

Right now, Kilkenny at least had closure, had whatever passed for justice in this modern era.

If they opened the door to doubt, how much more of his life would this case consume?

Was that fair to think? She should want to catch Shay's killer over anything else—if the second killer existed. But what Raisa really cared about was Kilkenny.

It took until midnight for Raisa to jump through all the hoops required to make her computer secure, but once she did, it was easy enough to pull up the official details.

Everyone thought of Kilkenny when they remembered the Alphabet Man case, but he hadn't actually been the agent in charge—even before Shay had been killed.

The man leading the investigation had been Xander Pierce.

Raisa had a flash of tall, dark, and handsome in her memory, a cowboy who'd wandered in off the range to strap on a badge and a firearm. She'd worked with him only a time or two, but she had come away from the investigations respecting him. He'd called Raisa in before shit had hit the fan. The same couldn't be said for many of the agents she'd had to deal with—ones who viewed her as a party trick at best.

Because of her particular skill set, she didn't spend a ton of time in the field. The most she had in recent years was in Everly hunting down Isabel, and that had been because she'd technically been tagging along with Kilkenny. Most of the time, she didn't even have to leave her apartment to do her job. Everything was digital these days—even communicated threats from criminals.

Agents who worked in the field tended to look at her as weak. Some of that was because she was a woman, she was sure. But she knew plenty of female agents who garnered respect. They were usually the ones clearing a building in a terrorist situation instead of the ones behind their computers figuring out which hate group wrote the threatening letter in the first place.

Add to all that the fact that she got shipped around the country more often than she worked out of any one particular field office, making it almost impossible to build a wide stable of allies in the bureau.

She got by fine. But she did tend to remember the agents who treated her well.

Pierce had been one of them.

He had also quickly assessed what was going on after the first victim was found in the Alphabet Man case. The tattoos, the naked body, the signs of torture—they had all pointed in one direction: serial murderer.

With that in mind, Pierce had dispatched local law enforcement and grunt agents to start scouring for more victims, both in cold-case archives and with search dogs at likely body-drop sites.

Two more were found within the week, which made Raisa think that the Alphabet Man had always wanted the bodies discovered and had simply caught "lucky" breaks on his first victims.

Morally, Raisa cared about all their names. But practically speaking, she didn't think they mattered much at the moment. She opened a fresh notes page on her tablet and wrote down only two of them.

Tiffany Hughes, the victim *found* first.

Sidney Stewart, the Alphabet Man's first kill based on time of death.

Raisa moved on to the tattoos, which were arguably the most unique part of his signature.

The Alberti Cipher was one of the simpler ones—each letter had another assigned to it to create two rows of the alphabet, one in order and one all jumbled up. *A* perhaps went with *T*, *D* with *S*, and so on. To encode a message, the author would simply need to know all twenty-six of those assigned pairs, but to decode it, someone would need to know which letter went with which. That was the hard part.

All Raisa kept thinking was that this case had been tailor-made for a linguist. She flipped through the file, searching for the name of a consultant.

Forensic linguistics as a science was decades old, but the FBI could often be decades behind the times. Until recently, the bureau had relied on experts from think tanks and universities, and outsourced any linguistic work that came in. With the rise in popularity of both the internet and texting—which played large roles these days in crimes ranging from bombing threats to terrorist attacks and school shootings—came two formal positions.

Raisa's East Coast counterpart was a fast-talking New Yorker named Emerson Bird. Bird specialized in international differences in idiolects. Raisa knew some of those basics, such as that native Spanish speakers didn't capitalize the days of the week or the names of the months. That could transfer over even if the person was writing in English, and could help narrow down a suspect list. But it wasn't her strong suit.

She and Bird barely spoke beyond emails divvying up cases. They had one department meeting every six months or so, and then sat through an awkward lunch with each other for exactly forty-five minutes afterward. Other than that, they were never in the same place at the same time.

Bird had come on after Shay's death, though. And if she was reading the notes correctly, the linguist who had worked on the Alphabet Man investigation *hadn't* been brought in for Shay's case.

Resources better allocated elsewhere, was the reasoning Pierce offered.

A budget decision.

Part of her wished she could look at the choice as suspicious, but it wasn't. Raisa's own involvement on task forces rested on the same calculations, and she pulled a salary instead of the per-day cost of a consultant. She'd been given that excuse multiple times during her three years with the bureau—usually when she went knocking on doors about why she hadn't been invited onto an investigation that had gone tits up.

Light washed her laptop screen white, and she flipped the rearview mirror up to avoid being blinded by the car parking behind her. She quickly x-ed out of everything she had open on her laptop and then shut it down completely. By the time she had shoved her tablet in her bag, Kilkenny was already halfway up the town house stairs.

He'd seen her, obviously. He was even probably going to let her in. But he wasn't happy about it.

"You can tell me to go to hell," Raisa said as she caught up with him.

Kilkenny didn't turn to look at her, just slipped his key in the door. "It's not your fault."

The reassurance came out through gritted teeth, like he was convincing himself, and she grimaced at his back.

In the technical sense, it was true. But she was the reason Kilkenny had brought emergency backup to that clearing three months ago. She was the reason Isabel was facing trial instead of rotting in the ground.

It was a little bit her fault.

Kilkenny waved Raisa into his living room and then reemerged a minute later with two beers in hand.

Even after what had to have been a long, rough day, Kilkenny looked effortlessly perfect in his expensively tailored suit, polished tan shoes, and slim tie that still sat snug against his throat.

Raisa simply sprawled on the sofa in an undignified lump, the stress of everything catching up to her, but he lowered himself gracefully into a beautiful midcentury modern recliner as if he were the model paid to sell it.

She eyed him, trying to get a read on what he was thinking. The problem was, Raisa didn't even know where *she* stood on this.

Isabel had been convincing. But she was a charismatic con artist; of course she was convincing. Why would Raisa believe anything that came out of her mouth?

Because the idiolects didn't match.

As much as Raisa liked to think of her work as an art, it came down to statistics and probability at the end of the day. Science didn't lie. The letters, the discrepancies, and the patterns—she was almost a hundred percent certain there was a second author.

She nearly giggled at the phrase, a little delirious probably. Would they have their own version of a grassy knoll as well?

Maybe they even had their own Zapruder film in the form of Kate Tashibi's miniseries. Would seeing the actual interview help them assess whether Conrad was lying? Kilkenny had hunted him for five years, but after he'd caught the killer, he'd famously turned down any and all chances to talk to Conrad. Did Kilkenny actually know him well enough to tell if he was lying?

Raisa realized then that she hadn't filled him in on her visit with Isabel yet. She did so, including her own analysis, which backed up what Isabel had said.

"Is there any chance he could have faked the idiolect?" he asked.

"It's possible," she said. "But why do that? No one ever talked about his writing style before. And then to go back to his old voice for the subsequent letters? That doesn't make sense."

He sighed in what sounded like agreement.

"There are other possibilities," Raisa offered. "Someone else wrote the letters for him, for example. Or . . . something I can't think of right now because my brain is a bit mushy at the moment."

"Yeah," Kilkenny said. He knew how to hedge just like she did. But he could tell beneath those *possibilities* her science and expertise were screaming one thing.

Conrad hadn't killed Shay.

"By the time Shay was taken, the public knew everything about the Alphabet Man," Kilkenny said. "There were articles every day. The media pored over every detail. His body-disposal methods. The tattoos. How long the victims were held for, the fact that they were taken in broad daylight. If someone wanted to fake it, they could do a decent job just by reading the newspaper."

"What did you keep back?" There was always something—a little detail that could mean the difference between deciding if someone who confessed was the real killer or not. It was standard operating procedure.

"The tattoo ink Conrad used was dark gray, not black," Kilkenny said, meeting her eyes. "Shay's was dark gray."

Well. That wasn't nothing.

Raisa chewed on her lip. "That would have been difficult to find out, huh?"

He scrubbed a hand over his face. "Yeah."

"Okay, so maybe I'm wrong," Raisa said, and held a hand up when Kilkenny went to immediately defend her to herself. "What if this is just all . . . Conrad trying to get into your head again? Some just-graduated filmmaker isn't necessarily going to be able to judge the veracity of the interview if a psychopath known for being charming sells the story well enough."

"Kate Tashibi." Kilkenny slid her a look. "Did she contact you?"

"Yeah," Raisa admitted. "She tracked me down in person, actually."

His brows shot up. "Ballsy."

"Stalker-y," Raisa countered, and he tipped his head in agreement. "You?"

"She reached out, I politely declined."

Raisa laughed. "You're a better person than I. I threatened to have her arrested."

Kilkenny's lips twitched. "It's easier to be mad on someone else's behalf."

"True," Raisa acknowledged.

"She would have had to prove the truth of what Conrad said in some way," Kilkenny said softly after a moment. "No credible company would buy her film otherwise. She must have some kind of evidence beyond his word."

Raisa deflated, knowing that was true. "Yeah."

"So, there it is, then. He didn't kill Shay."

He sounded entirely too calm. She didn't want him to fall apart, but she knew better than anyone that when someone kept it together this well, it usually meant they were headed toward a nuclear meltdown in the near future.

Raisa couldn't quite picture what a nuclear meltdown from the cool and composed Callum Kilkenny would look like, but she also didn't want to be able to picture it. Or experience it. "Maybe we should sleep on all this."

He glanced at the time; it was nearing one o'clock in the morning. "We have less than forty-eight hours until we lose our chance to speak with Conrad."

"You want to talk to him?" Raisa asked carefully, not wanting to sway his decision either way.

His eyes flicked to something over her shoulder. She glanced back and noticed the bookshelf for the first time.

On the middle shelf sat a framed picture of Shay.

Raisa swallowed hard and fought the urge to go get a closer look. She'd seen a few photos of the woman, but they had been ones that were provided to the police.

Here, Shay had been caught midlaugh, her eyes crinkled, her head thrown back.

Kilkenny's expression was so wistful as he rubbed a thumb over his wedding ring, Raisa nearly had to look away, unable to shake the feeling that she was seeing something private. Intimate.

"We have to go to Houston," Kilkenny finally said.

Raisa didn't blink at the fact that he'd included her in the plans. She had taken time off to attend Isabel's trial, and this was a much better way to spend those days. "Okay."

He smiled at her easy acknowledgment, but he didn't offer any other sign of gratitude. He didn't need to.

"You know what they'll all say, right?" Kilkenny asked, still staring at the picture. "If Conrad is telling the truth. If we prove he's telling the truth."

Of course she did. It might not have been her first or second thought—those had centered around Isabel and all the ways her sister had managed to continue to upend her life.

But it wasn't hard to reach the next conclusion. Raisa might be a linguist, but she was also an FBI agent.

It was always the husband.

"They're going to say you killed her," Raisa said, grimly meeting his eyes. "And that you framed the very serial killer you were famous for hunting."

EXCERPT FROM DECRYPTED ALPHABET MAN LETTER TO AGENT CALLUM KILKENNY

The sunlight kisses her skin, just like the blade of my knife does; and the more she screams, the more gentle I become. You thought I would say something different there, did you not Agent Kilkenny? You thought I would cut her deeper, to the bone even, when she cries because I like the way her voice reverberates off the stone walls. Oops. Did I give something away about myself? About my location, or worse, about my personality?

Do I have a personality, Agent Kilkenny? You must know the answer to that, as you say you know so much about me. Respectable, you have called me. At least on the surface. I have a good job, proper manners, a nice smile, maybe. That was in your profile, was it not?

So what lesson should the people of Houston learn? The Alphabet Man is trustworthy, so do not listen to your instincts that tell you someone is safe, harmless, good. Do you find that as ironic as I do?

Why you, why you, why you? I know you must wonder that in the deepest hours of a night as dark as coal. (Just like my heart, right?)

There is a reason, why you.

But it would give away all my secrets to tell you that one.

Why you, why you, why you? If you ever found the answer to that, you might also find me.

And I have spent my whole life making sure no one can ever do that.

CHAPTER SIX

Shay

September 2009
Four and a half years before the kidnapping

The dead girl was all anyone talked about for a month straight. And all Shay could think was that if people cared this much for the girls when they were alive, there might be fewer dead ones in the long run.

Shay couldn't focus too much on all that, though, because there was another complicating factor taking up most of her attention.

Namely, the fact that Callum Kilkenny was back at her bar.

He sat at the end, looking half-hopeful and half-shamefaced, like he acknowledged that she'd snuck out on him while he was still sleeping a month ago, but believed she had a reason for it.

She did, of course. It was just one that he could never know.

Shay was the only person working, and so she couldn't pawn him off on someone else. She took a deep breath, distantly wished she'd thrown on some makeup, acknowledged that thought as stupid, and then sauntered over to him, a bottle of Four Roses at the ready.

"You look familiar," she said, squinting at him, hoping it was obvious she was teasing him. "Do we know each other?"

It took a second, but then he grinned, a quick there-and-gone thing that she might have imagined. "I think I just have one of those faces."

Shay laughed and poured him the drink that proved that she really did remember the men she slept with. Not that there would have been anything wrong with it if she hadn't.

"Nah, yours is memorable." She studied it until the tips of his ears went pink. Adorable. "It's a good one."

"Wasn't sure it was to your liking," he said, *with the way you left* implied. He wasn't being a dick—she had a metric shit ton of experience dealing with passive-aggressive men, and this wasn't that. It sounded more like he was giving her an out. If she said, "Yeah, you're right," she was pretty certain he'd leave. In fact, he had one foot on the floor.

That was the reason she ignored the sirens wailing in her mind to tell him just that. Instead, she said, "It was very much to my liking."

The night was a repeat of the last time. Only, she didn't sneak out of his hotel in a mad dash to hide incriminating evidence that could send her sister to jail. Instead, she lingered, lounged even, as he got dressed in the morning.

"I, uh, might be in town a bit over the next few months," he said, as he knotted his tie. An excuse not to look at her, she was pretty sure. He was nervous. She hated that she found that endearing.

Then she remembered why he would probably be in town. The dead girl.

She sat up, tugging the sheet along with her. "Well, there's usually an empty barstool at Lonnie's on any given night."

He smiled at the ground.

Shay said no the next time he stopped by just to prove she could. As she'd predicted, he took the rejection easily. The next time he came in, he hovered instead of taking a seat.

"I can leave," he said.

She studied his face again. She had been right—it was a good one. And with the panic about Max and the gun long receded, she shook her head and grabbed him a glass.

"Stay."

He'd been back several times since then, but today was Shay's first day off in more than a week. She wasn't about to waste any more of it thinking about dead girls or Callum Kilkenny or the gun that hadn't been found yet.

That didn't mean she could spend the day at a swimming hole with a six-pack and a hot boy, like she would have done as a teenager. She had responsibilities, and Max had an appointment with her psychiatrist.

Her sister currently had her feet up on the dashboard of Shay's car, like she thought it would piss her off. Max was always doing crap like that—testing boundaries, some well-meaning social worker had told Shay. Max wasn't confident of her place in the house, and so she tried to push Shay to whatever limit she had just so she could see how bad the reaction was. A common tactic for traumatized and abused children.

But while Shay knew that Max felt like a burden to them, she also knew that Max could just be a run-of-the-mill bratty preteen who liked doing things to irritate people.

Anyway, it was Beau who cared about muddy prints in his precious truck, not Shay.

"Can we go to Galveston after therapy?" Max asked, still staring out the passenger-side window.

Shay jerked the wheel, nearly swerving into the oncoming lane of traffic. A pickup blared its horn at them, and Shay tossed a finger out the window because it wasn't like she'd meant to cause trouble.

"Jesus." Max was gripping the door handle for dear life.

"Don't be dramatic," Shay said, trying to sound normal. But there was only one way to get to Galveston. The thought of driving back down that same road, past the junkyard again . . . past the gun—with Max in the car, no less—had Shay's hands trembling.

"I almost just *died*," Max said, playing it up on purpose. Shay relaxed enough to laugh, because she always enjoyed Max's sense of humor.

"Yeah, they'll be building statues in your honor." Shay's heartbeat was still way above resting, but this back-and-forth was familiar. Easy to fake.

"So can we go?"

"We didn't bring any of our stuff," Shay said, and they both knew it was a delay tactic.

"You have a suit in the back, don't lie," Max said, thumbing over her shoulder to the mess behind them. Shay was 99.9 percent certain she was right. "And we can stop at the Bargain Beachware for a ten-dollar bikini for me."

Max asked for so little, Shay hated to say no.

"I'll pay for the ice cream," Max said, a wheedle in her voice.

And that did it, as Max had probably known it would. Beau and Shay tried giving Max an allowance so she wouldn't feel completely dependent on them, but they skipped more weeks than they followed through. For Max, two ice creams could wipe out half her savings.

It was moments like these that made Shay doubt herself. Doubt her memory of Max standing over a dead body, covered in blood.

"Okay," Shay said. But then shot Max a look. "If you promise to really try with Dr. Greene today."

Max went back to staring out the window, but she gave a soft "Fine," which was practically a pinkie promise from her.

As acknowledgment, Shay turned up the Eminem for the rest of the drive to Dr. Tori Greene's office.

Max pretended not to like the psychiatrist, but Shay was pretty sure Max kind of, almost, did. As much as she ever liked any adult.

When they arrived, Tori stuck her head out of her office, smiling when she saw them.

Tori was one of those hot older Texas ladies—one who looked so much like the wife on *Friday Night Lights* that Shay had to actively remind herself not to call her Tami Taylor. She was in her late forties or early fifties, and was proof that God had favorites. Even at her age, she still had luscious, wavy hair. While the strawberry-blonde coloring likely came from a salon, that kind of volume couldn't be faked. Her skin care routine must have been impeccable her entire life, because her face was smooth and glow-y despite the fact that she laughed easily and smiled even quicker.

Both Shay and Max—and Beau, really—had trust issues with mental health professionals, especially ones who were court mandated. But Tori Greene was tolerable, at least.

Tori didn't do any dumb crap like tell Max to just call her Tori or exclude her from conversations with Shay and Beau. She kept her office filled with dozens of real plants, and hung paintings that were actually interesting instead of the dull landscapes and color blocks that Max's first four psychiatrists had favored. She kept both candy bars and healthy snacks in the waiting room, as well as a floor-to-ceiling bookshelf full of romances, Westerns, thrillers, and all the latest YA fantasy heptalogies.

"We got the latest in that series you were reading," Tori told Shay with a little eyebrow wriggle. It was one of those *Fifty Shades of Grey* rip-offs, but Shay was hooked.

Max made gagging sounds as she sidestepped Tori into the office.

"Keep that up and you're getting a dramatic recitation at the beach," Shay called after her.

Tori laughed, a husky, well-used sound, and winked as she closed the door.

Shay grabbed the book, mostly to put on a show for Chrissy, Tori's nosy secretary. She couldn't focus enough to actually read, though.

Can we go to Galveston?

What had prompted Max to ask that? In her mind, Shay turned over every inch of her car, every inch of the night she'd made that junkyard trip. There was nothing incriminating for Max to have stumbled over.

Max could be eerily perceptive sometimes, too perceptive for her age. There was a cold calculation to it as well, that always set Shay on edge.

There was an old joke Shay had heard one time about how to tell if someone was a sociopath. You gave them a scenario: They had met someone they were romantically interested in at their mother's funeral, but didn't get the person's number. How did they find the person again?

For a sociopath, the answer was obvious. They killed their father.

Shay wasn't sure what Max would say, and she had no interest in testing it.

A lot of the time, Max could be incredibly caring, especially when it came to Beau and Shay. But she could flip the switch when she had to.

If Max weren't capable of that, Shay wouldn't be sitting in Dr. Tori Greene's office right now.

Shay tried not to shiver beneath the cool blast of the air conditioner at the thought.

―――

Beau was sitting at the firepit at the side of their house when Shay and Max got back from Galveston.

Max offered a halfhearted wave that didn't match the sheer joy she'd been letting seep out all day. Maybe her well was empty. That was fair. Shay's own rarely got past half-full.

When Shay sat in the second cheap plastic lawn chair, Beau held out a Miller Lite, the top already off. She took a long swallow, savoring the slight bite of beer after a day at the beach, which was one of her favorite sensations in the world.

"How come I didn't get an invite?" Beau asked, but he was just joking. He'd worked an overnight shift at the hospital and had likely only woken up in the late afternoon. "How was Dr. Greene's?"

Shay lifted a shoulder. Max was never particularly chatty after the sessions.

"Same old."

"Do you think she's helping?" Beau asked after a minute of staring into the nonexistent fire. It was too hot to do anything more than prop their feet on the stone pit.

"More than the others." Max had hated the previous therapists she'd seen and had spent more energy screwing with them than making progress. Although Shay wasn't sure what progress looked like for a kid like Max.

Were they all just trying to keep a boulder from tumbling down a hill? Had her fate been determined the moment she'd pulled the trigger?

Shay slid a look at Beau. He was wearing his curly hair styled these days—short on the sides and long and floppy on the top. Shay had started calling him *boy bander* for a few days, but when he didn't answer with a similar rejoinder or witty remark, she realized he cared. So she'd shut up about it.

He was relaxed now, in a way he usually wasn't—limbs loose, a small smile on his lips. They both worried too much. Beau had also been carrying around an extra dose of anxiety ever since his father had fallen off the wagon in spectacular fashion and slammed his car into a tree. The accident hadn't killed him, unfortunately. Instead, he'd ended up in long-term hospital care that insurance mostly but didn't quite cover. She was pretty sure the stress of it weighed on Beau every day.

So, no, Beau didn't need to know what she'd done with the gun, and he certainly didn't need to know about Callum Kilkenny. He'd probably have an aneurysm if he found out she had an FBI agent's number in her phone.

Or that an FBI agent had hers.

She took another swallow, and put it out of her thoughts. Callum Kilkenny had a lot more on his mind than the trashy bartender he was slumming it with.

"Thinking about visiting your dad on my next day off," she said.

"He'd like that," Beau said, but what he really meant was that Beau would like it. His dad was pretty much comatose most of the time, and high on morphine the rest. She doubted he could pick her out of a lineup if he was paid to.

Still, he was family in a strange, convoluted way. Or, more importantly, Beau was.

Hillary had imparted little in the ways of wisdom in the few years she'd stuck around to raise them, but she'd always made them appreciate the importance of that. Even though Shay could now see the irony of that particular lesson, it had also stuck for whatever reason. Maybe because Beau had. Even when the two of them had been saddled with a preteen with more attitude than vocabulary.

He'd stuck.

That was a truism she could always count on.

So she did her best to pay him back in little ways when she could. She sometimes bought him his favorite six-pack unexpectedly or shooed him away to the movies on her one night off. Or went and sat in a hospital room for an hour with no one for company but a man who drooled all over himself. Even though that same man had routinely taken all his aggression out on a ten-year-old's little body. Had broken Beau's bones, and bruised his skin, and then told him he loved him afterward, creating some kind of screwed-up feedback loop in Beau's mind about relationships and violence.

Shay would still do it, and smile the whole time.

The CD player cranked up inside, a heavy bass vibrating down into the ground where they sat.

"I'm filling in for a psych nurse," Beau said, breaking their comfortable silence. "She's going on maternity leave."

Beau was in oncology usually, but psych was where he wanted to end up. Sometimes she wondered if that had to do with Max. "Hey, congrats."

"Just a short-term thing," he said, ducking his head, bashful. She was the older of the two of them, but he always carried himself like he was twenty-two going on fifty. Until she was reminded in moments like these, Shay really did forget sometimes that he was just a sweet kid.

"It'll give you experience and networking opportunities," Shay said, like she actually knew what she was talking about. What the hell did she know about networking? What would she ever? Still, Beau tucked a smile away in the corners of his mouth, like anything could happen.

They drank the rest of the six-pack in silence, watching the sky go all sorts of colors in a gorgeous Texas sunset.

This had been a good day.

She wouldn't let herself catastrophize about the gun or even the possibility of Beau deciding to apply to other hospitals if he liked this psych rotation as much as she expected him to.

No one was going to find the weapon, and if they did, it would never get traced back to Shay.

And if Beau moved on, as he had every right to do?

Well, she'd survive, she supposed.

That's all she'd ever done. She was an expert at it now.

EXCERPT FROM PSYCHIATRIST DR. TORI GREENE'S PERSONAL NOTES ON MAXINE BAKER

Maxine Baker is a bright and astute child. Her IQ classifies her as a genius, but she does a remarkable job of hiding that intelligence. She was referred into my care by a colleague who realized she could not help the girl. I've found that's often the case with children as smart as Maxine—she does not want a psychiatrist and so she will sabotage any attempts made by professionals to connect with her.

Although I try to come to each patient with a fresh slate, it was imperative to understand Maxine's backstory before our first consultation.

There are unsubstantiated but believable reports that she was physically and sexually abused by her father, who will henceforth be known as James. James and Maxine's mother Hillary—a textbook narcissist—shared 50-50 custody, although it seems that Max was mostly raised by the two siblings who are currently her guardians.

They helped provide some stability in what appears to be a chaotic childhood for the girl.

None of this is the reason she is in my care.

At eleven, Maxine discovered James shot dead in the front entryway of their house. According to the police report, she checked for a pulse and then called emergency services.

Because of the traumatic event, it was recommended—strongly—to her new guardians that she should seek mental health services. In my experience, this was a highly unusual move. One, because it was not court-ordered, which is what I usually see. And two, because her path to me was with specialists who work with violent children. That had me trying to read between the lines.

I soon realized that everyone involved in Maxine's case, from the detectives to the custody judge, believed that she was the one who shot her own father. There was never enough evidence to convict, but they didn't want to miss an opportunity to intervene if needed.

Maxine is too young to be given a diagnosis of borderline personality disorder, but the psychiatrist who referred her to me suggested in her discharge files that she was on the watch for further developing symptoms, as a patient can receive a BPD diagnosis if she has shown symptoms for a year.

However, I see no signs of BPD with Maxine. Although she demonstrates a clear fear of abandonment to the point of self-harm, she's not showing any of the other major signs, such as severe emotional swings, explosive anger and impulsive decisions.

If she was involved in the death of her father, it was not because she has a personality disorder.

While I believe I'm making progress with Maxine, ultimately, I don't believe I'm the right psychiatrist for her. I will be recommending that she switch care to my colleague with PTSD experience once he has an opening.

In my personal opinion, Maxine is neither a danger to herself nor to others.

CHAPTER SEVEN

Raisa

Now

Everyone was capable of killing. Raisa had learned that long ago.

But even knowing that, Raisa couldn't imagine Kilkenny murdering Shay.

Of course, a lot of family, friends, and loved ones had thought just that before their family, friend, or loved one did the unimaginable.

Rage was a strong and terrible drug. There were plenty of normal, everyday people who snapped and then couldn't even remember what it was that had set them off. It was such a common phenomenon while driving that it had its own name.

It was also part of the reason domestic violence statistics were so high.

Was Kilkenny hiding fingerprint-shaped bruises and torn knuckles in his past? Was the myth of Callum and Shay just that—smoke and mirrors that covered deep wounds?

The picture was so easy to paint, so easy that it could become compelling.

Raisa glanced at the clock on the bedside table of the hotel she'd checked into for Isabel's trial. She'd come back to grab her bags while Kilkenny made flight arrangements.

It was three in the morning, an ungodly hour when nothing good happened. But that meant it was almost an acceptable time to call someone on the East Coast.

She slipped the hotel keys into the drop box in the lobby and then pulled up a contact she hadn't used in quite a long time. She hit the call button as soon as she pulled out of the parking lot into the mostly empty Seattle streets.

"Shit, this better be important," Matthew Nurse said when he answered, even though she could hear birds in the background and would bet money on the fact that he was already on his morning run.

Raisa's first year at the Bureau had been rough. She'd been young and a paper pusher in a job most people had never heard of before. Matthew Nurse had been a seasoned vet in the behavioral sciences unit with his eye on the exit, and zero interest in taking a rookie underneath his wing.

But for some reason they'd made allies of each other. Unlike Kilkenny, Nurse had never felt like a partner. He'd played the role of reluctant mentor pretty well, much to his own surprise and displeasure. He'd taken some job in DC after her first year, and they'd mostly lost touch, as Raisa did with the vast majority of people who came into her life.

That was probably something she should work on, but that was a problem for another day.

"You were around for the Alphabet Man, right?" Raisa asked without any preamble. It was six in the morning for him. If she started in with small talk, he'd hang up on her.

"Not on the case," Nurse said, panting only slightly.

"You were in the behavioral science unit, though," Raisa said, taking the highway toward the airport. "With Agent Kilkenny."

There was a long pause. "You want to know if he killed his wife."

Raisa couldn't hold in the surprised sound. "What? How did you get there?"

Nurse laughed. "Baby, I don't live under a rock. And I know you worked with him on that last case. You doing okay over all that, by the way?"

"Yup," she said, and she was sure that if he'd managed to intuit the reason she was calling, he was still sharp enough to tell that was mostly a lie.

"Sure."

"Anyway," she drawled. "Do you have an answer?"

"He didn't do it," Nurse said without missing a beat. "Someone with a grudge might plant some rumors over the next few days if you all don't handle this quickly, though."

"We're headed to Texas now," Raisa said absently. She'd had the passing thought as well—that even if no one really believed Kilkenny had murdered Shay and framed the serial killer he'd been hunting, it sure could throw a wrench in his career for some time.

"Good, you'll get it straightened out," Nurse said, sounding far more confident than she'd given him reason to be.

"How are you so sure that Kilkenny didn't kill her?" she asked.

"Because the head honcho of the BSU at the time ran an internal investigation," Nurse said. "I wasn't on it, but I heard that all the t's were dotted and i's crossed and Kilkenny was cleared quickly. It's not like we all lost our collective brains when the wife of an agent was killed. There are procedures in place."

Raisa exhaled in relief. She hadn't truly believed Kilkenny capable of such a thing, but that's how people got away with crimes for so long. "Then it can't be used against him."

"Please, you know that's not true." Nurse had come to the Bureau a cynic and left with all his worst ideas about humanity and government work proven right. At least how he told it. "I'll put a call in to make sure the report from the internal investigation surfaces, but you know the saying."

"A lie can travel halfway around the world while the truth is still putting on its underwear," Raisa said, echoing the sentiment he'd used at least once a week in that first year.

He guffawed, clearly pleased she remembered. "Being in Texas will help. Pierce is running the show down there—he'll offer Kilkenny some cover."

"Any tea on him?" Raisa asked, since she was already on the phone.

"Ambitious," Nurse said. "I've found with people like that, it can go one of two ways."

"What do you mean?"

"Either they follow every rule to the point of driving everyone crazy," Nurse said. "Or they slime their way to the top."

Nurse, who worked in politics, would know plenty about the latter. "Any thoughts on which one he is?"

"Eh, there are some rumors about him," Nurse said. "Nothing major, just enough for me to lean toward the slime."

Raisa perked up at that. "What kind of rumors?"

"The biggest one is that he uses questionable assets, sometimes off the record," Nurse said. "If someone can help him close a case, he's not exactly a stickler for policing the crime that helps them do it."

That wouldn't be great for his career if it came out, but it wasn't exactly the worst thing Nurse could have spilled about him. "Maybe five years chasing a serial killer wore down his ethics."

"Wouldn't blame him," Nurse agreed. "You go long enough with everyone thinking you've got your thumb up your ass, and buying off a few junkies to bump that closed-case ratio starts to look more appealing."

"Maybe he's all about the greater good," Raisa offered, the lights from the airport bright against the dark night.

"Never painted you for an optimist," Nurse said.

"I've turned over a new leaf," she lied.

Nurse laughed again. "Right. Come visit me inside the Beltway and I'll cure you."

"I'll hold you to that," she said, and he hummed, seeming pleasantly surprised. She'd forgotten how much she enjoyed talking with him. "Did you ever meet her? Shay Kilkenny."

"No," Nurse said. "Agent Kilkenny and I rarely overlapped. He was so busy with that case, he ended up in Houston more often than not." He paused. "He kept a picture of his wife on his desk, though. That doesn't mean much, but it doesn't mean nothing."

He still wore his wedding ring, too.

"An internal investigation means a lot more than that," Raisa pointed out, and Nurse laughed again.

"There's the realist I know and love," he said. "I was worried there for a second. I'll make some calls to get a head start on damage control."

"Thank you," she said, and he grunted in acknowledgment.

"You owe me a drink," he said.

"And dinner," she promised before hanging up.

She left her rental car in long-term parking—she'd deal with any potential fees when she got back.

The shuttle was empty except for the driver.

"Late night or early morning?" he asked in a way that didn't demand a response if she had no interest in giving one.

But she laughed, a little hysterically. "Both."

He nodded like he understood, and Raisa checked Kilkenny's latest text for the airline information.

They would land in Texas in time to meet with Conrad not long after visiting hours started.

Raisa wasn't sure what strategy they would take with him, but she figured she'd leave that to Kilkenny. After all, out of everyone in the world, it was Kilkenny who knew Conrad best.

That was a strange thought and a by-product of their jobs. Kilkenny's and Conrad's lives had become intertwined in a way that superseded even friendship. Enemies were always closer than acquaintances, hate being on the other side of the coin from love.

Conrad probably knew Kilkenny better than she did.

It took a half hour to get through security and find the gate. Kilkenny was already there. She gratefully snagged the soft pretzel he held out to her—it wasn't actually breakfast since she'd never gone to sleep—and then took the seat two down from him so she could see his face.

"Did you call this all in?" Raisa asked. She couldn't actually remember the name of his supervisor at the moment, her brain foggy with all the new information she'd read about the Alphabet Man case.

"There were a few people on the call, and they all believe Conrad is lying," Kilkenny said. "They expressed their distress that this is happening, but then suggested I rent a fishing boat until Conrad is no longer twitching on the table." He noticed her grimace. "Their words."

"Obviously," she said, the butter and salt and dough going a long way toward making her feel human again. "And you told them that you're going to Texas to talk to Conrad instead."

"They hung up before I could mention that."

Kilkenny, she thought.

"Okay," she said, and shrugged when he lifted his brows. "I'm not your mother. And if the head of the behavioral science unit for the FBI can't figure out that you're not about to go get up close and personal with the Puget Sound marine life right now, he probably shouldn't be in the position."

"I'm sure he'll see it that way," Kilkenny said dryly, but didn't actually sound worried. They both knew she was right anyway. Just because his supervisor told him to go fishing didn't mean he thought Kilkenny would listen.

She thought about bringing up the call with Nurse, but Nurse had said he would take care of surfacing the report clearing Kilkenny, and she believed him. She wondered if Kilkenny even knew about it.

They couldn't worry about it now; they had a ticking clock above their heads.

Raisa hid a yawn behind her hand as the announcement came for them to start boarding soon. Kilkenny glanced at the gate door, then seemed to make some decision.

"There's something I should tell you before we leave," he said slowly, and every muscle in Raisa's body tensed. Kilkenny never sounded completely lighthearted, but his tone left no room for interpretation. Whatever this was, he thought there was a chance it would make her stay in Seattle.

That it would make her abandon him so that he would have to go talk to Conrad alone.

Logically, Raisa knew Kilkenny's life must be similar to hers—constant traveling for a demanding profession making it almost impossible to build up a supportive social network. She didn't know much about his family, but considering he had never once mentioned them, she didn't think they were close, if they were still alive.

They were so alike, but it hadn't clicked until now that he might feel as lonely and isolated as she did. For some reason, she'd imagined this whole other part of his life, with bros over for football Sunday and close colleagues he considered friends. Even though what she'd seen and experienced around him didn't support that idea.

She had been viewing him as someone slowly and surely working his way into her inner circle. She just hadn't realized that she'd been doing the same.

Raisa was his support system. Maybe his only support system, as he was hers.

And she wasn't about to let him down now. "Hit me."

"I met Shay in a bar," Kilkenny said. Raisa almost relaxed on reflex, but then her brain caught up. Whatever had his shoulders as tense as they were, it was more than just embarrassment that he'd picked Shay up at some hole-in-the-wall.

"Okay," she said again, as neutrally as possible.

"It was during Tiffany Hughes's investigation," Kilkenny said. "The first victim we found."

Raisa blinked at him dumbly for a good ten seconds. "I'm sorry, what?"

"I met Shay when I first started working the Alphabet Man case," Kilkenny summed up, seeming to know she needed it repeated in easily digestible words.

When Raisa just continued to stare, the tips of his ears went pink. "She was a bartender at the place I went to unwind."

"Oh my god," she said, as the realization came to her. "Are you telling me you guys had a one-night stand? While you were working a serial-killer investigation?"

"I don't know how to break it to you, but that's not exactly an unusual occurrence," he said, the corners of his eyes crinkling.

Raisa covered her ears and shook her head. "No, my innocence has been ruined."

Kilkenny almost laughed at that, and she counted it a win. An almost-laugh from Kilkenny was a near guffaw for anyone else. Raisa dropped her hands and shot him a wry grin. "Okay, now that we've covered the fact that people have sex, that really wasn't my main concern."

Although, to be fair, when Raisa tried to imagine seeking that kind of relief during an investigation, she couldn't get past the idea that she'd probably pass out from exhaustion when her body hit the mattress. So maybe she was a little stunned by that aspect.

Still, there were more important things to focus on.

"Isn't that a wild coincidence that you met Shay while you were working the case for Conrad's first victim?" she asked.

"First victim we knew about at the time," Kilkenny corrected, a not-very-skillful dodge of her question. "He'd killed three times before that."

She narrowed her eyes at him. "Semantics won't distract me."

"The bar was in a different county. She didn't know I was an FBI agent," Kilkenny said, like he'd rationalized this to himself a million times. He probably had. "I watched for any untoward interest. She didn't care about the Alphabet Man."

"Ohh, *untoward*. Are we Victorian dandies now?" Raisa teased.

"My first day in town, everyone at the bar was talking about the case," he said. "Shay was working, and even then she barely paid attention to any of it."

"You remember the specific night well?" She'd had a million nights like that, all at different bars or hotels or in cars or airports. It was rare she could pinpoint exactly where she'd been when, let alone remember what those around her had been talking about.

"I met my wife that night," Kilkenny said with simple surety.

A lot of times she wondered how Shay could possibly live up to the reputation she'd gained as a tragic figure in Kilkenny's life—no fights or flaws, no personality or mistakes, just a ghost to be remembered as perfect. But right in that moment, a tiny part of her admired the stalwart devotion.

"In hindsight, though . . . ," Raisa prompted, because Kilkenny was too good of an FBI agent not to look at this coincidence and call it suspicious.

Still, he shook his head. "It's not some conspiracy. I met Shay in the area and then dragged her into the crosshairs of a serial killer. It's me that's the connection."

Raisa wasn't sure he was right, but she knew he believed he was. Eventually she was going to have to stop treading carefully. Kilkenny could handle it. "What if she wasn't collateral damage, though? You met her the first day you were in town. You have to think that's strange, looking back on it."

"She was a bartender with a tight-knit family and only a handful of close friends. Moving with me to Washington was the first time she'd left Houston in her life," Kilkenny said. "She didn't have enemies. She was killed because of me, not because of something she was involved in."

Sometimes there were stories that people told themselves so many times they became a cornerstone to who they were as a person.

They couldn't see that the stories weren't always true.

And at the heart of Kilkenny's story that he told himself was guilt. That was a far easier thing to live with than pure grief. If Kilkenny didn't have guilt to sustain him, what would he have? An empty house and pictures instead of the woman he'd loved.

Raisa understood that, she did. She had her own story she had been telling herself all her life, and it started and ended with two people she'd believed to be her parents. Two people she'd thought had died because of a silly mistake she'd made.

Raisa understood the simplicity of guilt, and how addicting it could become. Guilt at least implied some degree of control over your life. You became the driving force of terrible things, and so terrible things would never happen to you again if you were just a better version of yourself.

The universe was random, though. Bad things happened to good people, and all you could do was acknowledge that there was always a chance something devastating could happen again. And you might not have any control over it.

That was a pretty terrifying thing to sit with.

But if they were going to figure out what had really happened to Shay, they had to stop telling stories.

"Or maybe," Raisa said softly, so softly she wasn't sure Kilkenny actually heard, "you had nothing to do with it at all."

CHAPTER EIGHT

Shay

November 2009
Four years before the kidnapping

A strange man stood in Shay's kitchen.

Shay didn't stop to think or consider. She just reached for the wooden baseball bat she kept tucked into the corner near the couch.

The man hadn't heard her come out of her room. Or if he had, he hadn't turned. He simply stood at the sink, eating a piece of toast, shirtless and wearing nicely pressed khakis. The incongruity of it all broke the piece of Shay's brain that wasn't actively figuring out the best way to bust his skull in.

There was a small tattoo on his left shoulder blade, a design she couldn't recognize, and he was smiling out the window as if watching something amusing.

The man wasn't behaving like an intruder, but Shay wasn't about to drop her guard. That would be the kind of stupid that got someone killed.

Her bare feet sank into a sticky patch of carpet where she'd spilled her soda the other day. The sensation reminded her that she had to give the whole place a deep clean, and she immediately shook her head at the thought. She needed to focus.

Shay crept up close while his attention was still locked on the window. When she got nearly within swinging distance, she raised the bat to her shoulder in the perfect stance. She'd played all four years on her high school's softball team, not that there was a lot of competition.

Focus.

She shifted her weight, readying herself, but that's when the squeaky tile they hadn't gotten around to fixing gave away her presence. The man flinched, then turned, his eyes going wide. He held up his hands, palms out, in a universal gesture of peace.

Men lied, though.

"Who the hell are you?" Shay yelled. "You have three seconds before I crack your fucking skull open."

"Jes-us." That was Beau, the back door slamming behind him. In one smooth gesture, he plucked the bat out of Shay's hands. "He's going to think we're feral."

Before she could stop herself, she bared her teeth at her brother, snapped them a bit.

"Oh my god," he groaned, and then pushed her toward her bedroom. "Pants might be nice."

She glanced down to see she was in a T-shirt and boys' briefs, which, when it came down to it, were more modest than a bikini, but she didn't argue. She didn't exactly want to give the stranger a free show.

Beau was still apologizing for her when she walked back into the kitchen, pulling on a pair of jean shorts. She hopped up on the counter and assessed the strange man with a new eye, now knowing he was at least an acquaintance of Beau's.

He was objectively gorgeous, with thick honey-blonde hair that had lighter streaks in it from the summer. His face was that kind of symmetrical that scientists said babies came out of the womb preferring. His muscles had muscles, and she wasn't sure she'd seen abs like that outside of a movie screen.

The man's eyes—an incredible shade of blue that had probably inspired many a teen girl to sigh over her diary—dragged along her body in a similarly assessing fashion. Normally, she would prickle under that kind of gaze, but she'd felt plenty of stares in her life. His wasn't predatory. It was more like he was checking for hidden weapons.

"Sorry," she said, but she knew everyone in the room could hear she didn't mean it. "Maybe you shouldn't stand shirtless in random women's homes at the ass crack of dawn, though."

Beau groaned and ran a hand over his face. Again, he whispered, "Oh my god."

But the man just laughed, an appealing, self-deprecating thing. "I'm not usually in the habit of acting like a creepy serial killer, but that's a good note for any possible next time."

Shay's mouth twitched up, almost involuntarily. "Do you have a list, then? Of how not to be creepy?"

"One item so far," the man said. "I'm sure you'd be a font of advice, though."

"Here, drink your coffee." Beau shoved a mug into Shay's hands like a distraction but also like an apology. He'd made it just the way she liked it. "Sorry, I didn't think we'd wake you."

"It wasn't you," she said, gracious now that she had her caffeine. "Weird dream or something." She turned her attention back to the man. "Why are you shirtless? It's, like, nine in the morning."

Not early for the general populace, of course, but for Shay, who'd closed the bar last night, it might as well have been dawn.

The man's brows wrinkled. "Does the time have to do with whether that's acceptable behavior or not?"

"Ah, research for your list, huh?" she asked, tapping her temple. "Smart."

This sounded like flirting on the surface level, but it was the kind of flirting Shay did with the old men at the bar. Both sides knew there was no intent behind the teasing, so it became harmless fun.

"Shirtless is only okay in someone else's home if it's after noon and you're day drinking," Shay informed him. "It has to be both of those things together."

"Or your dumbass friend spilled coffee all over you on the way to work," Beau chimed in, rummaging through the closet that had probably been intended for coats. Instead, Beau hung all his nice shirts in there. He pulled one free and tossed it and an undershirt to his friend.

"My car's in the shop, and Beau's been giving me a ride, since I live about five minutes that way," the man explained, hooking his thumb over his shoulder in some vague direction. He pulled the undershirt over his head, covering up the work of art that was his six-pack. Shay sighed in general disappointment. She might not be attracted to him—and she refused to think Callum Kilkenny was to blame for that—but she could still appreciate beauty when she saw it. "Most days I wouldn't have minded the stain, but I have an important meeting. Beau said we could swing by here, though he didn't mention the baseball bats."

"Or crazy sister, I'm sure," Shay said, finishing her coffee. "You work at the hospital?"

"Sometimes," the man answered vaguely, and Shay shot a questioning glance at Beau.

But he didn't offer any more information. Instead, he jangled his keys. "Hey, since you're mostly awake, you want to ride in with us to visit Dad?"

Shay thought about what else she could do with the morning—namely, go back to sleep. But one look at Beau's hopeful expression had her agreeing quickly.

"Yeah," she said, hopping off the counter and heading to her bedroom to slip a bra on under her shirt.

"We're late," Beau called.

"Thirty seconds," Shay promised, shoving her feet into a cheap pair of flip-flops. The weather might bend toward cold soon, but it wasn't there yet. "Ta-da."

Beau was scribbling a note for Max, who would probably still be asleep by the time Shay got back.

"How are you going to get home?" Beau's friend asked, that same wrinkle between his brow that appeared whenever he was confused. It was weird that she knew something like that about him already.

"Taxi?" Shay said with a shrug. She didn't bother to think through logistics that often. Things tended to work out for her.

"I'll give you some cash," Beau said quietly as they all skipped down the steps to Beau's car.

She flushed a little at the idea that Beau's friend-slash-coworker had probably heard that. Shay had always prided herself on being good with money. But twelve-year-olds grew at a ridiculously fast rate, ate an absurd amount of food, and always seemed desperate for the coolest thing all their friends had. She could swing unexpected taxi fare, but Beau probably had a slightly cushier rainy-day fund than she did.

Shay took the passenger seat without bothering to check with either one of them, and propped her feet on the dash. The window was already rolled down.

They listened to music on the way in, and didn't talk at all. Shay wondered if that was their normal MO or if she was throwing off their dynamic.

She flicked her eyes up to the rearview mirror and found the man already watching her. Goose bumps bloomed over her skin, the fine hairs on her arms and neck rising as they went.

Shaking off the feeling, she slid her sunglasses into place and dozed for the remaining ten minutes.

Beau headed toward the psychiatric ward when they arrived, after some kind of complicated bro-hug thing and a wish of good luck to his friend. He ruffled Shay's hair as he passed, and slipped her a twenty for the taxi. She pocketed it. "I'll tell him you said hi."

"Thanks," Beau said, even though he'd probably visited Billy before leaving the day before, and honestly Billy was in no shape to understand even the simplest greeting.

Shay ended up riding in a painfully slow elevator with Beau's friend.

"You've been in the area long?" she asked. She wasn't the type who needed to fill silence, but she was actually interested. There was something fun about this guy, and the fact that he'd been able to easily banter with her even after she'd come after him with a baseball bat. Shay had always liked unruffle-able people. It was one of Callum's best qualities.

"About a year," he said.

"Where'd you come from?"

He slid her an assessing look. "Dallas."

"Not far," she said, leaning back against the elevator rails. The doors opened on the floor before Billy's for no reason. She'd gotten used to that at the hospital, though. "Miss it?"

"Yes and no," he said, turning toward her slightly. He didn't seem bothered by the questions, just truly undecided on an answer. "It's not . . . much different. The area."

"Texas is Texas is Texas," she murmured, though she wouldn't know. She'd only ever lived in Houston.

Still, he laughed. "True, true. And, well, I like the work here better. So."

"What did you do back there?"

"Still social worker," he said, with a little self-deprecating grin, seeming to acknowledge the fact that it couldn't be *that* different. Usually men that handsome didn't do self-deprecating well. "But it was with kids. I wasn't good at it."

"Really?" Shay asked, feeling like that confirmed the very uninterested vibes she was picking up. Had he wanted to hit on her, he probably wouldn't have admitted to being bad with children.

"They all knew too much about violence," he said, quietly, meeting her eyes like he knew her past. Like he knew Beau's and Max's as well. And maybe he did. How close were he and Beau? Or was it just obvious?

Shay looked away, and then the door opened. They both stepped off.

"I've got to run," he said, tipping his head toward the hallway that led away from Billy's room. "It was nice meeting you, Shay. Even under threat of baseball bats."

"Hey, same," Shay said, meaning it. "Maybe next time we'll try it without the weapon involved."

He laughed politely and then shifted toward one of the hallways.

"I didn't get your name," she realized, before he could walk out of sight.

"Oh." He smiled. "It's Nathaniel. Nathaniel Conrad."

CHAPTER NINE

Raisa

Now

"Tell me about Shay," Raisa said as the plane leveled out. She didn't have a sense for who this woman was. Just as she'd blamed Kate Tashibi for reducing the victims to names and numbers, Raisa had created a shallow stand-in based on murder-scene photos and myths for a flesh-and-blood person who'd probably had strengths and flaws and a personality.

That was the problem with the way they talked about these victims. They no longer belonged to themselves—they belonged, forever, to the person who had murdered them.

"You would never guess someone like her ended up with someone like me," Kilkenny said, with an incredible amount of fondness.

"What does that mean?" she asked.

"She was really fun," Kilkenny said, and Raisa lifted her brows in surprise. He was right; that wasn't what she'd been expecting. "Really fucking fun."

Raisa huffed out a laugh. "But you two clicked anyway."

"Against all odds," Kilkenny said, his mouth tilting up in acknowledgment of her little chirp. "She was hilarious and quick and smart as hell, though she didn't think so."

"Really?" She'd always imagined Shay Kilkenny as an academic type, though Raisa wasn't sure why. Or a model, the sleek and polished kind to match Kilkenny. All grace, no ketchup stains.

"You remind me a little of her," Kilkenny said, and from anyone else, Raisa would have taken it as a line and thrown up all her brick walls. But the two of them were on the same page about any potential romance. It had been a nonstarter from the word *hello*.

Instead, Raisa took it as a compliment. "She sounds awesome, then."

He laughed. "Yeah."

"What did she like to do for fun?" Raisa asked.

"The beach," Kilkenny said. "Put her near water and she was a happy camper. She even liked our Pacific Northwest beaches."

"Slightly different than Galveston's," Raisa said.

"Right." He smiled softly. "She'd talk me into taking a day off in the middle of the week, and we'd go down to Oregon. Eat good cheese and get drunk on cheap wine." He went quiet before admitting, "She made me remember there were beautiful things in the world. And it wasn't all just terrible trauma and death."

Raisa wondered how many vacation days he'd taken in the past ten years. She didn't think the number reached the double digits. "It sounds like she was good for you."

"She was." He rubbed his thumb over his wedding band. "I'm not sure I was good for her."

"I am," Raisa said.

"You have to say that," he said, predictably. Kilkenny always appeared so confident, and he was, in his job. But outside of that, he carried around the weight of Shay's death like it was an indictment on who he was as a person.

Even for the five seconds she'd wondered if he'd been the one to kill Shay, Raisa had always known he was *good*. At least, well meaning, which she put a hell of a lot of stock into even if it sounded like she was damning him with faint praise.

She thought about the way he had sent her texts every few days as his own version of a wellness check over the past three months, how he'd compiled a list of therapists but didn't nag her to go see one. How he'd met her at the courthouse door.

"I really don't." She exhaled before he could argue further, shifting the subject. "Okay, if you were approaching this case without any attachments to it, what would you think?"

"I would think horses and not zebras," he said. "Conrad killed Shay and is lying about it for attention or some other reason we haven't figured out yet."

"And if he's not?"

He shook his head, at a loss.

"Okay." She tried to force herself to think of the problem sideways. What if Kilkenny wasn't the reason Shay was killed? What if Conrad wasn't? "You said she was tight with her family. Tell me about them."

"A mixed bag," Kilkenny said. "Her mother, Hillary, was narcissistic and emotionally abusive. She had full custody of Shay, though sometimes pawned her off with Beau and his father, Billy. Who was also abusive and an alcoholic."

"Beau?" Raisa asked.

"Shay's half brother," Kilkenny clarified. "She had two siblings—that we knew of, at least. Beau was a couple years younger than her. They were incredibly close, and after Hillary left to places unknown, they became co-guardians of their sister, Max."

"Who also had an abusive father?" Raisa guessed.

"Hillary knew how to pick 'em," Kilkenny said, his lingering and warranted bitterness clear. "Max's father was killed in a robbery gone wrong when she was eleven, and Shay took her in. Beau moved in to help, since both of them had somewhat erratic schedules."

"What did Beau do?" Raisa asked.

"Nurse at the local hospital," he said.

"What was he like?"

"Old soul," Kilkenny said, without missing a beat. "Reliable. A little bit of a bastard, when it was warranted."

"It must have been hard for them," Raisa said. "Raising a kid. Especially when they hadn't had the best childhood themselves."

"Shay never complained," he said. "Which didn't mean it wasn't difficult. Max was . . ."

When he trailed off, Raisa bumped her knee against his. "What?"

"Challenging."

"Preteen challenging or . . . ?" She let him fill in the blank, and he did.

"When I met them, Max was seeing a psychiatrist who specialized in violent children," Kilkenny said.

"Oh-kay." Raisa drew out the word, processing that. "Violent as in she could kill her sister and frame a serial killer while doing it?"

"No," Kilkenny said, quickly. Maybe too quickly. "Nothing I ever saw indicated that she had a personality disorder that would lead to that kind of behavior." He paused. "Although I didn't spend much time with her. She might have been a very good actress."

"There must have been an incident in her past that would have led to her seeing the psychiatrist in the first place," Raisa said. He slid her a look, and her brain caught up with her mouth.

Robbery gone wrong. Abusive father. Dead father. "Ah."

"Just rumors," Kilkenny said. "Shay never confirmed it either way."

Everyone was capable of killing. Not everyone was capable of murder.

"It would have been like long-term self-defense," she mused.

"That's likely why no one pursued anything," Kilkenny said. "That, and there was no hard evidence beyond blood on her clothes. Which she said she got from feeling for a pulse. They weren't about to waste too many resources trying to lock up an eleven-year-old girl over the death of an asshole who'd made her life hell."

"How old was she when Shay was killed?"

"Sixteen," he said, and they met each other's eyes. Other people might say that was too young to commit a crime like the one that had been done to Shay. But they'd both just seen how dangerous Isabel Parker had been at that age—she'd murdered three members of her family to kick off a twenty-five-year killing career.

"Are you still in contact with her?" Raisa asked.

"No, she left Houston about a year after Shay died," he said. "She cut all ties with everyone here, and to be honest, I didn't try very hard to find her. She had no love lost for me."

"Is Beau still in the city?"

Kilkenny nodded. "Still lives in their house, still works at the hospital."

Yet both of his sisters were gone. "Was there ever any talk of Max coming to live with you guys when Shay moved up to Seattle?"

"No, Beau didn't want to leave Texas," Kilkenny said. "Neither did Shay, honestly. I put in a request for a transfer, but it was denied. Then Shay got pregnant and that forced her hand."

"Oh," Raisa murmured softly, surprised but trying not to show it. Kilkenny was staring hard at the seat back in front of him, his jaw tight and his hands clenched together. No one had ever mentioned a child, so it didn't take much to guess what had happened. There was no need to push him further on a loss that would have been made all the more heartbreaking for what had followed.

"It was hard on Shay," he continued. "Living in Washington, leaving them behind. And then we lost the baby . . ."

Raisa nudged his knee again, this time in silent support. "Did she want to go back to Texas?"

"At that point, no." He looked out the window, at the sunrise that was creeping along marshmallow clouds. "She was depressed. I'm sure of it, though she didn't receive an actual diagnosis. I was away so much, she was alone so much."

There was another story to tell. What had Shay been up to in that time period? If this were a different case, Raisa might have started digging. Had there been a lover? One who'd seen a way out of some complicated situation when he realized exactly who Shay's husband was?

Replicating the Alphabet Man's MO would have been brutal for any non-psychopath, though. The postmortem tattooing alone would probably dissuade the cruelest of them when they started to consider it. It sounded like anyone who wanted to kill Shay simply could have faked a suicide and had a chance of getting away with it.

"Why were you denied a transfer?" Raisa asked.

Kilkenny was like her—he got shipped around where he was needed far more than he worked out of any one office. Stationing him in Texas almost made more sense than having him on one side of the country.

"They never gave me a reason," Kilkenny said. "It always made me wonder, though."

"Did Xander Pierce make that decision?" Raisa asked, trying to remember how high he'd been in the chain at that point. "You would have thought he wanted you close by for the Alphabet Man investigation."

"I don't know," Kilkenny said, with a shrug. He didn't sound suspicious, though. "I suppose it's possible Pierce could have poisoned that well even if he wasn't making the actual decision, but I doubt it. We were good friends at the time. Why wouldn't he have wanted me down there?"

Raisa hummed in acknowledgment, not agreement.

She didn't know the answer to that, but she thought it might be a more interesting one than he seemed to want to consider.

CHAPTER TEN

Shay

January 2010
Four years before the kidnapping

Callum Kilkenny sat at the end of the bar.

Shay smiled at the sight of him, told herself not to, and then frowned for real when she saw the man next to him.

He was tall, broad shouldered, and dressed just like Callum. Not like Callum, she corrected. Callum wouldn't be caught dead in that tie or jacket with its too-short cuffs.

But the man was in a suit, and he had the distinct, watchful air of law enforcement.

Xander Pierce. She hadn't realized until that moment that Callum had talked about him enough that she could guess who he was without ever having met him before.

Shay ducked back into the kitchen, running into Melissa as she did.

"Hey," the new girl said, startled as she ended up with an armful of Shay.

"Can you cover for me?" Shay asked, already heading toward the back-alley exit. "Just for five minutes."

Just long enough to settle her nerves. She wasn't made for this life of hiding crimes, not when she was dating an FBI agent.

"No, it's Friday night," Melissa called, panic in her voice. She wasn't cut out for the bartending life, and Shay doubted she would last more than another few weekends. Lonnie had only hired her, off the books, because Shay had threatened to quit without a little extra help. In typical Lonnie fashion, he'd put in a half-assed attempt to make it look like he cared. Once the girl quit, Shay doubted he would fill the position again. And of course her threat had been empty. She needed the money.

But for now, in theory, Shay had backup, and she was going to take advantage of that fact.

The night air greeted her like a desperately needed slap in the face. Shay gulped in oxygen as she leaned back against the wall. The overhang protected her from the January rain, but her shoes were soaked in under a minute. Normally she loved a good torrential downpour, the water washing away all manner of sins.

Now it made her feel like she was drowning.

The heavy metal door slammed against the wall. Her racing heart stuttered and then revved, and spots popped in her vision.

When she got her breath back, she turned to bitch out Melissa for scaring the shit out of her.

Except that's not who stood there, haloed by the weak parking lot light in the distance.

"Nathaniel Conrad," she said, and his lips twitched up. As if she wouldn't have remembered him—he looked like Brad Pitt in his prime.

"I saw you fly out of there," he said, grabbing a cigarette pack from his back jeans pocket. "Wanted to make sure you were okay." He paused, ran a hand through his hair. "Beau would want me to."

He added that last part like he was feeling self-conscious about the decision to follow her.

She exhaled a shaky laugh and took the cigarette he'd lit for her. "I didn't even see you come in."

"It's busy," he said, with a careless shrug. "The feds spook you?"

"No." It came out too quick to be the truth, and they both knew it. She made a face. "So you spotted them, too."

"They might as well have been wearing neon signs."

"Right," Shay said, relaxing enough to laugh. "My mom gets into all kinds of trouble."

"Makes you nervous around law enforcement," he guessed.

"Yeah." It wasn't a lie. It wasn't the truth. It was what she could offer him. "And she's been calling around a lot lately. Asking for money we don't have. As if we're not raising her kid for her."

Beau hadn't been clear about how close he and Nathaniel were. Maybe she was sharing too many secrets with someone who was nothing more than a distant coworker. But there was something about the rain and the night and knowing so many people were behind them, locked away by that thick metal door, that had her wanting to confide in him.

And maybe there was something about Nathaniel.

"I'm sorry you have to deal with that," he said, which was essentially the perfect response. He hadn't offered to swoop in and save the day; he hadn't offered pity. Just gentle sympathy.

He flicked his cigarette to the ground despite the fact that it was far from done.

"Trying to quit," he admitted, staring at the butt for a second before bending to pick it up. He tucked it into his front pocket, a move she found incredibly endearing. "We all have our vices, I guess."

Shay gestured to her own, determined to savor it, and the nicotine, as long as she could. She rarely smoked, but when she did, she made damn sure the experience was worth it. "There are worse things in the world."

Something flitted across his face, but it was gone too quickly to tell what emotion it had been. Amusement, maybe. Or a distant cousin to it.

They stood in silence for a few minutes before Nathaniel dug in his pocket once more, reemerging with a set of keys. "I've got a full tank of gas and a map to Mexico if you want to flee the feds."

"Rain check," she said, and he laughed. The nervous energy had been burned out of her with amazing speed, and she knew who was responsible for that. "Thank you."

"Hey, it's a selfish offer. It would have made for a fun story," he said, deliberately misunderstanding her gratitude. But she knew he knew she was thanking him for more than just an escape plan.

"You headed back in?" she asked, going for the door.

"Nah, I've had enough fun, I think, for one evening," he said, the corner of his mouth quirking up with that same fleeting emotion from earlier. Again, it was gone before she could really process it. "You watch your back."

"Always do," Shay said, as she stepped inside, tossing a wink over her shoulder.

The door closed on Nathaniel watching her.

Melissa had tears in her eyes when she ran into Shay in the kitchen.

"They're animals out there," Melissa all but wailed, the heels of her palms swiping at her cheeks.

"Oh my god, take five," Shay said, knowing at this point Melissa would be more trouble than she was worth.

"I'm taking fifteen," Melissa said, as she headed toward the exit. Shay rolled her eyes at the girl's back, then put her out of her mind.

Shay took a deep breath before heading toward the bar.

Six customers in various states of irritation waited for her, so it took another ten minutes to work her way down toward Callum and the man she guessed to be his colleague.

"What's a guy like you doing in a place like this?" she asked Callum, leaning into the cheese of it to cover her nerves.

"Hey, don't talk shit about my favorite place in Houston," he said, the hint of a dimple teasing her, and she laughed, finally relaxed enough to turn her attention to the other man.

A cowboy, had been her first reaction, and she stood by it. He was all limbs, long and rangy, his face tanned, almost leathery, from a life spent beneath a Texas sun. He must be local or from the south, at least.

His build leaned toward skinny, but she could tell it was more than that—he'd lost weight recently, his cheeks hollow, his skin stretching over his bones. If he was who she guessed he was, then the answer as to why was obvious. By now these two had probably been hunting the serial killer for the past four months straight.

"Well, you look like you do belong in a place like this," Shay said to the man she assumed was Special Agent in Charge Xander Pierce.

That surprised a laugh out of him, some of the hard lines in his face going soft. Callum ducked his head and smiled, as if she'd made him proud with the banter but he didn't want to be obvious about it.

"Fair enough," the man said, and held out an enormous calloused palm. "Xander Pierce, pleasure to meet you."

So Callum had told him who she was.

"Shay," she said, skipping the surname. He probably already knew it, but there was no reason to just hand it over on the off chance he didn't. "Looks like you're ready for another."

"Nah, I'll head out," he said. "Early start tomorrow."

Callum still had half a drink left, so it made it easy for him to linger. He nodded to Pierce and then settled even more comfortably into the spot that had become his. Normally, he'd strike up a conversation with one of the regulars, but he was quiet tonight.

Shay was too busy to babysit him, but she made sure to pour him a club soda after he'd finished his whiskey. He smiled his thanks, his thumb brushing over the knob of her wrist in one of those tiny gestures of intimacy that Shay had always pretended she didn't want.

"Hard day?" she asked later. They were in his hotel bed, that same generic, budget place that was technically walking distance from the bar. She was glad he'd driven that night, though. The rain hadn't let up.

He wasn't allowed to talk about his work. Sometimes he alluded to it, and they both knew why he was in Houston. But he was professional to a fault.

There was an aura about him tonight that had her pushing, just a little bit.

"They gave him a nickname," he said. The room was dark, and the storm raged against the windows.

Shay rolled onto her back, staring at the ceiling. "I'm shocked it took this long." When he didn't say anything, she cleared her throat. "Is it 'the tattoo man'?"

He huffed out a breath. "That might be better. The Alphabet Man."

She made a face that he wouldn't be able to see. "Not exactly clever."

"Easy to say, easy to remember," Callum said. "It'll stick."

He sounded so resigned about it, she reached out and laced their fingers together.

"I just hate when they get names," he continued, the words spilling out like he couldn't physically contain them any longer. "It means people will talk about them forever."

From her tally, this serial killer had taken at least six victims. Nickname or not, he was going to be infamous. She didn't bother to point that out. Callum knew.

"He's killing so fast," Shay said.

Callum shook his head. "No, we're just finding bodies that were already dumped."

That made more sense. He must have felt her relax, because he rolled up onto one elbow so he could stare down into her face.

"You should start carrying Mace," he said, after a long moment. "Or a gun, if you feel comfortable with one."

"Mace," she said, as if it were a promise, though she wasn't sure she'd fulfill it. "Should we all be terrified right now?"

"No, you should just be smart," Callum said, like the professional he was. "Listen to your instincts, don't walk alone at night to your car. Things like that. Things you've been trained all your life to do as a woman in this world."

When he said that kind of stuff, Shay wanted to get up and walk away from him. Because if she didn't now, how would she do it after she'd already fallen hard?

And she had to walk away from him, because the only way this ended for her otherwise was heartache.

What was he going to do? Move his entire life down to Texas for a bartender who shared custody of a twelve-year-old girl who may or may not be a psychopath?

Normally, now was the time she'd get up and get dressed, flee the emotions that nipped at her heels. But there was a serial killer out there, and the bed was warm.

So she stayed.

———

Shay didn't expect to see Callum the next day, and she didn't. The bar was so busy she would have only barely noticed him anyway.

"Where's my help, Lonnie?" Shay yelled the one time the man deigned to make an appearance.

"Hey, get off my dick. I didn't fire her—she just didn't show up," he said, trying and failing to hide a smug smile. "No one can handle tough work these days."

Shay thought about Melissa's tear-streaked face, and how over-whelmed she'd been from a normal Friday-night crowd.

She rolled her eyes. She would never say it out loud, but just this one time she agreed with Lonnie.

TRANSCRIPT FROM "COLD CASE CUCKOOS" DISCORD CHAT
Five months before the Alphabet Man's execution

ICEICEBABY: Late night musings: Does anyone else think they missed some Alphabet Man vics?

COOLERTHANBEINGCOOL: Oh, a hundo percent. Give us ur thots tho vanilla ice

ICEICEBABY: OK, Melissa Sturgeon, 21, went missing right in that first six months they were finding all the bodies . . . she was getting a degree in fashion . . . friends describe her as fun, sweet, and outgoing.

OFICEANDMEN: AKA she liked to PARTAY

ICEICEBABY: Word . . . so anyway, like I said, she went missing in the right time frame the right county and get this . . .

COOLERTHANBEINGCOOL: are you waiting for a drumroll? 🥁

ICEICEBABY: 👇 so I have a friend of a friend of a friend

OFICEANDMEN: Of a cousin of a step sister of a neighbor of a friend . . .

ICEICEBABY: 👇👇 who says Melissa got an off-the-books job at a bar that CALLUM KILKENNY was known to frequent

COOLERTHANBEINGCOOL: 🫠

ICEICEBABY: There's more. Rumor is that's where he met Shay

COOLERTHANBEINGCOOL:

OFICEANDMEN: Are you saying the Alphabet Man was following Kilkenny from day one?

ICEICEBABY: I'm saying coincidences don't exist in serial killer cases. Melissa's body was never found, so we don't know if there would have been tattoos on it

COOLERTHANBEINGCOOL: But there was no letter with her name . . .

ICEICEBABY: Don't call me a tin-hatter here, but . . . I think sometimes he just killed because he was mad

OFICEANDMEN: wut?

ICEICEBABY: We know the first vic wasn't planned. He got upset about something in Houston when he was interviewing down there, remember? Sidney Stewart, the first vic, just worked at a random gas station between Houston and Dallas, where he had been living. The letter he sent about her wasn't dated . . . the sheriff's department didn't record when they received it . . . so maybe he sent it after and made it look like it was all part of his signature . . . What if his first killing—and others like Melissa—was just him throwing a tantrum?

COOLERTHANBEINGCOOL: gross

ICEICEBABY: I mean yeah, I know, I'm not making light of it . . . But what if he trailed Callum to the bar and then saw him and

Shay being all flirty flirty heart eyes and it set him off? Maybe he became obsessed with her that night and the timing to kill her just didn't feel right until years later? But he took it out on Melissa?

COOLERTHANBEINGCOOL: OR what if his crazy brain picked Melissa as a vic but didn't want her linked back to him in any way because he picked her up from the bar K was at? Im not a shrink, does that make sense? That he could kill her and not go through with his whole schtick?

ICEICEBABY: Seems possible! Maybe this new doc will dive deep on that ... but I'm not hopeful ...

OFICEANDMEN: me neither ... hey did anyone ever figure out what set him off in houston? Could be interesting. That first kill seems like a pretty big deal from what I've read (not a shrink, just an aficionado)

ICEICEBABY: I know some people think it's because he was interviewing for a social worker job, and it brought up memories of his *traumatic past*

OFICEANDMEN: you don't sound convinced

ICEICEBABY: He was a social worker in Dallas. What could he have experienced during the interview process that would have been worse than what he already saw in his day-to-day life?

OFICEANDMEN: OK vanilla ice, color me intrigued. What do you think happened?

COOLERTHANBEINGCOOL: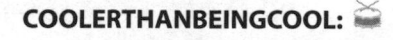

ICEICEBABY: I don't think it was some*thing* that triggered him—I think it was some*one*

COOLERTHANBEINGCOOL: duhn duhn duhnnnnnnnnnn

CHAPTER ELEVEN

Raisa

Now

FBI Special Agent in Charge Xander Pierce was waiting for Raisa and Kilkenny in the parking lot of the prison just outside Houston. As she'd remembered, he was lean and tall and handsome.

He and Kilkenny hugged like old friends. Considering they'd spent five years hunting down a serial killer together, she probably should have expected the greeting.

"You look old as shit," Pierce said, still gripping Kilkenny with one hand and slapping his shoulder with the other.

"Back at you." Kilkenny grinned. It was all very Male Bonding 101. "Thanks for coming out."

"Of course." Pierce glanced at the concrete walls behind him. "He's lying, though. You know that, right?"

"Yeah, I know," Kilkenny agreed, despite the fact that they both had doubts about that. "I just . . . I need to make sure. I would regret it the rest of my life if I didn't."

"I get it," Pierce said, though there was a sharpness to his voice that hadn't been there before. This had to be hard on him. He had been the lead agent on the Alphabet Man case, of course. But what was more important was that he'd led the investigation into Shay's death. The fact that Kilkenny didn't trust the results must hit like a personal blow.

If it got out that Kilkenny was down here because of the new information released by Kate Tashibi, it could tarnish Pierce's reputation as well. Cynically, Raisa wondered if that was the reason Pierce wanted to take a hands-on approach here. He could make sure he tilted this in a way that would reflect best on him.

Or maybe he just wanted to help an old friend, and Raisa was being a judgmental dick.

Probably it was a little of both, as most things were.

Pierce's attention slid to her for the first time. His expression turned speculative, and she didn't blame him. Her friendship with Kilkenny was so new, it hadn't made it to the Bureau's gossip grapevine. "Agent Susanto. A pleasure to have you in Texas again."

There was a question in the space following the greeting, but Raisa didn't rush to fill it. She didn't care if people talked or speculated. That was none of her business, and she had the track record to keep the whispers just that.

"Good to be back," she said. "Are you joining the interrogation?"

They moved as one toward the front gates.

"If you'll have me," Pierce said.

Of course they would have him. There had been a narrative built around the idea of the Alphabet Man versus FBI agent Callum Kilkenny. It had an appealing cinematic quality to it—a real-life showdown between an expert psychologist and a serial-killer mastermind. But as it often did, mythology had flattened reality into black and white. In truth, Pierce may have even known Conrad better than Kilkenny did.

After all, Pierce had been the point person receiving reports from the entire task force, not just Kilkenny. Kilkenny may have done a deep dive into the killer's psyche, but he'd also flown in and out of the case, coming to Houston only as needed. Pierce had probably lived and breathed the Alphabet Man investigation for five years straight.

"You think he's lying?" Raisa asked Pierce once they got through the prison's security process.

"Of course. Conrad loves getting attention from both the media and Kilkenny," Pierce said. "I'm sure he wants to have one last confrontation with Kilkenny." He paused, thoughtful. "Honestly, I think this might be the cherry on the top. He really just wanted back in the spotlight. Now people are buzzing about this miniseries. He might even think he can magic up a stay with this."

The idea slammed into her, not because it was shocking but because she felt a little foolish for not thinking of it herself. She could tell from Kilkenny's expression that he hadn't traveled down that path, either.

It made sense, though. If Conrad could convince Kilkenny that he had information on Shay's death, there was a chance in some universe that either Kilkenny or Pierce would want to keep him alive until they figured out the whole mess.

Would buying a day, a week, a month appeal so strongly to Conrad that he would lie about his victim count?

Still . . . there were the letters.

Her science proved that he was telling the truth, or at least part of it.

"Did any other suspects come up during the investigation into Shay's death?" Raisa asked, as they settled into the interview room they'd been assigned.

Pierce leaned against the wall closest to the door. He briefly met Kilkenny's eyes before returning his attention to Raisa. "The Alphabet Man left the first letter with her car."

"So you didn't investigate anyone else?" Raisa pressed, not to be antagonistic but because she needed a clear answer.

"No," Pierce said. "We knew we had three days to find Shay. We didn't want to waste time with anything else."

As much as field agents wanted to dismiss her experience sometimes, Raisa wasn't a newbie to task forces. The one in Houston would have been up and running for four years by the time Shay was taken.

There would have been a few spare men to chase down speculative leads, no matter how wild.

At least that's how well-organized task forces operated, and she'd always been under the impression that Pierce's fell under that category.

Perhaps she'd been wrong there.

"There was nothing to suggest someone could be framing the Alphabet Man?" Raisa asked.

"Everything matched his MO," Pierce said, a muscle in his jaw ticking.

She wasn't even interrogating him, not really, and he was getting annoyed.

"But all of that was public knowledge," Raisa said. "I know you wouldn't have been able to tell the letters were different at the time—"

"What?" Pierce cut in.

Shit, she was tired. She'd meant to keep that close to the vest. Still, when she glanced over to Kilkenny, he simply shrugged. So she explained the two-author scenario to Pierce.

"I was going to say, though, that you wouldn't have been able to tell that before decrypting it, of course."

Pierce rubbed his hand over his face. "I'm not sure that would have been enough to convince us anyway. He might as well have left a neon arrow pointing at himself."

Or someone else had. Raisa wasn't going to continue banging her head against that brick wall.

"Well, it's enough to convince plenty of judges," Raisa said, coolly. "Okay, just because we have time, let's go do some wild theorizing. Hypothetically, do you have any gut instinct on who would have killed Shay and framed Conrad?"

Pierce looked to Kilkenny, his eyes clearly telegraphing, *Can you believe this?*

But Kilkenny just stared back, waiting for an answer.

Something warm and pleased bloomed in her chest at his silence. She and Kilkenny? They were a team. They would provide a united front even if they disagreed, because that's what partners did.

She swallowed against her suddenly dry throat, and turned her attention back to Pierce.

He lifted one shoulder. "It seems like a pointless exercise."

"Does it?" Raisa asked, and then looked around the room, reminding them all where they were. They had enough doubt that they were currently tap-dancing to Conrad's tune. A little bit of brainstorming didn't seem like it would hurt.

Pierce exhaled, his nostrils flaring with his frustration.

"Her family was a mess." He grimaced. "Sorry, K."

Kilkenny shook off the apology. "That wasn't a secret. I've already filled Raisa in on some of it."

"Yeah, well, there's some of it you might not know," Pierce said. "Hillary, the mother, was into everything in the borderlands of legal. And most things over the line as well. Drugs, guns, prostitution. It was usually her boyfriends running the deals, but she didn't exactly object to the paydays."

"But Hillary was never arrested?" Raisa asked.

"No, that woman was Teflon."

Raisa gamed out a scenario where a mother could torture and kill her daughter. She knew better than most that familial ties didn't always matter, not to a narcissistic sociopath. But if Hillary'd had violent tendencies, it was doubtful she would have been able to keep herself out of jail her entire life. "Was she still in contact with Shay?"

"She didn't even come to the funeral," Kilkenny said, the bitterness as sharp as if it had happened recently. "She'd swing by every once in a while, try to steal some money, use the house as a place to crash, and then leave town again."

Even if Shay had gotten caught up in something Hillary was doing, it was hard to imagine a drug lord or pimp going to the effort of covering their tracks in such a way. When men like that had a body to get rid of, they had more efficient means than pretending to be a serial killer.

When she explained that, Kilkenny nodded, thoughtful.

"So, seems a stretch to say that had anything to do with it," Raisa said, and Pierce made a sound that was somehow both agreement and derision.

"Right, because Conrad is lying," Pierce said, as if talking about it for five minutes and dismissing the most obvious alternate theory were really proving his point. "He's the one who killed Shay."

"Maybe, but not necessarily," Raisa said. "What about the siblings? Did they have alibis?"

She was mostly thinking about Max, the half sister. But Beau interested her as well. He was a nurse, which meant he was more comfortable with the reality of death. The brutality of it. Maybe he'd become numb enough to be able to tattoo a cipher on his dead sister's arm.

Pierce rocked back on his heels. "Max was at home. No one could account for her whereabouts, but she didn't have a car."

That was hardly an issue for an ambitious young woman. "And the brother?"

"He worked at the hospital," Kilkenny chimed in. "Security footage puts him there for most of the window of her kidnapping."

"You can believe he wasn't happy that I checked that, either," Pierce said.

"Why did you?" With everything else he was saying, he hadn't even seemed to have considered anyone outside of the Alphabet Man.

"You always check family," Pierce said with a shrug.

"Are the hospital and mall close?"

"Close enough," Kilkenny said, grim now. "They were relying on witness statements, too, to place how long Shay's car had been there."

"Oh, jeez," Raisa muttered. Witness statements were as reliable as a broken clock—correct about one out of twelve times. "So, he's in play as a suspect."

"Maybe," Pierce said.

Raisa pretended not to hear the doubt in his voice.

"Okay, so Beau is one person to look at. Her father was . . . not in the picture?" Raisa asked.

"No, and she always said that was a blessing, considering what type of guy Hillary went for," Kilkenny said.

"Asshole?" Raisa asked, and he huffed out a breath.

"Exactly."

"And you said Shay didn't have any friends?" Raisa asked.

"No one close. She worked at a bar, so there were always people passing through," Kilkenny said. "But if this was just a random act of violence, well, I keep coming back to the point you made. There are easier ways in Texas to get rid of a body than framing a serial killer."

"Right, which was why it was Conrad," Pierce said, as if that concluded the conversation. "Once he has Kilkenny's attention, he'll overplay his hand. You'll see."

As if Pierce had planned it, the door swung open.

And Raisa got her first glimpse of the Alphabet Man.

KATE TASHIBI (VOICE-OVER): Long before Nathaniel Conrad was known as the Alphabet Man, he made headlines as the Survivor. That's because little ten-year-old Nate was the only one to make it out alive after Nathaniel Sr. poisoned his wife, his three children, and himself over Sunday dinner.

FIRST RESPONDER ETHAN JACOBS: I was the first person on the scene that morning. The neighbor called us after she hadn't seen anyone in the family outside for three days. Three days. Do you know what that does to a body? And the two kids . . . I'll never forget that sight for as long as I live.

NEIGHBOR MARIE D'NATA: They were *such* a lovely family. The two girls could have been twins, and their mother always dressed them in matching skirts and cardigans. They couldn't have been sweeter. The mother volunteered at every church function you can imagine, and had the best recipe for a yummy peach cobbler. Nate? How would I have described him? Well, now I know better. But I would have said, *Dennis the Menace*. Mischievous, maybe, but a good boy.

TASHIBI: You were the one who called the police weren't you?

D'NATA: Oh, yes. Paul, my husband, told me not to, of course. Told me I was being too nosy like usual. My whole family used to tease me about that. They never did once after that, though, mark my words. But the Conrads hadn't gone to church, which was already unusual. Come Monday morning, and Nathaniel Sr. didn't go to work. I went over and knocked on their door, but all their lights were out. By Wednesday, I'd had enough. I figured the most the police could do was laugh at me.

TASHIBI: No one laughed at you.

D'NATA: *[sniffle]* No. No they did not.

TASHIBI (VOICE-OVER): In the chaos that followed the discovery of the family, it took another four hours before anyone realized little Nate was unaccounted for. The sheriff's department assembled a search party, but they didn't need to look far. Nate had escaped into an abandoned barn behind the family property. He had a broken leg and was severely dehydrated, but otherwise he was in good shape. Children are resilient like that, the doctors said.

PSYCHOLOGIST HENRI OLIVER: Now, Conrad wasn't a patient of mine.

TASHIBI: Understood.

OLIVER: Even if Nate was fine physically, the trauma would have caused deep, deep wounds. Since he didn't return to the house, we can safely assume he realized what had happened, and that someone in his family had killed the rest.

TASHIBI: Looking back now, is there any chance that Nate might have been the one to poison his family that day?

OLIVER: I suppose anything is possible. The only hint of abuse in the family were three hospital visits for the two girls. The fact that the mother never sought care for herself might indicate that it was Nate who was causing the injuries instead of the father.

TASHIBI: Or they were simply childhood accidents.

OLIVER: Yes, we might never know. The fact that he rates highly on the Hare scale that measures psychopathic traits in individuals, though, means we can't rule anything out. But if it was his father, it's amazing the young Nathaniel survived. He was a small child to begin with. And then three days outside. He was lucky it was summer. He was lucky he threw up the poison. He was lucky for a lot of reasons.

TASHIBI (VOICE-OVER): Maybe so. But can the same be said for the rest of the world? It's chilling to think how many lives would have been saved had he been just a little less lucky.

CHAPTER TWELVE

Raisa

Now

Nathaniel Conrad was not immune to prison. Just like with Isabel, his shine had dimmed.

There had been a period of time after he'd been arrested that a small, but vocal, group of people had declared him too beautiful to be guilty. When he gave interviews, he was not only gorgeous but able to fake sincerity with incredible ease. His supporters simply played videos of him as proof that he couldn't have been butchering women for five years.

Now, he looked beaten down, his hair dishwater instead of golden, his skin sallow instead of tanned. He was missing one of his incisors and the front tooth beside it, so the smile he gave them was upsetting to look at rather than charming.

There was some magnetism left, Raisa realized as her body swayed toward him for no reason. Some people just had that within them—a current that even life inside these desolate walls couldn't take away.

As the guard went through the motions of chaining him to the table, Raisa fought off déjà vu from the day before. The entire time Kilkenny had been helping her hunt down Isabel, he'd kept returning to Nathaniel Conrad, the similarities in their puppet-master person-alities too strong to ignore. Seeing them both behind bars now drove that home.

"Agents, what a surprise," Conrad drawled in a way that made it clear it wasn't. Whether he was lying about Shay or not, he had been banking on the fact that Kilkenny would come down to make sure it wasn't true.

His attention slid to Raisa. "You're pretty."

"I am pretty, thank you. But you don't care about that, do you?" Raisa asked, and had the pleasure of seeing surprise flit in and out of Conrad's eyes. There were plenty of reasons that might explain why Conrad hadn't sexually assaulted his victims. But she'd found that most of those came from someone looking at the crime through a heteronor-mative lens. They talked a lot about him not wanting to leave evidence behind, as if that had never occurred to the majority of serial killers who raped their victims. Kilkenny had suggested Conrad might be impotent, and the killings could be some sort of outlet for his sexual frustration and shame. Even on some of the more open-minded mes-sage boards she'd checked out, people simply thought he was gay.

The speculation had never gone beyond the gay/straight binary.

Raisa had a broader frame of reference. She'd been friends with plenty of sex workers as a teenager living mostly on the streets and had gravitated toward people in college and grad school who were gender and sexuality majors.

If she had to guess, she'd say Conrad was on the asexual spectrum, perhaps even sex-repulsed.

"Mmm. You're a clever one, aren't you, Agent Susanto?" Conrad leered. "Which is something I *do* care about."

"That would be a lot more terrifying if you weren't chained to a table, less than two days out from execution," Raisa said, making sure to sound incredibly bored.

"Perhaps you should ask your sister how easy it is to get things done from the inside."

He wanted a reaction, but Raisa wouldn't give it to him. They already knew Isabel had a hand in this in some way. And like Isabel, Conrad hadn't been able to resist giving up information just for the sake of a jab. It was both something to keep in mind and further proof that Kilkenny had been right about their similarities.

"So, you're saying all this was her doing and not yours." Raisa knew how someone like Isabel would react if challenged like that. But he just smirked.

"Or maybe it was Kate Tashibi," Raisa pressed, "who orchestrated all this."

Conrad rolled his eyes. "Ms. Tashibi couldn't find her way out of a paper bag."

Raisa would never call herself Kate Tashibi's biggest fan, but the woman hadn't struck her as incompetent or stupid. Maybe it was pure misogyny speaking. But he had just admitted Raisa was clever.

So maybe . . .

Maybe he didn't want them to realize Kate *had* figured something out on her own, and whatever had helped her crack his code, metaphorically speaking, might be different from what Isabel had discovered. Maybe more evidence existed to prove that Conrad hadn't killed Shay, but it would give away something Conrad wanted to keep hidden.

Before Raisa could press further, Conrad continued.

"Your sister must have filled Ms. Tashibi in on the details, and so there were two people out there who knew my secret. By then, I knew my story would be told whether I liked it or not," he said. "If I gave Ms. Tashibi her interview, at least I would know it would be a good representation of what actually happened. God forbid, I go to my grave and have my documentary end up chock-full of those terrible reenactment scenes."

He shuddered theatrically. "Those are just cringey."

They *were* embarrassing, but Raisa wasn't going to agree with him. Not when she felt like he was leading them on a merry chase with his answers. She just couldn't figure out what he gained from lying right now, a day before his execution, when he'd already divulged the most shocking revelation he could.

Even as she had the thought, it occurred to her that this very confusion might be at the heart of it all—in theory, if he'd already divulged his most closely guarded secret, why would anyone think to probe deeper?

But if he was using the Shay confession as camouflage, that meant he was hiding a bigger secret than admitting he hadn't killed his most well-known victim.

That seemed impossible.

"This is all just bullshit," Pierce said. "Why are you lying about Shay?"

"What if I told you it was to get a stay?" Conrad asked.

It was Kilkenny who answered. "That's not the reason."

He said it quietly and with such certainty that the room dropped silent for a moment.

Conrad's eyes flicked to Kilkenny and then back to Raisa. It was only in that moment that she realized how little he'd looked at Kilkenny. If his primary motive for this stunt was to engage Kilkenny in one last confrontation, wouldn't Conrad be focused on him? Instead, he'd been talking mostly with Raisa, without any attempt to draw Kilkenny into the conversation.

"Believe me or not, I didn't kill Shay," Conrad finally said.

Something about that struck Raisa, and she parsed each word to figure out why.

Ms. Tashibi. Agent Susanto. He was formal in how he addressed them.

He lingered over Shay's name with a familiarity she found disturbing. Serial killers became attached to their victims, of course, but this seemed slightly different. He said her name like he was talking about a friend.

"You were framed," Pierce said flatly. "You and all your neighbors on death row, you guys are innocent, you swear."

Conrad sighed. "Not innocent. But not guilty of killing Shay."

"Why come out with the truth now?" Raisa asked. "Isabel said she figured this all out five years ago."

"Did she now?" Conrad lifted a shoulder. "I suppose I have a flair for the dramatic. And like I said, I wanted to set the record straight before I'm murdered myself."

Pierce's mouth pressed into a straight line of displeasure at the framing of that. Raisa agreed with Conrad in theory—capital punishment had always struck her as hypocritical and barbaric. But as she looked into Conrad's empty eyes while he made sure they knew just how many girls he'd killed, she could admit that, for her, there were exceptions to be made.

"Who killed her if you didn't?" Raisa asked.

"You think I'm going to do your whole job for you?" Conrad asked, amused. "I've already told you more than you deserve to know."

"But then you won't know," Raisa said.

His mouth pursed, not wanting to bite. But he couldn't resist. "Know what?"

"If we ever catch her killer." Human curiosity was a dangerous and beautiful thing. It was why people binged television shows and stayed up until 3:00 a.m. reading a page-turner, the words blurring beneath their eyes. Everyone felt that driving need to *know*.

But Conrad just smiled. "Oh, I already know. You won't."

Raisa sat back at that. A part of her believed him when he said he wanted to set the record straight. She'd been studying his file. He was a control freak. It would have been torture for him to die without ever knowing what Kate or Isabel would do with his story. And if he agreed to an interview, he could stipulate that he needed to see the final version of the documentary before he died.

There was something else she couldn't put her finger on layered beneath all that, though.

She couldn't help but think he was acting the magician right now, showing them enough to make it believable, utilizing misdirection to conceal his tricks, and knowing that it didn't really matter if they bought it as long as he could control where they were looking.

"Was Isabel the first person to realize you hadn't killed Shay?" Raisa asked, trying to sidestep her way toward whatever had set the itch to the back of her neck.

"I'm guessing Shay was the first one to realize that."

Pierce straightened out of his casual stance at that, shifting so he loomed over Conrad. "Keep her name out of your mouth."

Conrad peered up at Pierce through indolent, hooded eyes. "Or you'll . . . what? Kill me?"

Pierce exhaled through flared nostrils, then shifted ever so slightly to cup the back of Conrad's head. A second later, Conrad's face hit the table, a loud thunk of bone and metal.

"I can make your last forty-eight hours very painful," Pierce said, stepping back as if he hadn't just assaulted a handcuffed man.

Conrad touched his nose, which somehow, miraculously, wasn't broken or bleeding. Pierce seemed to know just how to cause pain without leaving a mark. Not that Raisa gave two shits about Conrad's health and happiness, but it was interesting to note. "I'd probably enjoy it more than you'd like, Agent Pierce."

Raisa wrinkled her nose. She could have gone her whole life without learning such a thing about Conrad.

"Why me?" Kilkenny asked into the tense silence that dropped. "You wrote that in a letter one time. That if I ever found out *why me*, then I would be able to find you."

It was a vulnerable admission from Kilkenny, an acknowledgment that Conrad had gotten into his head, at least a little bit. But for the first time, Raisa saw something like approval slip into Conrad's smile. Isabel had worn a similar expression when Raisa had finally stumbled on the right question to ask.

Whatever the answer was, it was important. At least to Conrad.

"I like the trope," Conrad said, a little too casually. "FBI psychologist, serial-killer mastermind."

As he said each, he waved first to Kilkenny and then to himself.

Raisa shook her head slowly. Conrad was watching her closely, seeing if she would get to the right conclusion. That meant he might have handed them enough clues in this interrogation that she could figure it out.

Why Kilkenny?

Conrad had given them almost nothing. But maybe it was what he *hadn't* given them that was the revelation.

Why Kilkenny? Why spend five years engaged in a cat-and-mouse game with an FBI agent? Why arrange for a shocking reveal in order to grab that man's attention, and then . . . barely talk to him when he flew all the way down to Texas?

If Conrad were obsessed with Kilkenny, she'd expect him to be reveling in his victory right now.

There was no reveling. Even the gloating seemed both toned down and, once again, directed at Raisa.

She didn't for a moment think that made her important—she was just a new piece in this chess match, and he seemed to like shiny objects.

In the end, Kilkenny was just an afterthought.

Raisa went over every word, then stuttered once again at that moment—that moment she'd thought, *Huh.* She remembered what she'd said to Kilkenny at the airport, in a bit of an exhausted daze.

"Or maybe you had nothing to do with it at all."

"You say Shay's name like you knew her," Raisa murmured.

Kilkenny made some kind of punched-out sound, but Raisa didn't dare let herself look over at him.

Sometimes there were stories that people told themselves so many times . . . they couldn't see that the stories weren't always true.

Conrad smiled, close-lipped but pleased. Another secret uncovered before he went to the grave.

"Kilkenny has spent ten years thinking he dragged Shay into the crosshairs," she said slowly. "But it was the other way around."

CHAPTER THIRTEEN

Shay

March 2010
Four years before the kidnapping

Shay found Beau sitting on the floor of the kitchen, in the dark, clutching a mostly empty fifth of rum. She didn't flip on the lights, simply slid down the cabinets until she was shoulder to shoulder with him.

He leaned his head against her. "Dad died."

"Oh." Shay grabbed for his hand.

They sat like that for an hour. Shay wasn't even sure where Max was, but right now she couldn't care. All she could think about was being a solid presence so that Beau could let go.

He didn't cry. She wasn't surprised.

Beau had a complicated relationship with his father, one that couldn't be summed up by weeping or rejoicing. It was best described as exactly this: a dark kitchen floor and a bottle of alcohol.

A tiny, traitorous part of Shay was happy they would no longer be on the hook for the man's medical bills. If the state hadn't been picking up most of the total, they would have gone bankrupt by now.

It was a relief.

And it was a crappy thing to think.

That probably made her a bad person.

"He died a long time ago," Beau finally said. "That wasn't Dad in there."

Shay nodded, her fingers finding a small, round scar on Beau's hand. If you didn't know the damaged skin was there, it could go unnoticed. She knew it was there. She'd seen it happen.

People were complicated, though. If Hillary cleaned up her act, if she put in time and actually tried hard to be a good mother, would Shay cut her out of her life anyway?

Clearly not. She couldn't even do it when Hillary was still a mess.

Billy had become something like a good guy for the last decade of his life. Maybe that wasn't enough to earn him a spot in heaven, but it had earned him a relationship with Beau.

They didn't say anything the rest of the night, but Shay stayed right there with him until morning.

In the coming days, Shay did what she could to help him with the funeral arrangements.

Do you want me to come? Callum had texted her a few days before. I can.

She'd stared at the message for too long. What were they doing? It had been seven months since that first night. Neither of them was seeing anyone else.

But Max was twelve. That meant six more years where Shay was her legal guardian. Even if Shay was ridiculous for thinking so far out—what would they do to move the relationship forward? She couldn't just drag her family up to Washington, which might as well be another country to the three of them. Callum couldn't move down here, either. Where would he fit into her life? Hell, where would he fit into her house?

The whole thing was too complicated for what had started out as a one-night stand.

Her thumbs hovered over the keys, until she finally sent just one word. Please.

On the day of the funeral, she was incredibly thankful for that weak moment. Beau hadn't reacted at all to the news that an FBI agent would be joining them, and Max had just shrugged. She never got as nervous around law enforcement as Shay did, and it made Shay doubt her own memory sometimes. But Max had been only eleven when everything had happened—maybe she didn't even fully realize what she'd done.

They all drove to the church in silence, Beau and Max in the front, Callum and Shay in the back.

Halfway there, Callum reached out for Shay's hand, and she gladly let him take it.

The service was poorly attended. Most of Billy's friends had mourned him already and moved on. Max's psychologist, Dr. Tori Greene, of all people, was one of the few to attend, and she looked somewhat uncomfortable once she realized the turnout was what it was.

At the end of it, she gave Shay a hug. "I'm glad he's at peace now."

Shay took the comfort, and when she drew back, she waved toward where Beau and Callum stood. Max was several feet away, looking horrified that her therapist had shown up.

"We're having a get-together at the house," Shay said. Tori's hesitation made Shay think it was a step too far. But she'd already started . . . "You're more than welcome to come."

"I have an appointment, I'm sorry," Tori said, her mouth twisting with regret. "I was only able to sneak away for a moment."

"Of course," Shay murmured. In the next moment, an old buddy from Billy's garage drew her attention, and Tori slipped out of the church. The buddy took them up on an offer for a ride, and then regaled them with fishing stories all the way back to the house. The place was already crowded with people who wouldn't make a drive to see a closed casket but would turn up in droves for free booze and food.

Nathaniel Conrad found her in the kitchen during one of her lulls in conversation. "I'm sorry I couldn't make it to the church."

Shay waved that away and pulled him into a hug. He was warm and soft and comforting in the same way Beau was. She'd gotten to know him slightly better over the past few months, though she'd quickly realized that ride to work had been an anomaly. Still, Beau had invited him to hang by the firepit enough for her to consider Nathaniel a friend.

He was lovely but also strange sometimes. She had a theory that as a child he'd taught himself to be socially charming—because he very much could turn it on. Banter came quick to his tongue, and he always went along with a good bit. But sometimes he would say something strange and intense that made her pause. When he noticed, he would almost immediately recover, offering up some self-deprecating explanation for the gaffe or misstep.

Thus, her odd duckling–to–gorgeous swan theory had been born. It would explain the gaps she sometimes saw in the persona he presented to the world.

"How's Beau?" Nathaniel asked.

Shay lifted one shoulder. "You know."

"Yeah."

There wasn't much else to say to that. She nodded toward the window in the kitchen, toward their backyard. "If you want to, go ask him yourself."

"Yeah," he said again, squeezing her arm as he passed.

Callum came up behind her, pushing a wineglass into her hand. "Hey."

Nathaniel stopped, midstride. He shifted back toward Callum and held out his hand.

"Nathaniel," he introduced himself. "I'm a friend of Beau's."

"And mine," Shay teased, and got a half smile.

"Callum. Nice to meet you."

Shay was pretty sure Callum would immediately forget Nathaniel's name. He had an incredible memory for the details of a case, but that seemed to take up all the room in his brain. Everything else got put in the garbage disposal.

"I'm gonna . . . ," Nathaniel said, gesturing toward the door. It slammed shut on its hinges behind him.

"Nice guy?" Callum asked, leaning against the counter. His eyes were scanning the room, and the hallway beyond. She used to hate guys who did that, assuming they were looking for someone hotter to talk to. But Callum did it in every room and every situation because of his training. She knew he was still giving her at least 90 percent of his attention.

She rested against Callum, an echo of when she'd found Beau in here on the day of Billy's death. "Hmm?"

"Nothing," Callum murmured, his hand slipping up to cradle the nape of her neck. "Not important."

His fingers worked at the tense muscles there, and she let herself enjoy it.

"You know what, I've never asked," Kilkenny said after a few minutes of silence. The partygoers seemed to sense their need for this private moment and were leaving them be. "Why was he in the hospital in the first place?"

"Billy?" Shay asked, though of course that's what he wanted to know. Her brain had gone a bit syrupy at his touch, and she needed a moment to come back online. "Car crash. He was plastered. They found two empty bottles of Jack in the footwell next to him."

It had been two years now since that 3:00 a.m. call. Max hadn't been living with them at the time, thank god for small mercies. Beau had woken Shay up, and they'd driven to the hospital in a daze. Billy was unresponsive, but alive enough.

Wasn't that a funny thought? Alive enough to fuck up their finances for two years.

That was uncharitable, of course. Especially at his wake.

They didn't often talk about the circumstances of Billy's car crash, because those little facts had a way of erasing anyone's sympathy for the man. But like Shay had thought a thousand times, people were complicated. How much should one night, one bad decision, decide the way a person was remembered?

"Did he hurt anyone?" Callum asked softly.

"No." And thank god for that.

"Just himself." Callum finished the thought. "Wasn't he sober?"

"Five years," Shay said. "He fell off the wagon, I guess."

There was a long pause.

"Were there any signs of that?" Callum asked, and she heard the new tone in his voice. The FBI agent.

She straightened, disentangling herself from him. "Why are you asking?"

He shook his head, a dog shaking off water. "Sorry, ignore me."

"Tell me," Shay said, making sure it came out a plea instead of a demand. She plastered herself against him, looking up through her lashes. "What are you thinking?"

"It's not unusual for someone to relapse, of course," Callum said. "But it also strikes me as an effective way to get rid of someone with a history of alcohol abuse."

Shay's brows drew together. "What are you talking about?"

"It's stupid—ignore me," Callum said, trying to brush it off again.

"No," Shay said, pulling him in tighter. "I'm not calling you crazy, I'm just not following."

Though maybe she was. Maybe she was following too closely.

He pursed his lips. "Where was he driving to?"

"What?" She felt so stupid, like a parrot who only knew one word.

"He'd drunk two bottles of Jack, you said?" Callum asked. "For a guy who hadn't had a drop of liquor in five years, why didn't that lay him out flat?"

Shay blinked up at him. No one had ever questioned that before.

"And why were the bottles in the car with him if not to paint a picture of someone on a binge?" he asked, and then he shook his head again. "Or he was slipping for a while and they were old and weren't actually what he drank that night."

"Beau swears he wasn't," Shay offered. "Slipping."

"Alcoholics learn to hide it really well."

"Not if he was leaving bottles around in the footwell of his car," Shay pointed out.

"True," Callum said, his eyes sliding past as if trying to assess the guests in the other room. "Did he have any enemies?"

Shay sucked in a breath. Because she'd known that's where this conversation was going, but his asking it outright made it all seem more real.

"You think he was killed?" It came out a hushed, too-gossipy whisper.

"No," Callum said slowly. "No, I don't. Parts of the story strike me as odd. Was there even an investigation?"

"No," Shay said, and wanted to add *Of course not*. But Callum was used to working with the FBI, not a stressed-out sheriff's department that saw a truck wrapped around a tree, a few bottles of Jack, and called it a day.

"Hmm."

She slapped him lightly on the chest. "You do think he was murdered."

He shook his head, but then asked again, "Is there anyone who would have wanted to get rid of him?"

The answer came before she even really had to think about it. Hillary.

Hillary.

This made ex-husband number two who had wound up dead. Some of that had to be attributed to the type of people she married—men who courted violence and/or made dumbass decisions because they were idiots. Her husbands tended to be men who put themselves in terrible situations, had terrible associates, and did terrible things for money and drugs.

She said all that to Callum and then asked, "Do you think it's related?"

"I don't know," Callum said quietly, but he sounded like he did.

"Maybe he was just a drunk who drove into a tree," she offered.

"Maybe." He ran a hand over his face. "Don't listen to me. I'm making trouble."

It had been a miracle Billy had survived at all. That's what the sheriff had told them and then the doctors, too. He hadn't been wearing his seat belt, and he'd flown through the front windshield. By some lucky stroke, the glass had missed his arteries; otherwise he would have bled out in seconds.

They would have gotten away with the perfect murder.

Just like with Max's father.

"Two is still a coincidence," Shay said, and she could hear the desperation in her voice. Like she was convincing herself.

"Yes, but should we really wait until it becomes a pattern?"

CHAPTER FOURTEEN

Raisa

Now

"Nathaniel Conrad knew Shay," Raisa said, perhaps unnecessarily. But she wanted them all to be on the same page.

Kilkenny was pacing in front of their rental car, and Pierce watched him with a concerned expression.

Raisa was just glad to be back out in the sunshine, the heat of it burning away the unpleasant residue of the prison. Fluorescent lights were really starting to wear on her.

"You're throwing spaghetti to see what sticks," Pierce said. She understood why he was being defensive, but she was tired of it. She wasn't his enemy, and unless he'd had something to do with Shay's death, he wasn't hers.

"Did you not see him all but confirm it?" Raisa asked, letting a little bit of snap come into her voice.

"I saw you throwing out a theory and him smiling because we're playing directly into his hand," Pierce said, as if she'd never dealt with a serial killer before.

"And what hand is that?" Raisa asked.

"He wants to muddy the waters," Pierce said. "That's all he's doing here."

"We looked," Kilkenny interjected. "We looked for a connection, of course we did."

"I thought you didn't investigate at the time," Raisa said.

"It was after," Pierce said. "The prosecutor's team was huge. They investigated each victim, found when he first contacted them, then documented any evidence, any signs that he'd been stalking them in the weeks before the kidnappings. They never found anything connecting him to Shay. Beyond Kilkenny, of course."

Raisa wished she could see those files. They sounded far more thorough than the ones from the active investigation. But that was because the FBI reports had been written when they'd had no idea who Nathaniel Conrad was. His name had never made it onto a single suspect list.

It was far easier to draw a map of connections when you had the name of your killer and all his personal details than when he was a faceless monster in a population of millions.

"I know you're probably thinking we did a shit job," Pierce said, the edge completely ground out of his voice now.

"I'm actually not." It was the truth. There had obviously been some missteps, but Raisa was never one to judge anyone for how they acted while the stakes were so high. Her own decisions had almost led to her getting killed no less than three months ago. And she might have had Delaney's blood on her hands as well, if things had gone just a little differently.

Pierce, who had seemed ready to defend himself further, was now at a loss. "Okay. Well."

"Raisa's just trying to help," Kilkenny said. He looked over to her. "I saw what you saw. Conrad wanted us to believe he knew her apart from me, but I can't say if that's the truth or not. If they were friends, it was in passing. He wasn't a big part of her life."

"She worked at a bar." It was one of the best places to meet someone, wasn't it? Especially if you wanted to do so with some anonymity preserved. "Maybe he was a regular. She wouldn't have thought to tell you about him by name unless he'd done something crazy."

"I was there all the time. I never saw him," Kilkenny said.

"But you can't say that for certain," Raisa pointed out gently. "You travel all over the country and have been to hundreds of bars and diners and clubs. Your brain has learned to filter out the noise. He could have been sitting on the barstool next to you every night and I doubt you would have remembered his face."

After a minute of consideration, he tilted his head. "Maybe."

"Tell me literally one thing about anyone at the airport yesterday," Raisa challenged him, and when he remained silent, she laughed. "I'm not insulting you. You're not unobservant, dude. You scan for danger and catalog your surroundings, but then you dump the information as useless. I've watched it happen—"

"This is pointless. So what if he knew her?" Pierce interrupted. "He probably started stalking her because of Kilkenny."

"Why would you assume that?" Raisa asked. "Why can't it have been the other way around? If he used this area as his base, is it crazy that he somehow knew Shay? And then if the FBI agent who was hunting him started dating her? Wouldn't he become more interested in Kilkenny than he would have otherwise?" She turned to Kilkenny. "Did you do anything to draw his attention? Did you offer some brilliant insight right off the bat?"

Kilkenny stared at the ground, but then he shook his head. "No. I offered a fairly standard profile. And while it turned out to be spot-on, it wasn't the thing that led to his capture. His own mistake did."

That mistake had been reusing a code—but that wasn't sitting right with what they knew about Conrad. He wasn't careless. Serial killers weren't evil geniuses who never made a misstep, of course. But there was something they were missing with that.

"Fine," Pierce said. "Doesn't that mean he's more likely to be lying right now? You really think it's possible she was friends with a serial killer, who was then framed for her murder?"

"I don't know," Raisa admitted, a bit helplessly. She was just trying to figure this out, too. It seemed wild to think that Shay might have known Conrad, one of the state's most prolific serial killers, and not died by his hand. She didn't have an explanation for it.

"What if she figured it out somehow?" Pierce said, persuasive now that he sensed her moment of doubt. "What if she figured out that her friend Nathaniel was the Alphabet Man? She didn't want to believe it was him, so she confronted him instead of telling Kilkenny. That's why there wasn't a sign of a struggle. She was meeting him in that mall parking lot."

Kilkenny stared at him for a long time, expression blank, and then his eyes flicked to Raisa. Because that scenario sounded incredibly plausible. In fact, that's probably what had happened.

Except . . . except there had been two different authors, one who penned the Alphabet Man messages and one who wrote the Shay letters.

That was the only real evidence they had that Conrad was telling the truth right now.

And it was based solely on Raisa's work.

Raisa was used to people dismissing her analysis as pseudoscience, no many how many graphs and statistical equations she threw at them. They didn't understand, so they thought it must not be as convincing as things like DNA and fingerprints. Only once before had Raisa questioned whether Kilkenny respected her work. He had explained away his doubt in a manner that had been mostly convincing. But in this moment, she realized the bruise remained—because she wasn't sure what he was going to say.

"He's not lying," Kilkenny said, and she relaxed, relieved. "He didn't kill Shay."

Pierce deflated. Where he would steamroll Raisa, he would at least humor Kilkenny. "Okay. We need Kate Tashibi's film."

"Can you convince her to let you watch the interview?" Raisa asked, dubious.

"I'm not leaking it to the press." Pierce shrugged. "There's no reason for her not to voluntarily share it."

Maybe no logical reason, but there were plenty of emotional ones. But if he wanted to try, she wasn't going to stop him. "That would be great if she turns it over."

"I'll get it." Pierce glanced at his watch. "I bet she's in town for the execution. We'll chase her down."

Raisa hadn't even thought about that, but of course Kate would want some final footage.

Kilkenny shook his head. "You must be busy. I can't ask—"

"Listen, buddy, I'm seeing this through to the end," Pierce cut him off. "Nothing else is as important."

That probably wasn't true. Pierce was the head of the entire Houston office. He probably didn't actually have time for coffee, let alone whatever it would take to chase down Tashibi and get her to hand over her precious film. But the loyalty earned him back a few points in Raisa's book.

"Thank you," Kilkenny said, holding out his hand. Pierce took it, and they locked eyes, years of experience passing between them.

She thought about what Kilkenny had said about Shay and her siblings. They'd been through war together. Hadn't Pierce and Kilkenny weathered the same? Didn't that create a bond that would last forever?

What would it take for that bond to be broken?

Pierce coughed, perhaps to cover up the fact that the big, tough men had been experiencing *emotions*, and dug into his pocket for his keys. "What's your plan?"

Raisa desperately wanted her hands on all Conrad's messages to Kilkenny, wanted to see the codes and the tattoos on the victims' arms. She was here to support Kilkenny, but the best way to do that was to analyze writing samples. "I need to see the letters."

"I'll call down to the evidence room. You'll just have to show your ID, but they'll have everything ready for you," Pierce said, jerking his chin back toward the field office. He turned to Kilkenny. "What about you?"

Kilkenny sighed and ran a hand through his hair, mussing it in a way she knew he would hate at any other time. "Beau."

Pierce grimaced at him. "Good luck."

Raisa lingered even as Pierce took off toward the office to wrangle Kate Tashibi into compliance.

"Why Beau?"

"If Conrad knew Shay, Beau might have as well," Kilkenny said.

"Do you need backup?"

Kilkenny shook his head. "You're right—you should analyze the writing. We really dropped the ball there."

"You could take someone else," she said.

"No, I can handle Beau," Kilkenny said, sounding confident enough that she stopped pushing. This was his former brother-in-law, after all.

"Will he talk to you?"

"Probably not," Kilkenny said with a sigh. "But I've got to try."

"Do you really think he might have something to do with Shay's death?" Raisa asked. He'd said the siblings had been tight. He'd described Beau as both an old soul and reliable. A bit of a bastard, too, but he'd said that part with fondness.

Kilkenny's mouth did something complicated, like he wanted to say no but couldn't. "I don't know why he would have lied about knowing Conrad."

Raisa pressed her lips together. Neither of them needed her to state the obvious.

"I'd always thought there was no way Beau could have tortured her, no way he could have tattooed her," he continued. "But . . ."

"If he was Conrad's accomplice, he wouldn't have had to. Maybe he simply killed her, and left the rest to Conrad," she said. "Did Conrad ever strike you as the type to have an accomplice?"

"Never. He was a loner."

"Okay, so maybe we're barking up the wrong tree with Beau," Raisa said.

Kilkenny sighed. "I hate that I have to think either of her siblings had anything to do with her death. Those three . . . Family was everything for them. The be-all, end-all."

Isabel had been the same way. She was obsessed to a fault with both Delaney and Raisa. They were her sisters, and that meant every other consideration went out the window.

Raisa had never experienced that emotion from her own end. For her, family was a destructive, terrible thing that led to death and grief and despair. She hated the way those ties that bound them together could be so easily used as puppet strings, as a noose, as handcuffs.

But in the right light, it could probably be appealing. That kind of devotion, unwavering and unconditional.

"We both know how rancid that kind of thing can turn, though," Raisa pointed out. Isabel could be exhibit A, Delaney exhibit B, and everyone they'd dealt with in their careers at the FBI could fill in the rest of the alphabet.

For a moment she was back in those woods, Isabel's gun pressed to her back.

Isabel would have killed both her and Delaney, even though she professed to love them. And with Delaney, it had probably been true.

"Yeah," Kilkenny said. "I think it's time we try to find Max."

EXCERPT FROM MAXINE BAKER'S JOURNAL

I went to see Billy today even though I wanted to smother him with a pillow the entire time. He was so vulnerable, just lying there like a hunk of meat. Beau wanted me to go, maybe like he could sense something. Like he wanted me to say goodbye before it was too late.

I never knew the bastard, but that's Beau for you. He'd do anything for the people he considers family. Shay thinks it's his best quality. What she never seems to acknowledge—or maybe even realize?—is that Beau is constantly testing us to see if we'll do anything for him.

Dr. Greene says I do that, too. Test boundaries, push limits. Abused kid syndrome.

At least I'm obvious about it.

Beau does it in that sneaky way that Shay never picks up on. Maybe it's because she wasn't abused, not like us. Not like me and Beau. Dr. Greene would say that's unfair, but it's my fricking diary I'm allowed to be unfair. Shay wears her bad childhood like a badge of honor but Shay forgets that out of the three of us, it was she who got to live with Hillary full-time. Maybe Hillary was a bitch to her, but she still chose her, still took her in and protected her. Beau and I had to live with the consequences of Hillary's bad choices for half of every month and then every other holiday. Even when Billy was using Beau as an ashtray. And when father dearest was using me *as a whore*.

Anyway.

Because it doesn't matter that Beau's a manipulative asshole, I really would do anything for him, I plotted every way I could kill Billy today. Tripping over a cord that somehow disconnects his vent? Oops, clumsy me. My favorite idea was to set him on fire considering that's how he hurt Beau so much. These assholes can always dish it out and never take it. I'd want him to be awake. I'd want to be able to watch as he screamed in agony. Burning to death seems like it would be really painful.

Can you imagine the note that would go in my file then?

They all already think I'm a monster anyway. Maybe they would actually arrest me this time.

But Billy isn't worth becoming a killer for.

Maybe someday someone will come along who will be.

CHAPTER FIFTEEN

Shay

October 2010
Three and a half years before the kidnapping

Hillary had never given Shay any guaranteed personal space. When she'd been a girl, she'd more often than not slept on some chair or couch in a tiny apartment's living room. Or in the second hotel bed in those weeks in between when they hadn't had a stable place to stay.

Shay had made a point to draw boundaries for Max when they'd brought her into the house. A direct contrast to all their childhoods.

That was all great in theory, but the real world existed, and so did Shay's cell phone battery, which was currently at 1 percent. Shay's charger had also decided to stop working for some goddamn reason, and the other day she'd seen Max shove their extra charger in a bag she kept in her room.

"Shit," Shay murmured. Hard boundaries existed for a reason, and she'd had hers obliterated too many times to make the decision lightly. But there was a serial killer on the loose, and she shouldn't drive home at two in the morning with a dead phone. She couldn't guarantee anyone in the bar would have her type of charger, either. The answer sucked, but it was also a no-brainer.

She took a deep breath, as if she were going into a room that was on fire.

Max was at school, so she wouldn't exactly walk in on Shay going through her shit. Moreover, Shay had no desire to go through her shit. She just needed that bag that she was 99 percent certain was in Max's closet.

"Okay," she said, exhaling and pushing the door open.

The shades were drawn, the lights out. Despite the fact that it was midafternoon, Shay had to give her eyes a moment to adjust to the dark.

As expected, the room was a mess. Max might be a mature preteen in some respects, but that didn't extend to making her bed. The laundry, at least, was mostly in the hamper, but Shay suspected that was because Max didn't want the threat of Shay coming in to collect it herself.

Shay tried not to look too closely at anything as she made her way to the closet. She'd caught glimpses inside the inner sanctum before, of course. An open door, a sick kid who needed saltine crackers or Gatorade. But she'd never gotten a really good feel for the room.

Shay wouldn't—she wouldn't—but she wanted to linger, wanted to get a peek into Max's world in this brand-new way.

She knew there were posters of rappers taped all over the walls, but which ones were Max's favorites? Which ones had earned spots closest to her bed? Shay knew there were sticky glow-in-the-dark stars scattered all over the ceiling, but were the constellations accurate? And if so, why had Max chosen the ones she had?

Teenagers had a right to privacy, but Shay wished they understood that a lot of the time, the adults in their lives just wanted to *know* them. To enjoy their budding personalities as they grew into who they were meant to become.

A picture on Max's dresser caught her eye—it was of Beau and Shay making ridiculous pouty faces at the camera. A hand squeezed around her heart at the fact that Max kept it in a place of honor.

She wondered how Max had gotten a printout version of it, and wished she could ask for her own copy. But then she'd have to admit she'd seen it at all, and Shay was still debating if she'd tell Max she'd gone into her room in the first place.

Shay was cowardly hoping she wouldn't have to.

The closet door stood ajar, and Shay nudged it all the way open with her foot. She spotted the corner of the bag at the back and knelt down to grab it.

It was pure bad luck that her arm hit a cardboard box on the way back out.

"Shit," Shay said, dropping the bag and shifting to put the top back on.

Her hand paused midair.

Then, slowly, she hooked a finger over the edge of the box, pulling it closer.

Articles. They were newspaper articles, all carefully cut out. The ones that had jumped from page one to other sections were pasted together on cardboard paper, like a school project.

Except Shay couldn't imagine that anyone at Max's school had directed her to collect all the articles that had been written about the Alphabet Man.

Shay riffled through them, her fingers becoming desperate and careless the deeper into the box she went.

There was nothing else in there, but every single mention of the Alphabet Man had been preserved.

She hit the bottom and then her ass hit the ground. In the next moment, Beau squatted in front of her, concern written in every line of his face.

"You shouldn't have come in here," he said, like she was to blame for this.

"I needed . . ." She trailed off, the excuse sounding so hollow now. Then she blinked up at him. "You're home."

"I got off early. I heard . . . something in here." His eyes slipped to the box, lingered. "You're freaking out."

"Yes," she admitted.

"There's no reason to," Beau said. He'd always processed things quicker than she had.

And what he said would be true if Max weren't who she was.

If she were just a preteen with a dark fascination with a serial killer terrorizing their part of the state, Shay would have shrugged. But Max wasn't like every other kid. She had a police file and a psychiatrist who specialized in violent children.

"I'm sure she just wants to solve the mystery," Beau continued when Shay just stared at him, incredulous. "She wants to figure out who it is. You know how curious she is."

"Curious. Right," Shay said with a nasty laugh. Anger burned bright, turning the panic to ash. Why was she the one who had to worry about Max? Beau always seemed to shrug off everything that had happened. Even when she'd finally admitted to him that she'd moved the gun, he'd simply nodded, said *Good call*, and proceeded with his day. In every other aspect of their lives, he carried his fair share, even more than his fair share sometimes. But he never did anything that would ensure Max wasn't a danger to herself—or, more importantly, others. "You think this is just weird twelve-year-old girl stuff?"

Beau's attention drifted to the box once more. "It's all the articles?"

"From what I can tell," Shay said, a little helplessly. "I haven't been following along all that closely. Maybe she missed some."

"But most," he said, and then sighed. He sat down and leaned against the wall, his knees drawn up. He looked tired these days, ever since Billy's funeral. Or maybe even before then? Had she missed the signs? All the anger that had flared up a minute ago died down. Beau had probably been tired since he'd decided to coparent an eleven-year-old girl. His father's funeral had probably just pushed him over the edge. "I don't know what you want me to tell you, Shay. I think it's probably an odd little hobby or something, but you're staring at me like we just found a body."

"A hobby—"

He cut her off. "It's not like she's the Alphabet Man. She's twelve."

"But—"

"Yeah, okay, she's had some violence in her past," Beau continued, steamrolling over her side of the conversation. "That still doesn't make her a serial killer. Not everyone who's been involved in a self-defense murder then goes on to tattoo stupid messages on dead girls."

Shay blinked at him. When he put it like that, of course it sounded absurd. All at once she deflated. "You're right."

"Oh, should I mark the day on the calendar?"

She kicked out at him and then dropped her cheek to rest on her upturned knees. Quietly, she admitted, "I worry about her, that's all."

"I know, bud," Beau said, knocking his head gently against her own. "But she's going to be fine. She's a good kid. You know she is."

"Yeah," Shay said, just a beat too slow for honesty. But the more she thought about it, the more she realized Beau was right. Max *was* a good kid—someone who would buy her sister ice cream with the last of her meager savings just because Shay had taken Max to the beach. There were a million moments like that. There was the photo on the dresser. There were those silly stars on the ceiling.

Max was more than what was in her past.

A few years back, a burly, hairy, ugly trucker had become a regular at the bar. He read poetry and spouted off ancient wisdom between downing half a cask of beer each night. On his right bicep he had a tattoo, a quote from Aristotle.

"One swallow does not a summer make."

When Shay had asked him about it, he'd told her about the year he'd spent in jail. And he'd told her about how that year didn't define his life any more than any other year he wasn't in jail.

One bad event did not doom a person to be evil. One good deed did not a hero make. It was all about a life built on moments and choices and actions.

"You know, she might also just be scared," Beau offered.

The suggestion shocked Shay. She'd always thought of Max as incredibly tough, almost brave to a fault. After all, she'd dealt with the asshole who was listed on her birth certificate under "Father." She wore her attitude as armor, and Shay had always imagined it covered just another layer of stronger armor beneath. And then molten lava at her core.

But she was just a girl, really. There was a serial killer in their area, and some of his victims were the same age as Shay.

"I'm officially a dumbass," Shay admitted. She had been on edge for a while, but then Kilkenny had arrived on the scene. With him came the possibility of scrutiny into her life, into her secrets. She could admit she was overreacting, but she could also admit there was a reason for that.

"Yeah, but you're *our* dumbass," Beau teased, his foot nudging hers to make sure she knew he was joking.

"I'm going to have to tell Max," she said.

"Yeah," he said again.

"What do you think this is going to cost me?" she asked, finally pushing to her feet again.

"If you're lucky, a bribe of no less than twenty dollars," he said.

She made a face, but agreed. That was best case. Worst was that she'd lose Max's trust. It didn't seem like something she could easily get back.

"I'm calling off from work," Shay said, and Beau raised his brows. "So that I'm here when she gets home."

"Oof, ripping off the Band-Aid, good for you."

"But you're not going to be here to witness it," she guessed.

"No, thank you," he said. "I have no interest in the shrapnel."

He dipped out of the room as quickly as he'd entered, and a minute later she heard the front door close.

Shay stared at the box of clippings and wondered if she should put them back how they were. Maybe not even ask about them.

She couldn't even remember what order they'd been in, though.

"What are you doing?"

Shay startled, banging her elbow on the door, looking all the more guilty for it, she was sure.

Max stared at her from the doorway.

"I'm sorry," Shay said. "I came in to get the phone charger. I didn't want to be without a phone tonight . . ."

As she trailed off, she waved at the elephant in the room.

A tiny, tiny, minuscule part of her watched Max's expression closely as her attention landed on the box, on the articles.

It gave away nothing.

After several terrible seconds that felt like hours, Max relaxed and shrugged. "Okay."

Shay opened her mouth, closed it. "You're not mad?"

"It's your house," Max said, in a terrible blank voice, and Shay realized her relief from moments earlier was ill founded. Max wasn't mad, but Shay had broken her trust. And that was a profound loss, no matter how subtle it was. Max no longer felt like this was her home.

"Max," Shay tried, her heart breaking a little, and Max just shook her head, too quickly.

"I get it," she said. "You needed your charger."

That was the problem, wasn't it? There could always be a valid excuse. Shay could have stopped at the gas station on the way in. She could have bought a replacement. She could have borrowed one of the three burner phones Lonnie kept on his person at all times. She could have done anything but barge into Max's room without her permission.

A twenty-dollar bribe wasn't going to fix this.

Shay didn't actually know if it was fixable at all.

So she asked what she wouldn't have asked if Max had given her any sign that this would blow over. "Why do you have these?"

In a box, hidden in a closet, like it's a bad secret, Shay thought but didn't add.

Again, she got a neutral expression. Shay hated that Max had enough experience with intense emotion that, even at twelve, she was able to hide hers.

Max just stared at her for a long time. And then she said in a flat voice, "You shouldn't ask questions you don't want an answer to."

CHAPTER SIXTEEN

Raisa

Now

The Alphabet Man's letters were spread out before Raisa, and for the first time all day, she relaxed. This was where she felt on solid ground.

Words. Writing. She had always been drawn to the patterns of language, even before she realized her biological parents had been world-class mathematicians. When she'd been thrust into the foster system at ten years old, everyone had wanted to talk at her. It was then she'd learned the power of words. They were something she could control, even as young as she'd been. She could withhold them or offer them up as she pleased, and no one could force her to do otherwise, no matter how persuasive they were.

So many people let their words fall out with abandon, as if they didn't have any power. But Raisa had known better.

And here they were in all their terrible glory.

In front of her, she arranged all the letters in chronological order, all the way back to the ones that had been tossed into file cabinets before anyone knew what they were.

When going through them piecemeal, she'd thought them incredibly long-winded for encrypted messages. But after reading the first six or seven, she noticed they were almost a template of each other.

They weren't the exact words repeated, but the structure was the same and could be broken down into parts.

1. An over-the-top greeting that over time became personalized to Kilkenny;
2. Taunts about being smarter than law enforcement, the task force, and then, again, eventually Kilkenny;
3. Taunts about the way he'd tortured his last victims to inflict as much pain as possible before killing them;
4. Personal information about someone on the task force to show how much he knew about all the members (though the first few letters deviated there, and were information on sheriffs at the departments he'd sent them to);
5. An over-the-top sign-off;
6. The next victim's name.

The exact details varied, of course. But they, without fail, stuck to that format.

Except for four of the victims: Shay, of course. And then the female victim where Conrad had been "sloppy" enough to use the same code twice. Finally, there were the two male victims.

Raisa ignored the buzz in her skull, like she always tried to do when her mind wanted to jump ahead of her careful work.

This wasn't about theories right now. It was about analysis. She went back to the beginning.

Each individual letter had its own evidence bag. And then attached to it was a decoded version of the message it contained.

She carefully handled the very first letter through the bag—modern-day paper was fragile and prone to tears. Although she couldn't actually read the message, it was impressive in length. Encoding something with an Alberti Cipher wasn't the most difficult thing in the world, but the ones she'd seen before tended to keep the contents limited to what was necessary.

The Alphabet Man—Conrad—had written an entire page.

She set it aside in favor of the decoded version. Attached to that with a paper clip was a photograph of the cipher tattooed on the first victim's arm. Raisa easily parsed through the first word.

Salutations.

Those grandiose greetings were a hallmark. Maybe that wouldn't hold up in court, but she'd found it on every one she'd analyzed. Except for the ones from those four victims.

Raisa pulled up her spreadsheet and labeled the Conrad letter as *A* and the possible second author's letter as *B*.

Her fingers worked almost independently as she created lists for both.

A

- *No positive or negative contractions (ex: I am and are not, instead of I'm and Aren't. Because it would give away code?)*
- *Excessive use of similes (ex: the knife sunk in like butter, the blood droplets spattered on my hand like rain; you might think I am crazy, but I am crazy like a fox)*
- *Excessive use of self-referential pronouns (ex: I missed you at the bar last night; My intrepid Agent Kilkenny; why will you not answer me?)*
- *Idiom misuse: One in the same (correct: one and the same. See: letters 3, 6, and 9)*
- *Word misuse, eggcorn: feeble position instead of fetal position*
- *Double space after periods*

B

- *Error: Dropped vowels before consonants in last syllable or a*

word (considerbly, entirly instead of considerably and entirely)
- *Error, likely typo: of instead of off*
- *Only grammatical error: used hear instead of here*
- *Positive and negative contractions (ex: they're and can't)*
- *Simple salutation: (ex: dear Callum)*

She went on until she had a good sense of both their voices. Her one asterisk that she would add to any report was that the two authors had been writing using the Alberti Cipher. Likely they'd composed the message and then encoded it, but the process might account for something such as a dropped letter from the word *off*. The same could be said about some of the punctuation.

Still, there was enough to tell that they were different writers, just as she'd thought during that first analysis.

Raisa did the same with the letters about the two male victims, and came to the same conclusion.

The second author hadn't even tried to mimic Conrad's idiolect. Raisa wondered if they'd dismissed the idea or if they just hadn't thought about it at all. They had probably thought that writing in a specific code was enough to make their letters seem like they were from the same person.

And she had to admit it had worked.

So why these victims? Raisa found it hard to believe that they simply had a much slower copycat serial killer on their hands.

One of the Alphabet Man's signatures was that he had such a short cooling-off period. If these four victims were excluded, he'd still killed twenty-three women over five years. That was nearly five a year for an extended period of time.

That last woman, the one who would have been the Alphabet Man's next kill, hadn't actually died. So that meant their second author—copycat or whatever they were—had killed three people over the span of four years. Shay and then the two male victims. The difference was profound.

The fact that the last letter was probably written by their second author meant that the person had likely saved the woman's life and ended a five-year-long manhunt for an infamous serial killer in the process.

The implications of that were big enough to send her pulse skittering.

Calm down. Go through the process.

She shifted through the files until she found more information about the last letter. It was directed to Kilkenny—or, rather, Callum, a notable departure from Conrad's letters—but it had been addressed to the FBI Houston field office.

The victim was Conrad's, but the letter was from their second author. So had their second author intercepted Conrad's letter, or had that person beaten Conrad to the punch?

And if it was the latter, how had their second author known who the victim would be?

Raisa sat back and the pieces of the case rearranged themselves in her mind, but all she came up with were more questions.

What the hell was going on here?

Her phone buzzed on the table. She jumped and then laughed at herself, her nerves frayed.

"Beau wasn't at home," Kilkenny said, once she answered. "Looks like he closed up house and left."

Dear Callum. How many people called Kilkenny that?

His brother-in-law, surely. His sister-in-law.

His wife.

"Do you think that means anything?" Raisa asked.

"I don't know," Kilkenny said. "I thought for sure he'd attend the execution."

"Avoiding you?" she offered.

"Maybe." He paused. "And obviously I didn't get Max's address."

Both of Shay's siblings, siblings who by all accounts would do *any-thing* for each other, were missing. That seemed . . . important. But she couldn't figure out how to fit it into what they knew about the case.

Kilkenny made some guttural sound that she could easily translate as anger and frustration and helplessness made vocal. It built into a tidal wave, crashing over both of them.

She let him ride it out, here in the safety of an open line, with her as the only witness. It was the best-case scenario, and of course Kilkenny had retained enough composure to wait until now to lose it.

The emotions retreated nearly as quickly as they had come, and Kilkenny dropped silent before uttering, "I'm sorry."

"Don't be?" Raisa tried quietly. "I've been worried you've been holding it together too well."

He laughed. "Well, I've gone ahead and disabused you of that notion."

"Nah, that was nothing," she said, her tone light. But she meant it. Isabel had thrown Raisa into such a tailspin, she'd barely been functioning. And here Kilkenny was taking thirty seconds to vent his frustration before pulling himself together again.

"Right," he said, not sounding like he believed her. "Right. Tell me what you've got."

"I don't know yet," Raisa hedged, not really lying. Her thoughts were scattered, and even if she tried to put them into words, she didn't think she could.

"Do you need me?" he asked.

Raisa stared at the letters. *Dear Callum.*

What did that mean? Did it mean anything? Did it mean anything that their second author had essentially turned the Alphabet Man into the authorities?

She didn't know, and Kilkenny didn't need to hear her talking herself in circles.

"Not yet," she said. "I'll have an update soon, though, I swear."

"You don't report to me," Kilkenny said, some amusement in his voice again. It made her shoulders relax to hear him closer to normal.

"Are you going to try to find Beau?" she asked.

"I have a BOLO out on him," Kilkenny said. "But . . . I don't know. He's used to hiding from authority. I'm not optimistic, and we have a ticking clock."

There was *some* truth to the fact that innocent people didn't run— but there were caveats, too. People like Beau, people who'd grown up looking over their shoulder for the next horrific thing to happen, ran as a default and then figured out the rest from whatever place they deemed safe.

"I'm going to get an update from Pierce," Kilkenny continued. "See if he tracked down Kate Tashibi."

Kate.

Raisa had all but forgotten the documentarian in the past hour. Where did she fit into this mess? Or was she just a bystander, capturing it all on film?

There were too many threads right now. They needed to start snipping some of them away. Hopefully, she'd been a little more cooperative with Pierce than she had been with Raisa.

The moment they disconnected, Raisa dismissed Kate Tashibi and Kilkenny and even Beau, and focused back on the letters, which was where she could actually be helpful.

Was this a partnership gone bad? That would explain how their second author knew so much about Conrad's MO that he managed to dupe the task force.

But why had the second author written letters for only four people? If it was a partnership, it was a lopsided one.

Which . . . could still make sense, even if Kilkenny had dismissed the idea. Serial-killer duos existed, and when they did, there was often a dominant personality and a submissive one.

She pulled the two male victims' files closer. She'd been focused on Shay and the last woman. But these were data points as well.

The only two men out of the bunch.

In the original investigation, they had stood out and they hadn't— mostly because the Alphabet Man's female victims differed from each other so much in terms of age, race, and socioeconomic status. And so the men had looked like just another variation.

But out of the three actual victims they had connected to the second author, two of them were these men. *That* was notable.

So what was it about these two that had been special?

Raisa had thought a lot about puzzle pieces during their hunt for Isabel. When constructing a puzzle that was just a blue sky, all the pieces looked too similar to tell apart in the beginning. But as you filled in the corners, the edges, the obvious bits, and the gradations started to emerge, it became more and more obvious when two puzzle pieces were in the completely wrong spot.

Those pieces could be what made the rest finally make sense.

Jason Stahl. Tyler Marchand.

Raisa stared at the two male victims' names and wondered if she'd finally found those pieces.

DRSHERLOCK: Let's talk body drop sites

MARPLESASSISTANT: You're going to talk about Jason Stahl again, aren't you?

DRSHERLOCK: Why Miss Marple's assistant, you know me so well. It's almost like you're a detective or something

MARPLESASSISTANT: It's almost like we're the only two people on at 3 a.m. talking about a stupid serial killer. Alright get on with it

DRSHERLOCK: I'm guessing he's anything but stupid. He's gotten away with killing more than a dozen people in the past three years at least. But OK, have you noticed that Jason Stahl's delivery routes go right by seven of the ten body drop sites we know of? That can't be coincidence

MARPLESASSISTANT: Circumstantial

DRSHERLOCK: Except that he fits the rest of the profile Kilkenny has given of AM

MARPLESASSISTANT: How did you even find this dude? He's just a random person and now he's being accused everywhere of being AM

DRSHERLOCK: He knew one of the victims . . .

MARPLESASSISTANT: Circumstantial

DRSHERLOCK: Someone posted a picture of him in the crowd that gathered after a *different* victim than the one he knew was found . . . and *don't* say circumstantial again!

MARPLESASSISTANT: As you just said, his delivery routes go by the body drop sites . . . if he was there at all, he probably just stopped to see what was going on. Have you ever heard of Richard Jewell?

DRSHERLOCK: The guy who got blamed for the Olympic bombing scare in Atlanta

MARPLESASSISTANT: Yupppppp . . . his life was ruined because he was falsely accused. Ruined, my dear Sherlock Holmes. Think about that before accusing someone off coincidental evidence

DRSHERLOCK: His name isn't actually everywhere, just on sites like this. And it's three in the fucking morning, Miss Marple. On a true crime discord where we shoot the shit about active crime cases. Who exactly am I hurting?

MARPLESASSISTANT: That's my point . . . you just never know

CHAPTER SEVENTEEN

Shay

October 2010
Three and a half years before the kidnapping

Shay hated lying to Beau, but she knew he wasn't going to approve of what she was about to do.

He would defend Max with his dying breath, even if their sister were the one holding the knife. Shay loved Max, but that didn't stop her from being worried about her. In fact, it just made her worry more.

She'd mostly talked herself out of thinking the serial-killer box meant anything but natural curiosity. But Max's blank *You shouldn't ask questions you don't want an answer to* still sent shivers along Shay's skin.

Max had been distant ever since, but Shay wasn't shocked by that turn of events.

"Shay?"

Dr. Tori Greene's voice broke her out of her doom-spiraling.

"I'm sorry, did we have an appointment scheduled?" Tori asked, looking between Shay and her secretary, who was, of course, sanctimoniously shaking her head.

"No, I'm the one who should apologize," Shay said, standing. "I was actually hoping I could chat with you real quick. Maybe off the record."

That got a small smile. "I'm not a journalist."

But then she gestured toward her office before turning back to her secretary. "We're done for the day, Chrissy."

Shay had been in the inner sanctum before, but never as anything other than Max's guardian. It felt different taking the comfortable—but not too comfortable—seat across from Tori.

It felt vulnerable.

Tori grabbed one of her notebooks, but kept it closed on the arm of her chair as she studied Shay. "I can't tell you what Max and I discuss in our sessions, if that's why you're here."

"No, no." Shay rubbed sweaty palms against her jeans. "Maybe I shouldn't have come, but . . ."

Like any good psychiatrist, Tori seemed to know how to wait out the awkward silences.

"I'm worried Max is a danger to herself or others." Shay had been told plenty of times in the past that saying those words would erase a lot of boundaries when it came to mental health privacy. The thing that made it palatable was that Shay really believed it.

Surprise flickered into Tori's expression, but she skillfully ironed it into blank curiosity. "Did something in particular happen?"

Shay took a breath and spilled out a somewhat disjointed retelling of the serial-killer-box day.

When she petered out to a stop, Tori was hungrily eyeing her notebook like she was dying to write out how crazy she thought Shay was being. But she refrained.

"I see. And the articles are the only reason you're worried about her hurting herself?" Tori paused delicately. "Or others?"

Because they both knew what Shay was saying, why she was here. She didn't think Max was suicidal or considering self-harm. She was worried about the second part.

"Her history, too," Shay said, cautiously. "And what she said after I found the box. How I shouldn't ask questions because I might not like the answer."

Tori inhaled, exhaled, and shifted to stare out the large window. The golden light poured into the room, making it cozy without being overly warm.

"There's a wine bar a couple storefronts over," Tori said, and Shay had to take a second to make sure she heard her right.

"Okay."

"I could use a glass, how about you?" Tori asked, eyebrows raised, clearly communicating something.

Shay could pretty much always use a glass of wine. "Okay."

Ten minutes later they were seated at a back table in a room with dark mood lighting and soft jazz music. The wine was expensive, and so was the cheese board Tori ordered without blinking at the price. All of it was delicious.

It was then that Shay realized she didn't have any female friends. No one to call when she wanted to hit up a fancy happy hour. All she had were the regulars at the bar, Callum Kilkenny, sometimes, and her family. How pathetic was that?

"Listen, I can't talk specifics with you," Tori said after their waiter left. "Hypothetically, though, what you told me doesn't worry me. I would expect a girl, a teenager, even a young woman, to show interest in a criminal that's known to be in the vicinity." She held up a finger to stave off whatever follow-up Shay had. "And I think anything that happened after you found a box like that might be that person trying to unnerve you."

"Why would she try to unnerve me?" Shay asked, not wanting to play along with hypotheticals.

"To punish you," Tori said, like it was the most obvious thing in the world. Perhaps it was.

Shay slumped back, the relief a palpable thing on her tongue right beneath the smooth cabernet. "Thank you."

Tori sighed. "I probably shouldn't have given you that much, but I do believe you're worried for no reason. If I thought anyone in my care was capable of harm, I would be obligated to report it."

"I know," Shay said. "Logically, I knew that."

"We're all a bit shaken up around here," Tori said. Her insanely beautiful hair was braided back today, but the tail end hung over her shoulder and she toyed with it. "I've started carrying bear spray."

That startled a laugh out of Shay.

"Hey, don't mock it," Tori said, with a smile. "That can take down a six-hundred-pound grizzly. I'd like to see a serial killer escape that."

Shay giggled and then glanced around. There were mostly women in the crowded little wine bar, and she wondered how many of them were having this exact discussion. How many of them had been having this discussion for their whole lives? If it wasn't the Alphabet Man, it was the rapist next door or the frat guy who couldn't hear no. Violence was a part of their daily lives—the Alphabet Man was just bringing it to the forefront.

"I feel like I'm burying my head in the sand," Shay admitted, like it was a shameful secret. "I am definitely not of the collecting-articles mentality."

Tori tilted her head in that way every psychologist Shay had ever met did when they found something you said interesting but didn't want to come off as diagnosing you. "Why do you think that is?"

"Noooo," Shay said on a laugh, tossing a peanut lightly in Tori's direction. "You're off the clock."

"Oh my god, sorry." Tori buried her face in her hands and shook her head. "I can't believe I just said that."

"I'll give you one—and only one—of those," Shay said, and then actually thought about the question. Because maybe it was interesting. "I don't know. Doesn't it feel like a slippery slope sometimes? Like you start paying attention to some of, and then all of, the articles. And then you get paranoid. You start triple-checking your locks every night. The next thing you know, you're carrying a gun or Mace."

"And that's bad because . . . ?" Tori prodded.

"It gives us a false sense of security." Shay shrugged. "It's probably a best-practice-type thing, but for me, I don't think that's actually going to stop a serial killer from taking me if he wants to."

Tori made a considering sound. "You're more alert because you don't have a weapon."

"Yeah. But I guess I should just get a weapon *and* be alert," Shay said with a wry smile. "And pay attention to his hunting grounds and all that jazz. It just seems like it won't do me any good."

"And his hunting ground is widespread," Tori pointed out. "Hard to just avoid the entire multicounty area."

"Right," Shay said, getting into it now. "And the task force talks a big talk but doesn't really seem to understand anything about the man or his choice in victims."

Shay made a silent apology to Callum, who probably did know more than she realized. Still, from the snatches of conversations and news reports Shay picked up at the bar, it didn't seem like they had a firm grasp on anything.

Tori's eyebrows went up. "It is strange that he doesn't seem to have a victimology that's easy to profile. I would imagine that makes him hard to pin down."

"Have you tried?" Shay asked, leaning in. "I would imagine you have a little bit more insight than the average person."

Tori blushed a little and looked away. "If I were the task force, I'd hate armchair psychiatrists coming in and trying to out-Sherlock me."

"But I'm not the task force," Shay said, a slightly distorted echo of Tori's earlier words.

"Ahhh, okay," Tori said, like she'd wanted to be talked into it, but still wanted to put up a token protest. "Okay. I don't think he's under-employed like most serial killers. I think he works in a fairly respectable position, where he would need to stay groomed and approachable."

"Oh, how can you tell that?"

"The fact that there isn't much sign of struggle at the scene," Tori said. "He's articulate, maybe even personable. He hides his psychopathy extraordinarily well in the short term. But he won't have long-term friends or relationships. He can't maintain them."

Shay didn't wince, but that did cut kind of close to what she'd just been thinking about her own life.

"He experienced some kind of major trauma as a child," Tori said. "Either extensive sexual and physical abuse, or something that completely rocked his world. But in a violent manner."

Like Max, Shay thought but didn't say.

Tori continued on for a good twenty minutes, laying out a psychological profile for their local serial killer. Shay ordered another glass of wine halfway through, enjoying the perspective. But a lot of what Tori was saying seemed to be things she could pick up on those popular FBI and cop shows. When she alluded to that fact, Tori made that same considering sound.

"I think looking from the outside in, abnormal psychology can seem chaotic, or at least how it presents looks chaotic," Tori said. "But there are familiar beats to it, like anything else. If a child is abusing an animal, that's not necessarily diagnosable by itself; setting fires, the same thing. The behaviors start to add up, and when they do, so do the similarities to violent offenders."

Her vowels were a little loose, a little twangy now. She'd had four glasses to Shay's two.

"I'm just glad the field is moving away from its obsession with mothers," Tori said, rolling her eyes. "There was a time there when the mother got blamed for everything."

"Shocker," Shay said dryly, and Tori laughed in agreement. "What are you seeing more of now?"

"The father," Tori said. She lifted her glass in a toast. "Parity."

Shay tapped her own against it. "For once."

"There's a theory about war veterans coming home without mental health treatment," Tori said more seriously. "They beat their kids because they had extreme PTSD, and then those kids go on to become serial killers."

"Do you think that's our guy?"

It was strange how both of them had started referring to the Alphabet Man as *theirs*. She'd noticed that at the bar, too, when her regulars spoke about him.

What a claim to make.

"I don't know," Tori admitted, her smile as loose as her vowels. "Can I ask you something I shouldn't?"

Shay leaned forward. "Always."

"What were you really worried about, with Max's box? It's not as if she's the Alphabet Man."

"You said there were patterns of behavior that could add up," Shay said. "Hypothetically, don't a bigger majority of the kids you see go on to get into criminal activity than the ones you don't see?"

Tori squinted at her. "Oh, I need either more or less wine to be able to follow that."

Shay huffed out a breath. "You can't stop serial killers from becoming serial killers, right? Once they're on a certain path."

"Now that's a fascinating question," Tori said. "To my knowledge, no one has ever really been able to pinpoint the moment in someone's life that sets them on an irreversible course. Is it the second they actually decide to kill someone? Is it when they put a tarp in the trunk of the car just in case? Or is it a moment when they were a child and they were hit, or burned with a cigarette, or locked in a tiny cupboard for seventy-two hours by an abusive family member?"

"Exactly," Shay said, and it reminded her of the quote she'd found comfort in: *One swallow does not a summer make.* Only in this case, those swallows turned into a pack of murderous Hitchcockian birds. "So, if you see one of those moments, in real time, wouldn't you try to intervene? Even if there was no current and present danger?"

"But what if you push it the wrong way?" Tori asked. "What if you create the very serial killer you were trying to prevent?"

"You know," Shay said, as she waved down the waiter to order another glass of wine, "that would be exactly my luck."

CHAPTER EIGHTEEN

Raisa

Now

Jason Stahl. Tyler Marchand.

Those were the men who might unlock their mystery.

Raisa started at the beginning of Stahl's file.

At the time of his death, he'd been working for a printing company that had locations all over the Houston metro area. One note caught her attention. The company had offices near several body-drop locations, and Stahl's route took him by all of them. People at the time had speculated about that fact on a few message boards. It was the kind of information low-level task force members in charge of monitoring social media put in to show they were doing their jobs. Raisa tried not to put too much stock into any of it, though, because it usually was just gossip.

When it came to big cities where lots of people lived, there were tons of ways to draw connections that didn't necessarily mean anything.

Instead, Raisa went further back, into Stahl's childhood, to the protective services section that had been included in his file. When Stahl had been thirteen, he'd been living with his mother and her boyfriend—who'd apparently had the habit of beating up on the kid.

There were three urgent care visits and two more ER trips in the space of two years. That should have warranted intervention quicker than it had, but Raisa knew that everyone in those offices was overworked. She couldn't blame them too much.

Then Stahl had turned thirteen, and of his own admission, he'd started hitting back. He'd been a big kid, and one night he'd landed some kind of lucky—or unlucky, depending on your point of view— punch. The boyfriend's head hit the curb just wrong. Because it was considered self-defense, and the judge had rightly seemed to realize Stahl should have been removed from the situation before it escalated to that point, he'd gotten probation and community service.

A social worker had been assigned to him—she quickly checked, no connection to Conrad—and the woman's reports from ages thirteen to eighteen had been glowing. Stahl barely ever acted out, and when he did, it was never violent. The mother moved them to a new neighborhood, got a stable job, and Stahl went on to become a responsible, productive citizen. At least on paper.

The system had worked, and Stahl was an example of why Raisa would never suggest harsh punitive sentences on underage children.

The success story might have been a little sweeter if he hadn't died at twenty-six at the hands of a serial killer.

Everything else about Stahl's case—the tattoo, the body drop, the fact that he'd been held for three days—all matched up with the Alphabet Man's MO.

Except there had been no hard evidence tying Conrad to the crime after he'd been caught. That wasn't a complete anomaly—the state had been able to tie him to eleven of his twenty-seven believed victims through both DNA and souvenirs he took from the women. That had been enough for the prosecutor to argue he'd likely killed all of them.

That was fair and consistent with other serial killers, and there didn't seem to be anything fishy about that or the lawyers involved in Conrad's case.

Raisa set the file aside and moved on to the second male victim.

Tyler Marchand. He'd worked at a nonprofit that helped foster kids transition out of the system. Raisa checked for obvious ties to Conrad, but couldn't see any beyond working in similar fields. Conrad hadn't even worked with kids in Houston, just adult cases. It would have been unlikely for them to come into contact.

She didn't have to go far to find the section for his child protective services file. Marchand had been a single kid of a single mother. He had some red flags for abuse—a couple ER trips, a note about suspected malnourishment from the school nurse—but nothing as obvious as Stahl's.

When he was eleven, his mother had died in an apartment fire. She'd been drunk and passed out with a lit cigarette in her mouth—one of the oldest stories of all time.

Marchand had been dumped into the foster system, but had been adopted by a wealthy couple less than six months later.

Another success story.

That was strange, though maybe Raisa was biased.

Raisa toyed with her phone for a moment and then texted Kilkenny.

What can you tell me about two vics?

Jason Stahl and Tyler Marchand

Dots appeared almost immediately, and she waited him out. What she got was a long list of facts that were nearly verbatim to what she just read.

Not what's in the files, she typed, rolling her eyes.

This time it took longer.

They disrupted the pattern, but not enough for me to change my profile.

Raisa chewed on her lip. Can I call?

A second later her phone rang.

"What's up?" Kilkenny asked.

"Are you with Kate?"

"No, she's driving in. She didn't want to send us the footage via any digital pathway," Kilkenny said, and she heard the frustration clear as day. The FBI had secure drop boxes that would have made it both safe and easy for Kate to send in whatever interview file she had. But the move didn't surprise Raisa. Kate seemed to want to be in control of every aspect of her work.

Raisa wasn't sure she could blame her for that. "Are you with Pierce?"

"Yup, putting you on speaker," Kilkenny said.

She quickly filled them in on her process with the letters and how that had helped her isolate the three victims she was fairly confident had been killed by their second author rather than Conrad.

"Shay was personal," Kilkenny said. "The last victim had to do with turning Conrad in."

Raisa smiled at the reminder of how well they worked together. "Yeah, those were my thoughts. That's why I wanted to focus on Stahl and Marchand."

"Stahl was the first male victim," Pierce chimed in. "We got a lot of questions then about copycats."

"Did you ever wonder that yourself?" Raisa asked delicately. She really didn't want to start an argument again.

"The ink Conrad used for the tattoo process was a dark gray, not black," Pierce reminded her. "Even if you saw a picture of the cipher, you would think it was black."

"Right." She had mostly forgotten that little detail. But it was incredibly unique. Their second author had either known that through Conrad or . . . or they'd worked on the task force.

She wondered how Pierce would react to that theory. From her experience with him over the past couple of hours, she'd guess *not great.*

"I think these two guys are key to something," Raisa said, sidestepping that land mine for now. She wouldn't be forgetting it, though. "Is there anything else we know about them?"

"Sasha," Kilkenny murmured, and Pierce made an agreeing sound.

"What?" Raisa prompted them with that feeling of being outside an inside joke.

"Aleksander Malkin," Kilkenny said. "He was the journalist covering the entirety of the Alphabet Man case."

"Why would he know more than you?" Raisa asked.

"He found the male victims intriguing as well," Kilkenny said. "I think he might have started writing a book on them, but it never got published. He's worth talking to, though."

"Okay, send me his number. I'll see if he's available while you guys wait on Kate." Hopefully, given Houston's traffic, she could get back in time for that interview. But she likely wasn't needed.

"Yup, will get it over to you," Kilkenny said, sounding like he was about to sign off.

She hesitated. "Kilkenny."

There was a pause, and then the distinct absence of ambient sound that meant he'd read her tone for the request it had been and had taken her off speakerphone. "What's up?"

"Profile-wise, what did you make of the anomaly at the time?" she asked, feeling freer now without Pierce's hairpin trigger hanging over the conversation.

He didn't answer for a second, and then she heard a door close behind him. "He was testing it out to see if he got the same thrill from killing men."

Raisa pulled a face he couldn't see. "Oh."

"I know that sounds crass," Kilkenny said. "Conrad wasn't attached to the victim type, though. We already knew that."

"So, the men were an experiment."

"That he didn't take to," Kilkenny said. "He went back to women only. And that became his only real constant. I know it looks strange now. Knowing what we know. But . . ."

"At the time it made sense?" Raisa guessed.

"Honestly, yeah," Kilkenny said on a sigh. She pictured him running a hand through his hair, leaning against a wall, maybe. He was tired. They all were.

"What would you say about someone who only killed three people and framed the Alphabet Man for it?" Raisa asked. "And then turned him in to the FBI."

"I'd say they had incredible self-control," Kilkenny said. "Which would have made them even more dangerous than Conrad himself."

———

Before Raisa could meet with the journalist, she had one pressing matter to attend to.

She couldn't stop thinking how strange it would be if their killer had taken three victims and then stopped completely. She paced in front of her car, the contact pulled up on her phone, but she couldn't quite make herself hit the "Call" button.

To say she had complicated feelings about Delaney Moore would be putting it mildly. Delaney hadn't exactly aided Isabel's killing spree—and she had enough plausible deniability to avoid charges on any of the murders—but she'd certainly known about it. Her silence and inaction had damned her in Raisa's eyes.

But her sister was incredibly skilled at research, primarily with finding patterns that other people couldn't see. She was also a computer guru who had written algorithms that the FBI would kill to get its hands on.

In Raisa's opinion, Delaney owed the world a whole lot of free public-service work, and Raisa was going to make sure she paid up.

Only . . . she didn't exactly relish talking to Delaney. Nor asking her for a favor.

"Do it, do it, do—" Her finger hit the screen.

"Hello," Delaney said after one ring.

There was no surprise—no emotion whatsoever—in her sister's voice, despite the fact that the last time they'd talked, Delaney had been holding a gun on Raisa.

"You need help with the Kilkenny stuff," Delaney continued before Raisa could find her tongue.

"Yes." If Delaney was going to make it easy on her, Raisa wasn't going to make it hard on herself. "I'm looking for more victims in the Houston area."

There was a pause. "No tattoos?"

And this was why she'd called Delaney even though half of her regretted having to. For some reason, she and Delaney had been able to follow each other's thoughts as if they'd worked together for years.

A more fanciful person would think their familial connection had something to do with it. Raisa thought it was probably just genetics. Their brains were wired similarly.

"No cipher," Raisa confirmed. "Unsolved murders, men in their twenties to thirties, Houston area. A wide net, though. Think four to five surrounding counties."

"Anything else?"

Raisa chewed on her lip. She had a gut feeling, but it wasn't strong enough yet to limit the searches. "No."

"Okay."

Delaney hung up, and Raisa was left staring at her phone.

She laughed, and it came out slightly hysterical. "Okay."

Her next call was Aleksander Malkin, who was an easy man to get hold of. He also suggested they meet right away. Sometimes she loved journalists.

When she told him where she was, he rattled off an address not far away.

Twenty minutes later she found herself across from the massive Russian at what had to be the only vodka bar within a hundred-mile radius.

"Call me Sasha," he told her, and then promptly downed a shot.

Raisa liked him immediately.

"You drink?" he asked, though he didn't seem to care much about the answer, already refilling his own glass.

"One," Raisa conceded. She wanted him to talk, and despite the fact that she couldn't remember when she'd last eaten, one shot wouldn't incapacitate her.

His lips twitched as if he'd heard that many times. Like he'd heard it and ignored it. The liquor splashed over her fingers when she grabbed hers.

They clinked their glasses together. The vodka slid like silk down her throat before warming her belly. She'd been expecting the fire earlier, in the way of cheap university-level drinking, and she didn't want to know how much this bottle must cost. Sasha looked unconcerned.

The place was dark and velvety and a nice respite from the warm weather.

"Did you ever try to figure out who the Alphabet Man was yourself?" Raisa asked, waving off his attempts for her to go again.

"No, not my job," Sasha said.

"But you must have been naturally curious," Raisa pressed. Reporters—especially crime reporters—were like bloodhounds, in her experience. "Never on your off days? Or late at night? You didn't come up with any possible scenarios?"

"My pet theory was always Pierce," Sasha said, with a casual shoulder lift, as if he hadn't just accused the lead investigator of being a serial killer.

Raisa blinked, trying to catch up. "Why?"

Sasha squinted into the distance. "Pierce's task force couldn't catch him."

"A task force couldn't catch the Zodiac, either," Raisa pointed out, as a shortcut to the plenty of serial killers who'd eluded authorities. That didn't mean every lead agent was the serial killer themselves.

"Zodiac was back then. This was now," Sasha said, and then tipped his hand back and forth. "Now-ish."

Raisa knew what he meant. He was saying that with modern technology and crime-solving techniques, Conrad shouldn't have been able to get away with what he got away with for so long. Except that mindset was influenced by movies and TV shows where every staff was well funded and had buckets of time to devote to the bad guy of the week. This was reality, and it certainly didn't make Pierce guilty.

The fact that the second author could have been someone on the task force meant Pierce might be guilty of negligence, though.

"Was Conrad ever on anyone's radar?" Raisa asked. "Even a fringe suspect?"

"Never once heard his name until he was arrested," Sasha said. "I wish I could say I'd thought it was him all along."

"He never tried to contact you? Anonymously, of course."

"No, he was laser-focused on Callum Kilkenny," Sasha said. "Always found that curious. Not Pierce." He paused and saluted her with his glass. "Which lent itself to my pet theory."

"Did you ever do any work to try to prove it?"

"Not my job," Sasha said again with a jaunty smile, before downing his fourth shot since she'd joined him. He was a large man, so she guessed he wasn't even feeling it yet. Meanwhile, the room had gone a bit wobbly since she'd had hers.

She gave him a look, and his smile widened to a grin.

"Maybe sometimes I tried to prove it, but then Pierce always had an alibi," Sasha said. "And I worried if I dug too deep, it would all fall apart. And I didn't want to let go of my pet theory."

"You still believe he was guilty?"

Sasha's bushy brows lifted. He had large features to match the rest of his build, and they were extremely expressive. She wondered how he ever bluffed sources, then thought that maybe he didn't. Maybe he was just honest with them and that's why they trusted him.

"The perpetrator was found guilty," Sasha said, like he was reminding her. "Should I have my recorder out?"

Raisa sidestepped that one. "Can I ask you about two of the victims in particular?"

He nodded once.

"Jason Stahl and Tyler Marchand," she said, and he nodded again.

"The first two men," he said.

"Yes," Raisa said. "Agent Kilkenny remembered you taking an interest in them."

His eyes crinkled. "Did he? Yes, yes, I did. I thought it a curious path, one that became even more curious when it was shot down by the task force."

"Was it something other than the fact that they were men?" Raisa asked.

"You have to picture what it was like at the time," Sasha said. "The city was on fire with all of this. Everyone terrified they would be next. And then a young man shows up dead. He fits the profile released by the FBI. He has a job where he drove by at least half of the body dump sites. What do you think? Just immediately."

"Someone thought he was the Alphabet Man," Raisa said, almost surprising herself with the answer. Though, of course, she must have been thinking it. Even Kilkenny had noted the similarities in their childhoods. "And they took matters into their own hands."

"Da," Sasha said. "I thought we might have a vigilante trying to chase down our serial killer. Now *that's* an interesting story. Then the second victim turned up. Similar situation."

"Though he didn't have a connection to the body drops."

"No, but he had a connection to three of the victims," Sasha said.

"What?" Raisa asked, sitting back.

"Because he worked with the department of social services," Sasha said. "As did Conrad, so it made sense later. But at the time, there was some low-level chatter that this was the vigilante again. Only on the most off-the-record basis, of course."

"How did you explain the fact that the supposed vigilante covered up the murders by framing the Alphabet Man?" Raisa asked. "That doesn't make sense, if they thought the person they killed *was* the Alphabet Man."

"You think vigilantes always make sense?" Sasha asked. "You're not from Russia."

Raisa laughed and he shook his head.

"The vigilante realized he got it wrong," he answered, seriously this time. "But he was already committed. Or the men saw his face. He gets it wrong once, he feels bad. War has its casualties, though. He gets it wrong twice, he worries he's becoming the monster he's hunting and stops."

And the next time, he'd simply offered the suspect up on a silver platter. He'd learned his lesson. It didn't completely fit, but it wasn't ridiculous, either. Grief or rage did strange things to people.

What it didn't explain was Shay, though.

Unless . . . unless Shay had figured out who the vigilante was.

It was still hard for Raisa to wrap her head around someone killing three innocent people when they were trying to, in theory, stop it from happening. But, again . . . people went mad with strong emotions sometimes.

"Was there anything else about Marchand and Stahl that stuck out to you?" Raisa asked.

"Mmm, well." Sasha looked around, but the place was empty. "Stahl killed the mother's boyfriend. Self-defense, yes, but he did it."

"Right," Raisa said.

"And then with Marchand," Sasha continued. "Cigarette and a drunk. And somehow he made it out alive?"

Raisa blinked at him. "You think he did it?"

"I think it's possible he might have," Sasha said. "Or he saw an opportunity and let it happen. The report says the firefighters found him outside. He said he went out his bedroom window. And it was open. So."

She tried to remember the details of Conrad's childhood. "Was there ever any chatter about Conrad poisoning his family instead of his father doing it?"

Sasha shrugged, his barrel chest rising and falling. "They said he was a child. But in hindsight it seems possible."

Raisa stared at their empty glasses as her mind tried to slot all this into something that made sense. But all she could think about was that while Marchand and Stahl had strikingly similar childhoods to Conrad, there were two other people who fit that bill.

Shay's siblings.

CHAPTER NINETEEN

Shay

December 2012
One and a half years before the kidnapping

It felt strange attending a Christmas party with attendees who were all trying to catch a rapidly escalating serial killer.

If this were a movie, they would be locked in some mood-darkened office, with weeks' worth of takeout debris scattered around them, the pictures of the victims taped up over every inch of wall space.

But here they were, getting boozed and stuffing their faces with tiny appetizers, and Shay couldn't fault them for it.

Especially since this was the first time she'd seen Callum without his permanent frown in months.

It had been more than two years now since that first body had been found, and at least from where she stood, they hadn't seemed to have made any progress.

Shay slipped Kilkenny his refilled whiskey glass, and smiled as his hand settled on the small of her back in thanks. The free bars stocked well liquor, but Shay had known one of the guys serving the drinks, and talked him into a couple of splashes of the good stuff hidden away from the masses.

Callum sighed in appreciation after the first sip.

Shay wasn't drinking. She hadn't told Callum why yet, hadn't told anyone why, but he sometimes looked at her with a softness in his eyes that made her think he'd guessed. He wasn't dumb.

She smiled as she tucked herself fully into his side and tried not to think about their future. Callum had put in a request to transfer down to the Houston office—he was there so much anyway, he literally got invited to their Christmas party. But he'd been denied.

No one had given him a good reason.

Her eyes found Xander Pierce, and she wondered.

He was a schmoozer, and she'd known too many of them to be charmed by his outgoing personality. He had his eyes locked on the director position, even if that was decades away.

Callum liked him, and he tended to be an excellent judge of character. This one time they'd have to agree to disagree.

Part of her wondered if Pierce was threatened by the attention Callum was getting because of this case. Pierce was the lead agent, and yet most of the profiles that talked about the hunt for the Alphabet Man focused on Callum instead. That was the nature of the narrative, and it was one the Alphabet Man himself had set up. But that didn't stop Pierce from resenting it.

If she had to guess, that would be why Callum hadn't gotten the transfer. Pierce wanted to keep him in Seattle, away from his own spotlight down here.

"Okay, give me the goss," she whispered in Callum's ear and got a little thrill when his lip twitched into an almost-smile. Sometimes she thought about that first night they'd met, how he'd laughed when they'd had sex, how he'd smiled so freely afterward.

That laugh, that smile, had been why she'd agreed to go back to his hotel against her better judgment the next time. And now they both made such infrequent appearances, she celebrated at the hint of one.

She touched her lower belly. Would he laugh with the baby?

Would he smile when she told him?

Would Beau? Would Max? They had to know it meant her leaving Texas. She'd be back; she could just travel along on some of the dozens of trips Callum took down here. But it wouldn't be the same. She'd have a baby to contend with.

Neither of them would come with her, either. Callum had made sure Shay knew Max could live with them if they ever moved in together. But Max was like a cat—more attached to the place than the person who loved it.

"Those two are having an affair," Callum said, subtly jerking his chin toward a couple on the other side of the room. He liked the image of himself as hovering above the fray, but really, he enjoyed drama. "Both married to other people, who are both here."

He inclined his head toward another couple, also standing too close to each other.

Shay spotted both pairs and laughed. "No, babe, it's a foursome."

Callum choked on his drink and then studied all of them for a minute. "Or they're cheating to get back at their respective partners and being as obvious as their spouses are to rub it in their faces."

"I like my way better," Shay said. And then nudged him to give her more details about these people he'd worked so closely with for so long. As he did, the tension slowly bled out of his shoulders, and she got two almost-smiles out of him.

It was a good night.

Shay began making noises about being exhausted around midnight, despite the fact that this was pretty much afternoon for her normal schedule. Still, Callum got it, because, inexplicably maybe, he got *her*.

"Just let me pop by my office. I have a file I want to get," he said. "Five minutes."

She nodded and then tried to blend into the wall so no one would talk to her. Despite being in a yearslong relationship with an FBI agent, she'd never grown comfortable around law enforcement. She couldn't imagine that changing just because they were all toasted.

"It was nice that you guys could come," Xander Pierce said, slipping into the spot Callum had vacated.

Shay cursed quietly. She hadn't even noticed him crossing the room. "It was nice of you to invite him. He doesn't really have steady colleagues otherwise."

"Hate the circumstances, but love the silver lining of being able to work with him," Pierce said, and he sounded genuine. But men like him tended to sound genuine even as they lied to your face. Maybe he didn't think of it as a lie. He just didn't want to admit, even to himself, to throwing a wrench in Callum's life. Maybe she was creating drama where none existed.

"I know he feels the same," Shay said, both diplomatically and truthfully. Callum didn't suspect Pierce had been the one to block his transfer, after all.

"This probably isn't any of my business," Pierce said, and Shay fought a wince. No conversation that started like that ended in any other way than Shay wanting to punch someone. "But are you carrying anything?"

Shay reeled back, her hand on her womb. Then her brain caught up with the fact that he was *not* asking about her pregnancy in one of the weirdest ways possible. "Uh . . . no?"

He nodded like that was what he'd expected. "I know Kilkenny likes to keep his work separate, but if you ever need guidance on getting a gun license . . ."

"Um . . ." She was nearly married to an FBI agent. If she needed help, she'd ask him. But Pierce was watching her with an intensity that made her want to step back. "Okay. Thanks."

"I know you leave work late," Pierce continued, and Shay did shift back this time. Of course, he'd come to the bar—he knew what her job was. It was still strange to have him reference it like that. "The attacks are ramping up. I just want everyone to be vigilant."

And she wanted this conversation to end. "Right."

He leaned in closer, and she could smell the alcohol on his breath. "Look, Kilkenny would never say this. But. I think it might be wise to distance yourself from him a bit."

"What?" Shay said, moving from scared to angry as she slowly realized what this all was. He was hitting on her.

"No one wants to talk about it, but it happens. Wives, girl-friends . . . they get targeted by these monsters," Pierce continued. He didn't sound drunk, but he must be. "I'm just saying, you might want to think about your own safety. It might be easier to end things now before you get hurt. Or worse."

"I don't think that's any of your f—"

"Hey." Kilkenny stepped up behind her, his hand resting on the small of her back, as it had all night.

Shay stared at the floor so she wouldn't have to meet Pierce's eyes. The conversation had unnerved her more than it should have. There was nothing strange about the agent in charge of a serial-killer task force warning the women in his vicinity to be vigilant. And probably he'd crossed the line there at the end, but she'd experienced much worse on a normal Wednesday at the bar. If he remembered this tomorrow, he'd probably be mortified.

"Are you ready?" she asked, trying to force a smile for Callum.

"Yes," Callum said, before shaking hands with Pierce. "See you in the New Year."

"Hopefully not too soon," Pierce said, seeming to settle back into himself. He didn't look at Shay, just turned to the group of people behind them, all of whom welcomed him with raucous greetings.

The drive back to the hotel was quiet, and Callum kept shooting her curious glances. Finally, just as they were about to turn into the parking lot, he asked, "Did Pierce say something to you?"

Shay debated telling him. But what would she say? *Yes, he told me to be careful and it creeped me out?*

"No," she said. "Nothing important."

———

Shay and Callum's relationship had never been about grand romantic gestures. So it made sense that Shay finally confirmed the pregnancy in a small moment.

She'd just finished the one cup of coffee she allowed herself a day, while flipping through the style section of the actual-to-goodness hard-copy newspaper Callum still received.

He cupped the back of her head as he stepped closer, holding the coffeepot with his other hand. He was moving on autopilot clearly, half-asleep on this rainy Sunday morning.

Right before he poured her a refill, he stopped himself. "Oh, right."

Callum didn't even seem to realize he'd said anything, just shifted back toward the counter while Shay gaped at him.

Of course, she'd known he probably knew. But she'd expected him to pretend he didn't until she told him.

"You knew," she accused, with fake outrage.

He froze, coffeepot midair. "Ah, shit."

And it was just . . . so them that Shay couldn't stop herself from laughing.

Callum turned around with a sheepish smile. "I thought you were planning some kind of reveal."

Shay loved a lot of things about their relationship. It wasn't all sunshine and rainbows, of course, but in a situation like this one, Callum could have jumped to the worst conclusion, could have thought she wouldn't ever tell him about the baby, or that she regretted it had happened at all. And yet, he simply gave her the benefit of the doubt. They trusted each other. Always.

And that's why, even though this was unplanned and scary, she had faith it would all be okay.

She stood, crossed to him, wrapped her arms around his waist, pressed her cheek to his heart. He rested his chin against the top of her head, holding her tightly.

"Are you happy?" she whispered into his T-shirt.

"So happy," Callum said, and sounded like he meant it. "And."

She waited, knowing his rhythms by now.

"Terrified," he admitted. "With my job, I wasn't sure I ever wanted kids."

With her childhood, Shay hadn't been sure she would, either. She also felt like she'd been raising Max, and doing a mostly shit job at it. Still, she hadn't been disappointed when she'd taken the test and it had come back positive.

"I see all the ways the world can be cruel. I see the evil in people, so much more than I get to experience the good in them," Callum continued. "But even though I'm scared, I still want to. Because it's with you."

"We'll protect them," Shay said, even if she knew she couldn't actually promise that. She could promise that she would do anything in her power to try. Just like she had for Max.

Callum hugged her tight and then lifted her off her feet, spinning her around. She clutched at him, surprised by the silly gesture but laughing the entire time.

When he set her down again, he pressed his smile against her own. "We're having a baby."

There would be time to talk more about all the reasons this was a frightening thing.

Right now . . . right now was for joy.

"We're having a baby," she whispered back.

———

Shay and Max had never recovered completely solid footing in their relationship after Shay found the serial-killer box. They were close, but the easy trust had been shattered, and for someone who'd had an upbringing like Max, people didn't get second chances.

Max was never more outwardly hostile to her than any other teenager would be, and most of the time Shay couldn't even sense the rift.

But she was nervous now. Telling Max about the baby and getting only polite, lukewarm congratulations was going to make that void seem vast, dark, and deep.

Inspiration struck when she was driving Max to her first therapy session of the year. Dr. Greene had long ago shifted Max off to a colleague who specialized in PTSD in abused children. It made it easier for Shay to be friends with Tori, and Max seemed to like her new therapist—as much as she could—so it worked out for the best.

They still took the same route, and Shay remembered that day in Galveston. It had been one of their last great days together. Suggesting they take the trip again could tarnish the memory or it could recapture its joy, and Shay decided to go for optimism.

"It's winter," Max said, but Shay knew her sister and that wasn't a no.

The ice cream shop wasn't open, but it didn't matter. They sat on the mostly empty beach and watched the ocean in contented silence.

"You're pregnant," Max finally said, and Shay laughed and laughed and laughed until she fell back into the sand, breathless.

"What? You are," Max said, her lips twitching. Sometimes she reminded Shay of Callum that way, scared of her own amusement.

"I feel like I'm wearing a sign or something," Shay said, pushing back up into a sitting position. She took a risk and scooted close enough that her shoulder pressed against Max's. Max stiffened but didn't move away. "I've been building up to tell you for a week, and you already knew."

"You stopped drinking, girl," Max said, with a sly look. "You might as well be walking around with neon."

Shay buried her face in her hands, but laughed.

"Does this mean you're leaving?" Max asked after a few more minutes of silence.

"Yeah," Shay said on a sigh. "Callum tried to get moved down here even before I told him about the baby, but . . ."

"Red tape," Max finished the thought.

"You can come with us."

"Ha, our own fucked-up little *Brady Bunch*? No, thank you," Max said, as expected.

"Not to be, like, an after-school special, but you're always welcome with us," Shay said. "I just needed that said once, and now I'll drop it."

"You said it twice," Max murmured, but without any bitterness.

Shay nudged her shoulder. "I can say it as many times as you need to hear it, too."

"Beau would be lonely without me," Max said, and Shay didn't know if that was true. She thought Beau might be like one of those trees that flourished after you cut its invasive neighbor down, finally able to get full sun for the first time in years. It wasn't a flattering thought for either her or Max, so she kept her mouth shut. "Is Callum going to put a ring on it?"

"Yeah," Shay said with a laugh. She wasn't necessarily into the idea of weddings or marriage, but she was into the idea of promising herself to Callum for a lifetime. And he was a little old-fashioned in that regard. Not that he would have forced the issue, but she knew he wanted to marry her. "It won't be anything fancy. But you can be my maid of honor."

"Oh, yippee, an ugly dress," Max said, with such fond amusement that Shay nearly hugged her.

"You can wear pants," Shay promised. "Jeans, even, if you want."

Max pressed her cheek into the top of her knees and looked at Shay through one squinted eye. "You know that serial-killer box you found?"

The change of topic surprised her, but Shay cautiously went with it.

"Uh, yeah." As if she would ever forget about it.

"Do you think I'm capable of hurting someone?" Max asked. "Is that why you were so worried? Because you love me. You trust me to be your maid of honor, but you don't trust me not to kill someone."

"I didn't think you were going to kill someone," Shay protested.

Max made some disbelieving sound. "You think I'm capable of violence, at least."

Shay stared out into the ocean. Max's bullshit meter was off-the-charts good. If she lied, she'd ruin whatever this fragile thing was that had been repaired between them today.

She inhaled and told the truth. "I think you're a survivor."

Max nodded and looked toward the water as well.

Long after Shay had given up on a response, Max whispered, "I learned it from you."

CHAPTER TWENTY

Raisa

Now

A text message from Kilkenny was waiting for Raisa when she left the bar and Malkin behind.

> Come to Pierce's office when you're done.

It should have taken her twenty minutes to get back to the office, but she made it in fifteen.

The secretary waved her through, and she walked in without bothering to knock.

Pierce sat behind his desk, but Kilkenny leaned against one of the full-wall windows, half turned to the view as if the conversation were of no import to him.

And then, of course, there was Kate Tashibi, looking essentially the same as she had on the street in Tacoma. Although this time, Raisa noticed a slinky black tattoo that slithered down from her hairline into the collar of the men's white button-down she wore over black leggings.

"Agent Raisa Susanto," Kate said, breaking the silence first. "I'm hoping I can escape without any bruises today."

Pierce made an inquiring sound at that, but Raisa ignored him.

"That seems like it will be up to you," Raisa said.

Kate smirked. "Oh, now that sounds promising."

Raisa rolled her eyes and took the second chair. "Did I miss much?"

"Nope," Kate answered for the men. "We were negotiating."

"What is there to negotiate?" Raisa posed the question to Pierce, but it was Kate who answered.

"Well, I have my own agreement with Mr. Conrad. And, you know, you might think I shouldn't act as if that's binding because he's a terrible person, but I have a reputation to uphold," Kate said with a shrug that said *It can't be helped.*

"I thought this was your first film."

"Right, that's exactly what I'm talking about," Kate said. "I go back on my word now as a documentarian, as a journalist, and no one ever trusts me again."

"What did you promise Conrad?"

"That I'd get Agent Kilkenny down here before the execution date," Kate admitted, with a little grimace tossed Kilkenny's way. He still hadn't turned from the skyline, but Raisa could see every bit of tension in his body. And he'd already been strung too tight before this. "Which, sorry, but, you know, greater good."

Kate even had a way of talking that reminded Raisa of Isabel. "Greater good? Really?"

"Yeah. Of Conrad finally admitting he didn't kill Shay," Kate said.

All three of them shifted at her easy use of Shay's first name. Like they'd been friends. Like she had any right to her at all.

"Okay," Pierce drawled out, clearly sensing that he should control the conversation or something was going to snap. "And how exactly did you figure it out?"

"The letters didn't match," Kate said, blinking innocent eyes at all of them. Somehow, Raisa knew she was lying. "You really should have hired a forensic linguist. Saving a few bucks is *never* worth it."

Raisa glanced at Kilkenny, who had relaxed enough to meet her eyes. Neither of them was going to argue that point, no matter how grating Kate was on both their nerves.

"And we're supposed to just believe that Conrad confessed after you showed him the discrepancy," Pierce said.

"Yes," Kate said. "He did. That footage you can watch right now." She patted the oversize messenger bag at her feet.

"What footage can't we watch, then?" Raisa asked. It seemed strange that what they wanted—the interview where Conrad admitted his guilt—wasn't what Kate was interested in protecting.

"The rest of it," Kate said, with a fake, apologetic smile. "Sorry!"

Kilkenny finally spoke. "You drove in here after giving us the impression we could watch the footage."

It was quiet, damning.

"You can," Kate said, her tone still upbeat and helpful, despite her actions being anything but. She reached for her bag again, but Kilkenny held up a hand.

"You drove in here, you 'got stuck in traffic,' you killed the clock until it was after five p.m.," he said, now fully turned. Raisa had never seen such anger, such disdain, on his face. "You wanted to make sure we couldn't get a warrant today without calling in some favor from a judge, who certainly won't grant it on an emergency basis."

Kate sat back in her chair, her innocent expression dropping away. In its place was something hard, that same something hard that Raisa had glimpsed in their confrontation in Tacoma.

"It's my film, Agent Kilkenny," Kate said, her voice cold and empty of any emotion. "And the person who gets to decide who else watches it early is me—not you and certainly not a judge who would rubber-stamp a warrant."

"We'll get it first thing tomorrow. You bought yourself fourteen hours, congratulations," Kilkenny said.

Kate stared back, impassive.

She would have known that, Raisa realized. If Kate had needed longer, she would have figured out a way. She could have easily dodged Pierce's calls for a few days, then pretended to be traveling from out of state. No one would have been surprised if it had taken a while to get the footage.

But all she'd needed to do was buy herself fourteen hours. Or, fourteen plus the time it would take them to go through the documentary.

Raisa ran through their conversation again.

I have my own agreement with Mr. Conrad.

"He's giving you something tomorrow," Raisa realized. "Some part of your agreement, it's happening tomorrow."

Kate's expression flickered just enough that Raisa knew she'd hit the mark.

Pierce dialed his secretary. "Please call and find out if Ms. Tashibi has an appointment with Nathaniel Conrad scheduled for tomorrow."

"You don't have to make that poor woman go through all that work just to make your point," Kate said, rolling her eyes. "Okay, you're right. I have an appointment with Mr. Conrad in the afternoon. What brilliant minds you are. I'm essentially his biographer, and it's the day he's dying. Of course I have an appointment with him."

That didn't quite sit right for Raisa. Of course, it made sense. But if Kate wanted just one more interview with Conrad, why was she being so stubborn about handing over her footage? Raisa didn't buy the artistic-principles excuse, especially since Kate seemed happy to let them watch the part with the biggest bombshell.

Kate's documentary revealed something she didn't want the FBI to know before Conrad died, Raisa was sure of it.

She just couldn't imagine what that *something* was.

Meanwhile, Pierce called off his secretary. "Never mind, thank you."

Then he turned his attention back to Kate. "What you don't seem to understand, Ms. Tashibi, is that we can get that appointment canceled."

Kate inhaled sharply enough for them all to hear, a misstep when she'd been so composed until then. "You can't do that."

"Oh, I assure you, me and my brilliant mind can and will," Pierce said, the resolve in the words clear. He wasn't bluffing.

This was a different side to him. From what Raisa had seen of him working, he usually went on a charm offensive. But this was just as effective, at least in her book. She was perhaps slightly more impressed by him now.

The moment that followed was fraught. Kate was trying to scheme her way out of showing them the footage, and the rest of them were staring at her, probably wondering the same thing: Was she being protective of her work, or was this something else?

"Fine," Kate said, reaching for her bag a third time. "You want the footage. Here you go."

She set a backup hard drive on Pierce's desk.

"You know, there's a rule of thumb while making a documentary," Kate said, with one of those fake, sweet smiles. "For every minute of film you use in the final version, you need an hour of raw footage. Good luck."

And with that she sailed out the door.

"You could call her back in and make her turn over the edited version," Kilkenny said.

"It's still going to be too many hours," Raisa said, standing. "I'm going to try to reason with her."

"She didn't exactly seem—" Pierce said, but Raisa was already headed through the open door at a jog.

The elevator was on her side, and Raisa managed to sprint out of the office in time to watch Kate beep open the doors on an old Honda Civic not unlike Raisa's own.

"Hey," Raisa called out.

Kate glanced over her shoulder and narrowed her eyes when she spotted who it was.

Raisa slowed to a stop not even out of breath, all those mornings running paying off.

"Are you going to try to use the fact that we both have tits in an effort to bond now?" Kate asked, hands on her hips, ready for a confrontation.

"Look, I mastered the abrasive thing just as much as you clearly have," Raisa said. "I get it, you're tough and don't take shit from anyone."

"So that's a yes?" Kate snarked back. "That might have worked better before you threw me up against a wall."

"Please, a stranger was stalking me three months after I got shot," Raisa said, annoyed that she was forced into playing this game. "What don't you want us to see on those tapes?"

Kate barked out a laugh. "Oh man, I thought you would at least try to be subtle. You got me. With one direct question I'm going to tell you all my hidden secrets. Fed."

"You don't care that we're trying to figure out who killed at least three people?" Raisa asked, letting go of that information to see if she would get a reaction. She didn't.

So Kate knew the second killer had likely struck more than once.

"I do care," Kate said. "Is that all? I have dinner plans."

"You care, but you're not going to help us figure it out?" Raisa asked.

"Who? Them?" Kate waved to the building. "It took them five years to catch Conrad. Like, I'm no Monday-morning quarterback, but don't think you're going to convince me Pinky and the Brain are going to solve this before Conrad rides the lightning."

"They do lethal injection down here," Raisa said absently as she parsed through that. "You think *you* can."

A dimple flashed in her cheek, a blink-and-miss-it tic. "You seem smarter than them, but just barely. What do you think?"

"I think you made some kind of deal with the devil," Raisa said, riding her gut instinct. "And that you think he's going to tell you something that will help you figure it out."

Kate smirked but said nothing.

"But I'm still stuck on why you don't want us to view the raw footage," Raisa said. "If he hasn't told you what you need to know yet."

Some of the arrogance dropped out of Kate's expression, as she stared off into the distance at nothing. Then she swiveled her jaw, a decision made. "He'll know if I tell you anything."

"And if you tell us, he won't give you the information you think you need to solve this," Raisa followed. "You could have told us that."

Kate rolled her eyes. "You've had an easy life, haven't you? You just think everyone can trust law enforcement?"

Raisa didn't argue. She knew why people didn't trust them better than most. "We can act like we don't know anything."

"I don't trust any of y'all, sorry," Kate said. "One of you might be in cahoots with the wrong person. I'm going to go ahead and do my best to keep my word. Tomorrow, we'll all be better for it. You can thank me later."

"You really trust Conrad?"

"I'd trust a killer's promise quicker than I'd trust that the Bureau could handle this without fucking something up," Kate said, lifting one shoulder. "And if he's screwing with me, I'll be no worse off in thirtyish hours. Then I'll tell you everything I know."

Raisa stared at her, knowing when she'd hit a brick wall. Whatever was going on with Kate and Conrad, she wasn't going to sway Kate to abandon the course.

"There's no way we can get through . . . what? Two-hundred-forty-some hours of footage," Raisa said in a Hail Mary. "Give me a scrap. The tits connection has to count for something."

Kate laughed. "Being funny counts for something." She paused. "Okay. I'm guessing you don't watch a ton of true-crime shit."

Raisa gave her a dry look. "I live it."

"Right, well, sometimes when you're *living it*, you forget the obvious tenets that we mere mortals know as gospel." Kate studied Raisa's face, as if expecting her to intuit what she meant. When Raisa didn't,

Kate continued with exaggerated patience, "The first victim always matters."

"Right." Raisa had even written the woman's name down when she'd been familiarizing herself with the facts of the case, sitting in her car outside Kilkenny's house. But they weren't hunting the Alphabet Man. They were hunting his impostor.

And apart from the letters matching his idiolect, they had hard evidence that it had been Nathaniel Conrad who had killed Sidney Stewart.

This wouldn't help them find their second author.

"It doesn't matter who Conrad's first victim was," Raisa said.

"Really? Are you sure about that?" Kate asked. "Because our two killers seem pretty intertwined."

"You could just actually tell me," Raisa said.

"If you don't figure it out—which I'm guessing you won't—I'll tell you once I no longer have to worry about pissing Conrad off," Kate said.

Raisa shook her head. "You have to give me something."

"I don't have to do anything," Kate said, sliding back into annoyed. But she crossed her arms and thought for a second. "You know where Conrad's first victim worked, right?"

"Yeah, she was a gas station attendant," Raisa said. "Up near Dallas."

"But not quite in Dallas, right?"

Raisa hadn't exactly memorized the location. She'd have to trust Kate on that one. "Okay."

"So why was he in that area?" When Raisa stared at her blankly, Kate made a frustrated sound. "You're smarter than that brain trust upstairs, but that's a low bar, darling."

"I've been on this case for twenty-four hours, tops," Raisa said. She wasn't actually sure that timeline was accurate, but the point was valid.

"Okay, well"—Kate shrugged—"if you can figure out why that's important, you might actually get yourself on the right track." And then she turned and slid behind the wheel of her car. She revved the engine until Raisa stepped back, and then tore out of the parking lot.

If Conrad had been stopping at a gas station outside Dallas—back when he'd lived there—he'd been headed somewhere out of town.

Raisa pulled out her phone and texted Kilkenny.

Where was Conrad driving to when he stopped for gas? For the first victim.

The typing bubbles appeared immediately. **Not to, from.**

Raisa rolled her eyes. **Okay, where was he driving from?**

Nothing popped up for a few moments, but Raisa guessed that was more because she'd surprised him with the question than because he didn't know the answer.

He had been interviewing for a job.

Raisa closed her eyes. She didn't need to ask where, but his next text answered it anyway.

In Houston.

Then he'd driven back to Dallas and murdered his first victim along the way.

So, what had it been that had triggered the serial killer waiting beneath his skin?

TRANSCRIPT FROM *THE ALPHABET MAN* DOCUMENTARY

KATE TASHIBI: Let's talk about Sidney Stewart.

NATHANIEL CONRAD: Oh, yes please. She was a delight. My first girl.

TASHIBI: Did something happen to make you choose her? For all your other victims, you picked them ahead of time. You learned their schedules and habits, their friends. Sidney was . . .

CONRAD: Spur of the moment. Yes, you are correct. First, you have to understand, the girls, they have an aura surrounding them. It's a golden hue, it's difficult to explain.

TASHIBI: I think that explains it pretty well.

CONRAD: With Sidney, it was the first time I'd ever seen it. It's beautiful, it's transcendent almost. When they die it changes to a soft, shimmery pink before extinguishing altogether. It's my greatest wish to see that one more time.

TASHIBI: Yeah, I think you're sold out of luck there, buddy.

CONRAD: No. Sadly not. You have an aura, did you know? I would love to get a knife in you and watch it go pink.

TASHIBI: Cool, yeah. That's not going to happen. Did Shay Kilkenny have an aura?

CONRAD: She did not. That's why I didn't kill her. There's no pleasure in killing someone without that golden glow.

TASHIBI: All of your victims had it?

CONRAD: Yes. I had no interest in anyone who didn't. I think . . . I think that's why women tended to like me. I had no predatory intent toward them unless they had the glow. And those girls were few and far between.

TASHIBI: How did you know, that first time that you saw the glow, that it meant you were supposed to kill the girl?

CONRAD: That's a fascinating question, but I have no answer for you, I apologize. I just . . . knew.

TASHIBI: What happened that day? Before you met Sidney.

CONRAD: Are you trying to psychoanalyze me?

TASHIBI: No, I'm trying to tell your story.

CONRAD: I don't think you are. But the end result will be the same. So. Let me think, I was coming back from Houston. I wanted a change of scenery. I was tired of Dallas. A spot had opened up with their social services office down there.

TASHIBI: How did you feel about working for an office that protects vulnerable people when you were killing women?

CONRAD: I felt fulfilled, believe it or not. I did not have a positive experience when I went through it all after my father murdered the rest of my family.

TASHIBI: Did you not? What was that like?

TASHIBI: Mr. Conrad?

TASHIBI: All right, we can move on from that topic. Back to Dallas. You wanted to leave the city?

CONRAD: I realize now that I was searching for my girls, and they were all in Houston. But at the time I simply felt restless.

TASHIBI: I assume the interview went well since you got the job. Who did you talk with?

CONRAD: Any manner of people. I even met with some of the staff at the hospital.

TASHIBI: And who else?

CONRAD: Like I said, a number of people.

TASHIBI: Any that made a lasting impact on you?

TASHIBI: Mr. Conrad?

TASHIBI: Okay, let's move on.

CHAPTER
TWENTY-ONE

Shay

December 2013
Four months before the kidnapping

The doorbell rang.

Shay looked around Kilkenny's condo—she still thought of it as his instead of theirs—as if someone else would be there to answer.

She didn't have friends in Seattle, didn't even have acquaintances. She certainly didn't know anyone who would drop by unannounced.

A delivery, her foggy brain supplied. It had been six months since they'd lost the baby, and she still felt a step behind in her thinking.

Of course—it was a delivery.

Pulling her cardigan tight to hide her stained T-shirt and lack of bra, she shuffled to the door and opened it without bothering to look through the peephole. In the back of her head, she heard Kilkenny scolding her for lax security, especially when he was being targeted by a serial killer.

But she couldn't really make herself give a damn.

Instead of a deliveryman, though, she got a dripping-wet Max.

"What on earth," Shay said, because all other thoughts escaped her at the moment. She hadn't seen her sister since the early summer, at her courthouse wedding to Callum. It had been the longest they'd been apart since Max was born. But Shay hadn't felt like traveling after her miscarriage, and that had happened only a week later. "How did you get here?"

"What a way to greet your sister," Max said, teeth chattering. "Aren't you going to invite me in?"

"Yes, yes, get in here," Shay said, tugging her inside and positioning her on the welcome mat so that she wouldn't slip on the floor from the puddle she made. "Hold on."

Shay grabbed her fluffiest towel from the linen closet, threw a mug of water into the microwave, and then wrapped Max up, rubbing her arms in that way mothers did for little kids when they came out of the pool.

Through sheer muscle memory, Shay dug out tea bags, dropped a couple in the boiling water, and settled them onto the couch.

"What's going on, babe?" Shay asked once the threat of hypothermia had passed.

"I took a bus," Max said, answering the first question that had tumbled out of Shay's mouth. "I slept in a bus station in . . . Colorado? Maybe. I don't know, it doesn't matter."

"I would have bought you a plane ticket," Shay said.

"That would have been a whole thing."

"And this isn't?" Shay asked, trying to keep her voice as light as possible. Her fingers itched for her phone. Did Beau know where Max was?

"You know what, you're right. This was a mistake," Max said, shrugging off the blanket Shay had draped over her.

"No, no, no." Shay grabbed her wrist, stopped her. Again, she asked, "What's going on?"

Max hesitated, but then relented, reaching for her bag. "You can't tell Callum about any of this."

"Oh, Max," Shay murmured, picturing the worst—another gun? That would explain why she hadn't wanted to fly.

"How many times do I have to tell you I'm not a psycho?" Max muttered, but she was distracted, pulling files and articles from her bag. Once she had everything on the table, she began rearranging them. "You have to promise not to tell Callum, or I'll leave."

"All right," Shay said, a little reluctantly. But what was she supposed to do? Just let Max walk out of here in the midst of some kind of emotional emergency?

"Okay," Max said, as if the agreement weren't monumental at all. And of course, it wasn't to her. She'd known what Shay was going to say. "Remember the beach?"

When Shay had told Max about the baby she'd thought had been a new beginning. She swallowed back tears and managed a "Yeah."

"When I asked if you thought I could hurt someone because I was interested in the Alphabet Man"—Max forged ahead—"you said yes."

That jolted Shay enough to get hold of her emotions. "Hey, I didn't say yes."

"Close enough," Max said, rolling her eyes. "You said, 'I think you're a survivor.'"

"Well, I do think you're a survivor. It wasn't just a dodge," Shay said, a little huffy at being read so easily.

Max laughed. "It's fine, dude. I get it. Anyway, I was kind of asking because of a reason."

Shay tensed. "Okay."

"I'm not having violent fantasies or anything like that. Unclench," Max said. "I wondered if you could believe I was violent on such little evidence. It kind of . . . validated a theory I had."

"A theory?"

"Stay with me," Max said. "You're going to want to argue, but just wait for it, okay?"

Shay didn't know if she could actually promise that, but she nodded.

"You know how I've read every article printed on the Alphabet Man case?" Shay just stared at her, until Max rolled her eyes. "It was a rhetorical question. You used to be quicker than this. Anyway, in addition to all those, I went to the library and found some people online who were discussing the case."

"Max," Shay couldn't help but chide. "Stranger danger, babe."

"I didn't ever talk to them," Max said. "I just, you know, lurked."

"Still." Shay had been born in the era where it had been drilled into their heads that every stranger on the internet *could* be a pervert, but it was different these days. The thought alone made her feel incredibly old.

"Oh my god, you're so old," Max said, both reading Shay's mind and sounding her age. Shay had wanted nothing more than for Max to have her bratty teen years, and here they were. "Okay, okay. So between the articles and the lurking, I started seeing a recurring thing."

"A thing?" Shay asked.

"Don't sound so skeptical," Max said, pulling out a map. There were purple x's all over it. "These are the body drops for all the known victims."

Shay couldn't help herself, she leaned forward. She knew a lot of people loved digging around in serial killers' brains, but Shay usually hated this stuff. It was why she'd been so panicky about that stupid goddamn gun years earlier. People might have looked down on her job at the bar, but she had gotten to chat with people, joke with people, make them happy and then go home and turn her mind off. She'd take that any day of the week over what Callum did.

And she would *never* do anything like this if she wasn't being paid for it.

"They look pretty random, right?" Max said. She held up one of those pencil-metal things that every kid used in sixth-grade math. A compass. She stuck the point in the center of the map and then drew a circle using the tool.

Whatever radius she'd set it to was perfect, because it went through about 40 percent of the body drops. And while the line didn't touch all the x's, there were *none* inside the circle. "What?"

Max's finger touched the small indent left behind by the pointy end of the compass.

Shay squinted. "The hospital?"

"At the very center," Max said, as if she were saying something monumental.

"You really think he took a compass and measured out from, what, his home base?" Shay asked.

"No, but I think he made sure he didn't come within a certain distance of anything that could be tied to him," Max said, and then held up a finger. She put the compass down once more and drew a second circle. That picked up about another 30 percent of the body drops. Max tapped the two indents. "I think he lives somewhere around here, and works at the hospital."

"That could be said of half of Houston," Shay pointed out. She was exaggerating, of course. But the circles were large, especially if you took in the area covered by both of them.

"Not really," Max said, calling her on the hyperbole. "You *could* say a lot of people who work at the hospital also live close to it."

Shay randomly thought of Nathaniel Conrad. He'd said he lived only a few minutes away from their house. And while he might not work at the hospital exclusively, he was there enough to have been recognized by security that one time they'd gone in together. The thought itself was foolish, but it just went to show how many people could fall within the two circles.

"This isn't exactly going to convince a jury," Shay said. There had to be thousands upon thousands of employees. It wasn't just hospital staff who used the campus. It was cafeteria workers, gift shop employees, janitorial staff, anyone with admitting rights.

"Right," Max said. "That's why I don't think you can dismiss the Dallas victim."

"The Dallas victim?" Shay asked. She should know all this stuff. She was sure she had at one point. But tuning out the details had kept her sane.

"The first woman, chronologically. She wasn't found first," Max clarified.

Something changed in Max's demeanor, and Shay felt her own body tense in response. Whatever Max was going to say next was the reason she'd hopped on a bus and crossed half a country to see Shay. Some part of Shay knew it must be serious, and she fought the urge to slap her hand over Max's mouth. Why couldn't she just swallow back whatever words were about to change their lives?

Max licked her lips, suddenly looking so nervous and so young. "Sidney Stewart. Her body had deteriorated because of the elements and the time it took to find her. But they were able to give a seventy-two-hour time window for when she died."

"Okay."

"Shay," Max said, her name so soft. "That window? Was only a week after Beau went up to Dallas to meet with that doctor. Remember that? To talk to that specialist who thought he might be able to help Billy."

"No," Shay said, though she must have known this was what Max was leading up to. She'd known and hadn't wanted to acknowledge it. "Beau is not the Alphabet Man."

"You've heard him talk about his grandfather, right?" Max asked. "He was in the war—he taught Beau about ciphers and codes. And Beau used to always be obsessed with those puzzles in the paper."

"Max, no, hon." Shay was actually feeling calm about this. There was no way Beau was the Alphabet Man. "Lots of people like word puzzles. Lots of people have relatives who fought in the war." She tried to remember the rest of the profile Callum had put together. "Lots of people look professional and are employed in positions that garner trust. That doesn't mean they're serial killers."

"He was abused," Max continued, her certainty growing stronger in the face of Shay's denial. "He had major trauma in his childhood. That's one of the hallmarks of Callum's profile."

"Again, as sad as that is, it covers a lot of people," Shay said, trying desperately not to sound condescending. How many people had had these conversations with families over the past few years? Sending each other sideways glances as each new detail was delivered from the task force. *That sounds like Uncle Bob.* Or, *You know, if you squint, our dad fits that mold.* And then they would all laugh and call themselves crazy, and some tiny part of them would think, *Well, maybe.*

Someone had to be right. Someone had to recognize their loved one when enough information had been gathered about them.

This was like horoscopes, though. She respected Callum and what he did, but his profiles could always fit a large swath of people. It was a design feature, not a bug.

Shay took Max's hands in her own and held tight as her sister tried to yank them back. She looked Max in the eyes and said, "I don't think you're crazy for thinking this. I just can't believe Beau is a serial killer. And if you look inside yourself, if you actually think through all the implications, you'll realize that, too. This isn't a book or *Unsolved Mysteries.* This is our brother, who is caring and loving and kind and generous." Shay drew in a breath but squeezed Max's wrist to keep her silent. Where the emotional appeal might fail, the logical one might actually change her mind. "And beyond all that, he doesn't have a basement to hold the girls in for three days. He's not renting one, either. We barely ever had enough money to pay the electricity bill."

Max stared down at their locked hands.

"Why did you get so worried about my serial-killer box?" Max finally asked.

That was one of the last questions Shay had been expecting. The surprise had her blinking at Max, a little dumb. "You know why."

"I need you to say it."

She didn't want to. They hadn't ever acknowledged the fact out loud, had only ever danced around it. But if Max could drop a bomb, so could Shay.

"Because you killed your father," Shay finally said.

And Max? Max smiled. "I didn't shoot him, Shay. Beau did."

CHAPTER TWENTY-TWO

Raisa

Now

The hotel sheets were scratchy against Raisa's back. It was late, past midnight. Less than twenty-four hours until Conrad "rode the lightning," as Kate Tashibi so eloquently put it—as wrong as she'd been about the method.

Raisa couldn't sleep despite the fact that she also hadn't slept the night before.

She considered breaking into the minibar to try to numb her brain into complacency, but instead she swung her legs over the bed. She stared into the darkness for a moment, then headed for the door in her sleep shirt, shorts, and bare feet.

Kilkenny was exhausted. She would feel incredibly guilty if she woke him up, but she promised herself she would knock softly. He opened his own door three seconds after her knuckles touched wood.

He still wore his dress pants and button-down but had shed his jacket and tie, at least. His hair was ruffled, like he'd run his fingers through it too many times.

They'd spent most of their evening focused on the footage Kate had turned over, zeroing in on any mentions of Dallas, or Conrad's early victims.

There was just too much for any one thing to stand out. Pierce had recruited a couple of young agents to keep at it through the night, but Kate had effectively rendered her evidence useless.

If so much weren't riding on this, Raisa would have admired her grit.

Kilkenny didn't say anything in greeting, just stepped back to let her inside. By some unspoken agreement, they moved to the tiny balcony—a little luxury Raisa enjoyed whenever she was in warmer climates.

She curled her legs up onto the plastic chair as Kilkenny handed her a beer and then took his own seat.

"Do you own pajamas?" she asked.

Kilkenny laughed, probably in surprise more than anything. "HR wouldn't approve of this conversation, but I sleep naked."

"You cannot tell me you lounge around in that," Raisa said, waving toward his suit. She was the type to strip out of anything confining before her front door swung fully shut. Kilkenny had always come across as perfectly poised and polished, but she'd imagined that when he went home, he unbent enough to put on comfy sweatpants and ratty T-shirts. This new image was just too sad to bear.

"I have been known to don the garments of the peasants on the odd occasion," Kilkenny said, the corners of his mouth twitching. Raisa laughed fully for what felt like the first time in twenty-four hours.

They settled into comfortable silence, and she took a swallow of her beer as she stared out at the city lights. "Would you have been happy living here?"

"I would have been happy anywhere Shay was."

Two days ago, Raisa might have believed that completely. Now, because she was just so tired, she asked, "Do you ever think you buy into the mythology?"

"Of me and Shay?" Kilkenny asked, following along as usual. "Sure, of course. It's easy to love a ghost. They never change. All their faults fade, while everything you adored about them stays."

"Maybe not easy," Raisa allowed. "But less complicated."

"We weren't perfect," Kilkenny said. "I never said we were, though. I let everyone else fill in their own blanks."

That much was true. This was the most she'd ever heard him talk about Shay.

"It was hard, us, our relationship," he continued. "I was away so much, and she was so isolated. And sad, toward the end. Something would have broken—but not us."

"You have such faith," Raisa said, not doubting, but envious, maybe. She wasn't sure she'd ever believed in the strength of any relationship—romantic or platonic—to that extent. To know that no matter what, it wouldn't break.

Kilkenny lifted a shoulder, as if having that kind of faith were easy. As if it were a given.

"Do you know what was the hardest part?" he asked, and continued without waiting for an answer. He seemed to want to talk tonight, and she was game. "Not being able to share anything. That created more space between us than the distance itself."

There were plenty of jobs out there that were either sensitive or boring enough that a spouse might not be able to or even want to share details about. But the work they did was taxing. It was seeing the worst of the world and then having to keep that locked up inside. Raisa knew that Kilkenny wasn't thinking about sharing details like what color ink the Alphabet Man used, but not being able to talk about having to see those tattoos and think about the man who pressed a needle into dying flesh was difficult.

"Is it strange when people talk about your relationship?" Raisa asked, almost shocked by her own boldness. But it was past midnight, and her tongue had been loosened by a number of factors. And Kilkenny was a big boy as well as a master at dodging questions he didn't want to answer. If he wanted to end the conversation, he would.

"Yes," Kilkenny admitted. "Like you said, it's become myth now. She's been deified, and, honestly? Shay would have hated how they've made her into this perfect person. She was just . . . she was just a woman. A flawed and funny and hot and smart and stubborn woman. And that's reason enough to mourn the loss to the world. She didn't have to be perfect to be missed."

It was strange how people only liked certain types of victims. Good, pure, honest—white and blonde. Otherwise they deserved to die for one reason or another. They wore too short a skirt, or they drank too much at a strange location, or they ran when they should have complied.

Shay was one of those perfect victims. A pretty body that became a blank slate to be written on. Over.

"I never get to talk about her," Kilkenny said softly.

"You can now," Raisa offered.

Kilkenny huffed out a breath. "I'm too rusty."

"I can wait."

"It might be a while," Kilkenny said. "Maybe not tonight."

"I can wait," Raisa repeated.

They sat in silence for a while before Kilkenny shifted toward her, his eyes clear and sharp now. She braced herself.

"You're keeping something from me."

He was probably right, but Raisa couldn't for the life of her remember what it was. "What?"

"I don't know how I know with you," Kilkenny admitted. "We haven't worked together enough for me to tell. But you're keeping something from me."

She squinted at him for a minute before it hit her, and she almost laughed. "Oh, Jesus. Right. I brought Delaney in on all this."

"Delaney," Kilkenny said, his voice completely neutral, not judgmental at all. He felt fonder toward Delaney than Raisa did, though. Or was at least more understanding.

"If we have a second killer, which we both agree, yes we do?" Raisa asked, checking in. He nodded. "Then it's weird that they only killed three times. Delaney's looking for patterns."

"Patterns and logic," Kilkenny murmured, like it was an inside joke. "You trust her?"

"Enough."

"You weren't doing well with it," Kilkenny pointed out. "Everything."

That was a gentle understatement. Raisa thought back to what she'd been forced to tell Isabel.

Do you have nightmares about me?

Most nights.

She thought of the list Kilkenny had sent her of therapists who could help her work through the trauma of her entire life being upended. She hadn't wanted to talk to any of them, but this wasn't Kilkenny the psychologist asking.

This was Kilkenny the friend.

And turnabout was fair play. She'd just spent a half hour pressing on his bruises; she couldn't balk when he did the same back.

Raisa said, "Yeah, well, when your sister turns out to be a psychopath serial killer, and your other sister turns out to be someone who aids and abets said serial killer . . . well, you have to start to wonder about yourself."

"Do you come down on the nature side of psychology?" Kilkenny asked. "Your life didn't shape you at all, or not enough to win out against blood?"

"No. Maybe. I don't know," Raisa said. She didn't want to think she was someone who believed there were those who were born to be serial killers. Or born to be evil. But . . . maybe she was. "It's terrifying, though. Looking at the sliding-door image of yourself, of what you could have become under different circumstances. To know that's within you, only a traumatic life event from being unlocked. And it wasn't just my sisters—from what it sounds like, my brother wasn't exactly proving the theory wrong, either."

Her brother hadn't been the one to kill their parents, like everyone had thought for twenty-five years, but in his short sixteen years, he'd left other kinds of victims behind.

"But none of them are sliding-door images of you," Kilkenny pointed out. "They're their own people."

Raisa nodded not because she believed it but because she wanted him to think she did. "When do you think it happens? That point of no return? What age was it that Isabel and Delaney and Alex became what they were going to become? What moment?"

Kilkenny shook his head. "If we knew that . . ."

"Right. We might not be here today, talking about Nathaniel Conrad," Raisa said. "Do you think he would have turned out any differently if his father hadn't poisoned his whole family?"

"No," Kilkenny said. "I think he's wired to be evil and nothing could have stopped him."

That was not the Kilkenny she knew. He was an optimist. He believed in the good in people, even when he saw the monstrous in them day in and day out. "Nothing?"

"No, I'm being a dick," Kilkenny admitted. "We're learning more every day. You know they've found a link between head trauma, psychological stressors at a young age, and serial killers? Maybe that means intervention is possible." He paused. "I have to believe it's possible."

"It would be pretty grim if it wasn't," Raisa said. She herself had often wondered about budding psychopaths. If you could identify them, how did you protect both them and the world from themselves? If they hadn't done anything yet, you couldn't just lock them up. And yet, could you live with letting them roam free until they killed? "And, hey. Maybe my parents dropped the three older children on their heads, but learned their lesson when it came to me."

"That's the way to look at it," he said, holding his beer bottle out to her so they could clink necks.

"You seem . . . 'better' isn't the right word," Kilkenny observed. "But something like that. This case has been good for you. To get back in the field."

He was right. Raisa felt more settled in her skin than she had in months, tired and brain-hazy as she was. It helped to move forward. The past three months she'd been stuck in that clearing, Isabel's gun pressed to her spine. The memory had kept her paralyzed. "'Better' is the right word. I needed a reminder that monsters can be beat."

"Yeah."

"And your monster is about to be yeeted out of this universe," Raisa said.

"Yeeted," Kilkenny repeated. And then he lost it. Absolutely lost it. Full-on bellyache laughs, then giggles, back to bellyaches until he finally tapered into erratic hiccups of amusement.

"Wow. That was . . . that was glorious," Raisa observed as Kilkenny wiped at the corners of his eyes.

"Jesus," Kilkenny muttered. "Yeeted. That's terrible."

"Maybe, but no less true," Raisa pointed out. "Are you going to see him tomorrow?"

"Of course," he said without hesitation.

"What are you going to ask him?"

Kilkenny opened his mouth, closed it. "Something."

Raisa cackled. "Brilliant. Practically Sherlockian."

"Shut up," Kilkenny said, completely out of character and endearing. "Honestly, though? I don't know. When we were chasing him, I had a million questions I knew I'd ask if I ever got to face him down. But now, I'm so uninterested in anything he has to say. He killed those girls because his brain is wired wrong. We're killing him because that's how we've figured out how to deal with people like that."

He shrugged. "And I'll continue to try to keep the cycle going."

"Hey," Raisa said, because she didn't want him to go grim about the mouth again just yet. "Tell me something about Shay that no one else knew."

"She loved being a bartender," Kilkenny said, without hesitation. "Everyone thought she was just doing it to make a wage, I guess. But, God, she loved talking to people. About things that interested them. That was her favorite thing—to really get someone going about something they loved. No matter how trivial or foolish it might seem to anyone else. All you had to do to see someone at their most beautiful was to ask them a question. That was her philosophy."

"What did she ask you about?" Raisa realized after the words had already tumbled out that it might have been mean. Kilkenny had interests, she was sure. Most people didn't know about them; she didn't know about them. That didn't mean they didn't exist.

"Wine," Kilkenny said. "I'm a big wino."

"You are not," Raisa said, but she didn't push for a real answer. There was one, she was sure. But it was private. Raisa wouldn't intrude where only ghosts dared tread.

"Have you ever loved someone like that?" Kilkenny asked.

"No." She would have danced around it with someone else. But here, wrapped in the protective bubble of night, she was truthful. "There was grad school and before that college and before that, you know, surviving. There's always an excuse, always a reason to be too busy."

"But?" he asked, because he was a psychologist before he was anything else.

"It's always an excuse, isn't it?" Raisa said, with a shrug. "I don't want to be hurt anymore. So I make sure I won't be."

"Mmm. Sometimes I worry," Kilkenny said.

"About what?" Raisa asked, hoping the answer wasn't about her.

"That I can't ever be hurt again."

CHAPTER TWENTY-THREE

Shay

December 2013
Four months before the kidnapping

I didn't shoot him, Shay. Beau did.

The words trembled in the air between Shay and Max, the aftershocks of an earthquake. Shay concentrated on just breathing as Max watched her.

"You thought Beau told you everything, didn't you?" Max asked. "He has so many secrets. You're just so easy to lie to because you always believe anything he tells you. He loves that about you."

"Don't be cruel," Shay snapped.

But Max was Max. Even if she hadn't ever killed anyone, she still had a mean streak. "You really think his father went out on a joyride at three a.m.?"

Shay pictured Callum in their kitchen in Houston after Billy's funeral.

Where was he driving to?

Did he have any enemies?

"Do you really think it was a coincidence that two men connected to our family died like that?" Max asked, relentless. Heartless. "I walked in on Beau just after he pulled the trigger, you know. He was still holding the literally smoking gun."

Shay's world rearranged itself. She had always imagined the scene in reverse. Max holding the gun, Beau walking in on her and the body. Beau taking and stashing the gun as he told her to go call 911. They would suggest it was a robbery and let the cops take it from there.

But then she thought of the way Beau had defended Max. He had always insisted that Max was fine, that she was normal, that she wasn't going to turn into a vicious criminal. Shay had thought it sweet of him to have such faith, but that had never been the case. He'd simply been lying to her all along.

Or . . . she tried to remember. Had he ever said Max was the one who'd shot her father? Had he just implied it? The three of them had never addressed the incident head-on, and both her siblings must have been going out of their way to protect the other.

So had she. She'd been the one who'd driven nearly to Galveston in a panic that night after meeting Callum the first time. She'd just been protecting a different person than she'd thought.

And it would have been important for Max to be the one to find the body if they wanted to keep Beau out of jail. If Beau had been the one to call the police, the cops would have been far less likely to go with the far-fetched story of a startled petty criminal. Max had been eleven—no one would have wanted to prosecute, even if they were shaky about the truth of it all. Beau was a different story.

But Shay wasn't the cops. They could have told her.

Then there was Billy.

How had Callum been the only one to sense something was going on beneath the surface there? And why had Beau done it?

Even if Max was being cruel right now, painting Beau as something he wasn't, Shay knew him.

She *knew* him. He would never kill just to kill. And he'd forgiven Billy long ago, so it wasn't revenge.

Should Shay even believe Max? What if Max was the one lying to her?

"Just remember how old I was when Billy had his little accident," Max said. She must have read Shay's mind.

Max would have been young, too young to pour two bottles of Jack down Billy's throat and then manhandle him into his car.

That didn't mean she wasn't lying about her father. Shay chewed on her lip. Maybe it didn't matter either way.

"I never actually thought you were the Alphabet Man," Shay said, directing this conversation back to the present. "Just because you were collecting all that stuff about him. Even when I thought you'd already killed once."

"I was, like, twelve when he started killing," Max said, the eye roll obvious in her voice. "I'm not saying twelve-year-olds can't kill people, but even if you think I'm both totally psychotic and also incredibly mature for my age, I still would have struggled to do all this."

She waved a hand at the articles, at the maps. "The tattooing alone should have ruled me out."

"I'm saying I never thought you were a serial killer," Shay said again. "And I don't think Beau is, either."

"But you're less sure than you were ten minutes ago, aren't you?" Max said. "I've been following this for years. How do you think *I* feel?"

"What was the first thing?" Shay asked, because her brain had started working again. "That made you think: *Beau*."

"You weren't home at night. You didn't realize Beau doesn't always come back when he tells you he does," Max said. "It wasn't intentional. I just noticed that anytime a victim was found, the night before, Beau came in late."

"That's a coincidence, not evidence."

"Good thing I'm not a jury that needs convincing," Max said. "It happened seven times, Shay."

Three times is a pattern, she thought.

A memory came to her. Her first night with Kilkenny, getting the gun, driving toward Galveston. That morning, when she'd arrived home, Beau had called her out on hooking up with someone and she'd fired the accusation right back.

He had flinched.

Shay's eyes tracked to the room Callum had turned into a home office. Did he have files in there? Real files, not Max's cobbled-together Nancy Drew effort. Real evidence, maybe, that Shay could point to and say, *No, see, Beau can't possibly be a serial killer.*

She halted that train of thought as soon as it left the station. "Say you're right about your father and Billy. Beau took care of them because he was protecting you. And maybe protecting himself, I don't know. He loved Billy at the end . . ."

"Billy was dating a woman with a son who was about ten," Max said. "They were getting serious. Beau met them. The kid had a bruise the size of Billy's hand on his wrist. Turns out it wasn't just the booze that made him mean around kids. Two days later he drove into a tree. The woman didn't stick around after that."

"Why didn't I know any of this?" Shay asked, her voice shaking.

"Because you're just . . . different than us," Max said. "You're . . . nice."

"Beau's nice," Shay said without thinking.

Max stared at her for a long time, then started laughing. "Jeez, girl, tell me what you really think of me."

"You know you're not nice," Shay said. "Doesn't mean I don't love you."

"It means you don't like me," Max countered.

"Not true." Shay plopped down on the couch beside her. "I like you a lot. I was just always worried for you."

"And all the psychologists who said I was fine?" Max asked.

"You'll understand if you ever have a kid," Shay said, and for the first time in six months didn't tear up at her own careless words.

Max nudged her knee, her version of a comforting hug.

"You always worry about your kids," Shay said, her smile wobbly, but there.

"Awww," Max drawled out, mocking her but only because she didn't like to show any real emotions. "But you're proving my point. You're too nice. Beau's not going to tell you he killed two guys—you'd freak the frick out."

She thought again of her nighttime flight to that junkyard. And the time she'd run out of the bar when Xander Pierce had shown up unexpectedly.

"Okay, fair, I would have," Shay admitted. Her world had become solid again, because Max hadn't really dropped as big a bomb as Shay was expecting. Beau might have *taken care of* two people without telling her, but he'd done it for family.

You killed for family. You helped hide the body.

None of that changed who Beau was as a person.

"But you're also proving my point," Shay said. "Beau doesn't kill for fun. He did it to protect you, and then he did it to protect that kid. He's not kidnapping girls, torturing them, and dumping them naked in random fields all over the city."

Max slumped back against the couch. "Have you ever read Beau's DFPS file?"

"No, and you shouldn't have, either," Shay said. This was getting too much. Max had taken it upon herself to play amateur detective, and that kind of behavior got people *taken care of.*

"You've both read mine," Max countered.

"We're your legal guardians," Shay said, exasperated. "Please tell me I don't have to explain the difference."

Max smirked. "No, but it still makes me feel less guilty about it." She searched among her paper pile and pulled out a manila folder. "The good stuff is on page seven. The psychological evaluation."

Shay refused to take it, so Max shrugged, opened it herself, and started reading out loud.

"'Given his inability to control his violent impulses, further counseling is recommended,'" Max said.

"That evaluation was given when he was eight years old," Shay countered. "Eight-year-olds have a hard time controlling any of their impulses. And Beau wasn't just any eight-year-old."

"Fine, I'm not going to convince you," Max said. "I had to try, though."

"Why? You don't want me to tell Callum."

Max rolled her eyes again. God, she was so young. "No. So that we could stage an intervention."

"For our brother, who you think is a serial killer," Shay said, an edge of amused hysteria creeping into her voice. "Hey, Beau, want to stop torturing and violently killing girls? Please *and* thank you."

"Well, I didn't think that far ahead," Max admitted.

"Yeah, you just thought far enough ahead that you snuck out, bought a bus ticket, and crossed the country because Beau's grandfather liked ciphers." No matter what Max said, Shay could be a little mean, too. "Why now?"

"Three days ago he came home late," Max said, eyes narrowed like she wanted to slap back but also wanted to actually give a real answer, too. "I was waiting for him."

"Oh, Max," Shay whispered. "If he actually was dangerous, that was incredibly risky."

"I don't think he would hurt me."

"People are always certain of that right up until they get hit," Shay countered.

"Not me," Max said, the hardness that defined her on full display. "I always knew . . . *he* . . . would hurt me. I just couldn't get away from him."

"Until Beau," Shay said softly. You killed for family. You hid the body.

How could Max think Beau was anything but an old knight born into a too-modern era, trying to protect those he loved? An old knight who'd had only so-so success trusting the judicial system. Shay didn't condone his actions, of course. But she would never, ever regret that Max's father was dead. She couldn't.

"I don't want him arrested," Max said, sounding defensive for the first time. "That's why I came here instead of the cops."

"Okay," Shay soothed her. "You were waiting for him."

"I asked him where he'd been. He told me it was none of my business," she said.

"Well, that was fair." They tried to treat Max with respect, but they were the adults in the house, and that meant something even if it didn't always seem that way.

"Technically, he's in charge of me, so it was my business," Max pointed out. "I pushed. He kept saying no. Then I saw the blood."

Oh, Beau. Shay just shook her head, though. "He could have gotten that anywhere."

"It was on his shirt. Just a few spots, but nothing he'd get while shaving," Max said. "And it wasn't from a patient, because I asked, and he didn't think quickly enough to lie."

That was hardly real evidence, not without a DNA test on the blood. It could very easily be his.

"What did he say?"

"That it was none of my business," Max said again. "And when I asked for the fiftieth time, he said he was helping out after a bar fight. Some guy broke his nose while slipping on beer, and Beau got in the splash zone and helped him plug up the blood."

"Then that's what happened," Shay said with finality. It was almost believable. Beau would have, of course, helped in that situation, his medical instincts kicking in.

"Fine—you want to explain all that away, fine," Max said. "But Shay. Where's Callum right now?"

"Houston," Shay said, without really thinking about it.

"Because they just found another Alphabet Man victim," Max said. "Who was probably killed around the same time Beau came home with blood on his shirt."

Shay shook her head.

"One thing is chance," Max said, in a leading voice.

Shay had looked up the original quote back after that conversation in the kitchen with Callum. It came from Ian Fleming—a James Bond saying of all things—and then it had gotten bastardized as it entered common language.

Once is happenstance, twice is coincidence, three times is enemy action.

But with all due respect to both Fleming and Callum, Shay wasn't convinced. People liked to draw connections where none existed. And like she'd thought earlier, all this was about as convincing as horoscopes. She could even prove it. "I fit the profile just as well as Beau does. I'm a child who experienced trauma—no matter what you think, living with Hillary's rotating cast of boyfriends wasn't exactly a treat. I work in this area." Shay tapped the bar's location, near the hospital, now that she thought about it. Funny, that. Then she tapped the second. "I live in this one."

"No blood, no missing nights when girls have disappeared," Max pointed out.

"You don't know that," Shay challenged. "You're asleep when I get home. The bar has a cellar. I could be holding the girls down there. They aren't sexually assaulted—that could be explained by the killer being a woman."

"You didn't fly to Houston a few nights ago."

"And you know that how?" When Max didn't say anything, Shay kept going. "I'm sure you can dig up some damning psychological evaluation from when I was eight. I like word puzzles, too."

"No you don't," Max said, but she sounded uncertain for the first time all evening.

Shay started to relax.

"Max, the blood could be from a bar fight," she said, conciliatory now, not mocking. "He might be dating someone and not want to tell us, which would keep him out late. He went to Dallas *a week* before the outside TOD for that first victim. Beau might kill for family, but he doesn't kill for fun."

Max just stared at her for a long minute before pressing the heels of her hands to her eyes. "Oh my god, I really thought he was the Alphabet Man."

Shay chewed her lip, but then Max let out a little hiccuping giggle, and Shay couldn't help it. The next minute they were laughing, tears running down their cheeks, clinging to each other somewhere between hysteria and relief.

When they finally settled, Shay kept her arms around Max, feeling closer to her than she had in years. She kissed the top of her sister's head. "I never thought you were a psycho killer."

"You said that already."

"I'll say it as many times as I need for you to believe it," Shay said.

"Shay?" Max asked after a minute.

"Yeah?"

"I think you should know something," she said, and Shay braced herself, pushing away a little, though just enough to be able to look into Max's eyes.

"What's that?"

"I *would* kill for you," Max said. Some people might say that as hyperbole, but this was a promise.

You killed for family. You helped bury the body.

Shay nodded and said, "I wouldn't hesitate for even a second."

CHAPTER TWENTY-FOUR

Raisa

Now

Raisa managed about three hours of sleep, but she was up with the sun. Kate Tashibi had said to focus on Dallas and the interview day, and Raisa believed her.

It was a long shot, but she called the social services office Conrad had worked for while he was in Houston. Of course, no one answered at the butt crack of dawn, but she left a message with her badge number and details about the case.

What she wanted was a list of the people Conrad had met, even briefly, during his day in Houston. Kate was right—he'd been triggered into killing his very first victim only a day later. It seemed like too much to be a coincidence.

No more than a minute after she hung up, a call came in.

Delaney.

Raisa closed her eyes for one beat. And then answered.

"What do you have for me?"

"Good morning to you, too," Delaney said, dryly. "I found one more male victim in the Houston area that might match your list."

"Can you—"

"It's sitting in your inbox as we speak," Delaney cut in. "Time frame is right, age is right. Mother seemed like she was Munchausen by proxy. But she died when our vic was nine."

"Sounds like exactly what I was looking for," Raisa said. "Thanks."

"Hold your applause," Delaney said. "I could have sent that all to you yesterday. But I got curious. This seems like a definite pattern with our killer. So I broadened the search to all of Texas."

Raisa hummed in approval. "You found something."

"Three more cases. The victims all had some kind of violence in their past," Delaney said. "When they were young children. But what was more interesting was that they were also then freed from that situation in some manner. So Munchausen guy was being abused, and then his mother died a mysterious death. Same goes with the other three."

"It's both. They were abused *and* escaped it," Raisa said. Like Max. Like Beau, almost, even if it was delayed. Like Isabel and Delaney and herself, though she might have been too young for it to match up perfectly. Was she looking for patterns? Or maybe they just lived in an incredibly cruel world, where people who were exposed to trauma and crime at a young age tended to be the ones, statistically, who experienced it throughout their lives.

"Yup. And one of the other interesting things of note is that they weren't all men," Delaney said. "There were two women as well."

"Interesting." Raisa couldn't see the bigger picture yet, but she felt like they were closing in.

"I'm sending you information on all of them," Delaney said. "You might be able to find more through the official files, but it doesn't appear anyone's made the connection between the victims. And they all died in different ways, so I probably wouldn't have, either—except that I knew what to look for."

"Like with Isabel," Raisa murmured, not sure she'd meant to say that out loud. "How she killed."

Heavy silence greeted her, but then Delaney made a thoughtful sound. "Exactly like Isabel, actually. Only one of the deaths was even suspicious—a mugging gone wrong.

"There was a single-car accident and then an apparent suicide," she continued. And for one ridiculous second, Raisa had such intense déjà vu that she wondered if they were somehow looking at Isabel's trail of death. She had been killing for two and a half decades before she'd been caught, after all.

"Isabel?" she tried out, hardly believing it, but needing to put it into the universe.

"I don't think so," Delaney said, and Raisa relaxed slightly. Delaney would know. "I think Isabel was in the Pacific Northwest when a few of these occurred."

"La la la la la, I didn't hear that," Raisa said. Ignorance was bliss when it came to Delaney's knowledge of Isabel's crimes. For all anyone was supposed to believe, Delaney hadn't talked to Isabel since they'd been teens.

But Raisa couldn't get on her high horse if she was using Delaney for her services.

"There are similarities to Isabel, though," Raisa said.

After another moment of silence, Delaney asked, "Did she ever tell you how she figured out that Conrad didn't kill Shay Kilkenny?"

"She said the letters sent during that time didn't match the ones Conrad had sent earlier," Raisa said. "And she was right."

"Hmm."

"What are you thinking?" Raisa asked.

"Well, for all her strengths, Isabel is quite the liar," Delaney said delicately, and Raisa snorted.

"Her strengths?"

"She does have some," Delaney said. "But she has no relationship with the truth."

"You think she lied to me?" Raisa asked, dubious despite the fact that she'd just had that thought. "But she was right."

"The two things aren't necessarily mutually exclusive," Delaney lectured. She had a tendency to do that, but it was actually a good reminder, so Raisa couldn't begrudge it this once. "Maybe she knew Conrad hadn't killed Shay, but she didn't want to tell you how she knew. She needed to convince you, though, so she found something that would." She paused, and then repeated the sentiment from earlier: "It's easier when you know what to look for."

"Why lie, though?" Raisa asked, not expecting an answer.

She didn't get one. "I don't know. But it might be worth figuring out. I know you have limited time . . ."

Raisa rubbed her palm against her forehead, the pain brewing there just a wisp now. But she could see it becoming a thunderstorm. "I've got quite the list going."

"Let me know if I can help with anything else," Delaney offered, then seemed to stop herself from hanging up. "Oh, but I found one more thing to add to your plate."

"Oh lord," Raisa muttered. "Okay, lay it on me."

"I got curious."

"Yes, you mentioned that," Raisa said.

"One of the extra things I did, because I'm brilliant, was run a check on any kids that might have fit Conrad's trajectory. So, a child who was a sole survivor of a mass-casualty event," Delaney said without acknowledging the interruption.

Raisa made an approving sound. It was similar to their other search.

"The match wasn't perfect," Delaney continued. "But it was interesting. There were two survivors, but four other family members died in the incident. It was close enough that my filters caught it. And then once I saw who it was . . ."

"Am I going to recognize the name?" Raisa guessed, bracing herself.

"Yes, ma'am," Delaney drawled. "It was Kate Tashibi."

Kilkenny knocked on Raisa's hotel room door ten minutes later, holding out a coffee with a chain's logo on the cup.

Raisa took it gratefully. She could never drink the cheap swill hotels provided. "Bless you."

"I don't think I've thanked you for coming down here," Kilkenny mused as she grabbed her bag and headed into the hallway. "I owe you a lot more than coffee."

"You don't have to," Raisa said. "But I'll never say no to coffee."

"Or Four Roses," Kilkenny said, nudging her shoulder. She laughed softly.

"Or that," she agreed. She'd wondered if they would be awkward with each other, a twist on the morning after, where the vulnerability had come from sharing emotions rather than sharing a bed. But Kilkenny looked loose, almost relaxed, and she thought she might have actually helped.

She grinned into her cup and then filled him in on everything Delaney had shared.

"Kate," Kilkenny murmured when she wrapped it all up. They were by his car now, and he fiddled with the keys. "Might explain her interest in Conrad."

"Yeah," Raisa said as they climbed into the SUV. They were headed to the prison for one last talk with Conrad.

Once Kilkenny settled into his seat, she slid him a look, trying to assess if he'd had the thought she had when she'd heard Kate's name. The woman's red flags were starting to add up. She'd manipulated them yesterday, lied to them, wormed her way into Conrad's life and into contact with the original investigators—something Raisa knew Kilkenny had suggested might happen in his original Alphabet Man profile.

And now this.

Kilkenny's expression remained thoughtful, but not shaken.

"So, do you think she's our second killer?" Raisa asked when he didn't say anything.

"The first victim that we think is from our second killer was found . . . thirteen years ago?" Kilkenny asked, obviously doing quick math.

"Yeah."

"That puts Kate at ten or so," Kilkenny said. "Probably rules her out."

"You have to be all logical," Raisa teased. She waited until he pulled out onto the road so that she wouldn't have to worry about him scrutinizing her expression. "I'm getting shades of Isabel with all of this."

"You do have PTSD," Kilkenny pointed out, and they both knew he was being serious. "And a true-crime documentarian is a close cousin to a podcaster."

Which Isabel had tried her hand at with the intention of getting close to the investigation back in Everly. Raisa silently admitted he had a point.

"I do think it means something that we keep seeing similarities in all these people," Raisa said, shifting them away from her trauma.

"And that Conrad himself fits the pattern," Kilkenny agreed.

She almost hesitated to say it, but right now, no theory was too wild. "So when I met with that reporter yesterday? He suggested a vigilante. Someone who killed people who matched the profile for the Alphabet Man."

Kilkenny grimaced, as she'd known he would. "We always take that risk when we make the information public."

Putting a target on a particular type of person was more of a safety issue when the profile included details that would attract bigots, but there were always loose cannons you had to worry about whenever including a wider audience.

"A vigilante would have to square up with the fact that he was killing innocent men, though," Kilkenny said.

"That's what I mentioned as well, and Mr. Sasha Malkin chided me for trying to make sense of a madman's mind," she said, and Kilkenny laughed before tipping his head in acknowledgment.

"Well, that's fair."

Raisa chewed on her lip. This would be the moment to bring up something she'd been thinking about. But she wasn't sure she wanted to lob the bomb.

Of course Kilkenny could tell. "What?"

She inhaled. And then ripped off the Band-Aid. "Do you want to hear the reporter's other pet theory?"

"Pierce."

"How did you know?" she asked.

"We all worked together closely for five years," Kilkenny said with a shrug. "You end up picking up some things. Toward the end, it became kind of an inside joke between Pierce and Malkin."

"You never suspected Pierce, then?" Raisa asked.

Kilkenny glanced over, taking his eyes off the road to do so. He was usually such a careful driver, that alone telegraphed his complete surprise. It was as if he hadn't realized this conversation had been serious until just then.

"I suppose I considered everyone at some point," Kilkenny said. "There was a strange moment between him and Shay at the Christmas party we went to one time."

"A strange moment?"

"I went to grab a folder from my office, and when I came back, things were tense between them," Kilkenny said. "I assumed he made some drunken pass. She wouldn't say anything. That's the only time I've ever questioned him being a good guy, though."

"I mean, not to excuse his behavior, but drunken flirting and serial killing are two pretty different levels," Raisa said.

He nearly smiled. "Exactly. I could never seem to land on him as suspicious."

"Why?"

"Timing mostly, I guess. I knew where he was when the Alphabet Man would have had to be somewhere else," Kilkenny said.

"Okay, but now we know Pierce wasn't the Alphabet Man, he could fit the vigilante theory, right?" Raisa offered. "He got tired of chasing Conrad through official channels, and took matters into his own hands."

"But . . . Shay," Kilkenny said. "If he was after the Alphabet Man, and only him, he wouldn't have killed Shay."

"She found out and he was covering his own ass."

"Okay, I can't believe him capable of that, but let's say he was. That doesn't account for the last victim," Kilkenny said. "If Pierce had somehow finally identified Conrad, why not stage it to make himself look like a hero? None of us got much glory for the capture, not with how everyone thought it was Conrad's mistake."

"Yeah, you're right." They kept coming back to these roadblocks. She had to have faith that one of these times they'd bust through them, but they were running out of hours.

Before she could push him for more wild theories, she saw the crowd. Then the vans, then the reporters and cameras and lights. She saw the protesters, pressed up against the prison's wired fence, most of them holding signs with anti–death penalty slogans scrawled across them. There were several people with bullhorns, standing on crates to lift them above the sea of people.

When Kilkenny rolled down his window to talk to the security guard, the noise rushed in. They were chanting something Raisa had no interest in deciphering.

She very much supported these people's right to be here, but she wished she could somehow shield Kilkenny from them. He had to have enough conflicting feelings about what was happening. He didn't need this extra stressor.

Raisa hadn't needed to wonder what the protesters would do. Someone caught sight of Kilkenny, and they all turned like sharks scenting blood. They pushed toward the SUV, hands reaching out as if to beat on the windows, on the doors.

"Go, sir," the security guard yelled, but Kilkenny couldn't just gun it without risking clipping someone.

"Kilkenny," Raisa said, eyeing the group, which was transforming into a mob before their eyes.

"Yup," Kilkenny acknowledged, jaw tight. He slowly pressed on the gas, moving forward even as someone cried out.

Raisa unbuckled, lifting out of her seat to check. No one appeared hurt. "They're fine."

The gate closed behind them and Kilkenny breathed out. "Jesus."

Even though she'd had a continuous clock ticking down in her head, it was almost like she'd forgotten.

It was execution day.

EXCERPT FROM THE *AUSTIN AMERICAN-STATESMAN*

4 DIE IN ATTEMPTED CARJACKING

May 10, 2006

A tragedy rocked the quiet neighborhood of Brentwood over the weekend when an attempted carjacking turned fatal. Haruto and Mio Tashibi were driving home from a family reunion just past midnight on Sunday with their two young daughters and two teenage nephews. Haruto Tashibi, who was driving, was forced to a stop by a car parked in the middle of the road. According to video obtained by the Austin police, three masked men confronted Haruto Tashibi. After a short discussion, they fired into the car, approximately thirty times.

Neighbors called emergency services once they heard the shots.

Haruto and Mio Tashibi and their two nephews were pronounced dead on the scene. Their two daughters survived, but both are in critical condition at St. David's North Austin Medical Center.

CHAPTER TWENTY-FIVE

Shay

January 2014
Two months before the kidnapping

Shay didn't tell Callum about Max.

She didn't know why precisely. As her husband, Callum was family now. But she liked the memory of Max in her arms, both of them seeking comfort in the other. Sisters had a bond that couldn't be rendered null, even by husbands.

Callum was tired. Shay had pretty much been thinking that since they'd met, but it had settled deep into his bones now. She finally talked him into taking a Friday off a few weeks after Max's unexpected visit.

They woke up incredibly early and made the four-hour drive to Cannon Beach. With the sun in their eyes and the window down on the unseasonably warm day, it almost felt like Texas. Spiritually, at least.

By the time they made it to the small Oregon town, the parking spaces had pretty much filled up. They managed to find something outside a small café, and they ordered cappuccinos and drank them at the two-top folding tables on the sidewalk.

Shay had packed them a lunch, which they took to the beach, the haystack formations looming large in front of them.

There were tourists everywhere, which was fine because they were tourists, too. Shay always hated people who complained about the very thing they were contributing to. They found a section in the back corner of the beach and laid out the blanket and cracked open the canned wine Shay had packed, each taking one. It was barely lunchtime, but vacations were for booze and sea mist in your hair—Shay would never be convinced otherwise.

Shay stared out into the water and wondered why all her best days revolved around the ocean. Was it the endless expanse, the opportunities it offered? Was it the salt-scrubbed feeling she left with, her skin raw but clean? Was it just the quiet, even with people buzzing about everywhere, that soothed the battered part of her that always worried about everything?

Maybe it was a combination.

"Tell me about something you love," Shay said, shifting to get a better view of the sprawled Callum. He was uncharacteristically disheveled, and she loved it. He wore his polish as armor, a way to keep people from finding any imperfections. But now he was relaxed in jeans and a polo. For anyone else, that was barely dressing down, but for Callum, it was progress.

His eyes were closed, his lips tipping up. "I love you."

"Stop." Shay shoved at his shoulder and he barely moved. He was lean but incredibly strong, something she'd always found hot. "You know what I mean."

"I love to keep score at baseball games," Callum said. "It's kind of looked at as an old-guy thing. But my mom used to take me, and she taught me how to do it. Three weeks before she died, we saw a no-hitter together. I have our cards framed in storage."

Shay breathed in, breathed out. It was strange the things you learned about someone after years of being together. "That must have been a pretty clean card."

He huffed out a breath. "Yeah."

"We should hang them," Shay said, nudging his thigh with her knee. "The scorecards."

Callum chewed on his upper lip, the way he did when he didn't want to smile too big and give away all his messy emotions. "I'd like that."

"Why did she start liking baseball?" Shay asked. She didn't want to stumble into stereotypes, but she would have been less surprised had he said his father was the one to take him.

"Her father played in the minor leagues," Callum said. "He was awful to her. He hated his life, wanted to be better than he was. He took it out on my mother and my grandmother. And for some reason, my mother walked away from that loving baseball."

"You're the psychologist, you must have theories about why that was," Shay said.

"I think if I was telling anyone else, I'd say it was because the game is predictable in a way," Callum said, staring up at the sky. "And there's ways you can track it, control it, and make it make sense. You can't do that with abuse."

"But it's me . . . ," Shay prompted.

"And so I'll say, I think she loved baseball because her father loved baseball," Callum said. "Sometimes it's as simple as that. Family's complicated."

Shay flopped onto the blanket and thought about her own circumstances. She hated Hillary, and yet, when Hillary asked, she gave her a place to stay and then looked the other way when she dipped into Shay's wallet.

You could love something and hate it at the same time.

"She changed what it meant," Shay said. "For you."

"The fingerprints are still there, though," Callum said. "The bruises. I like that part of it, too. That she found her own way into giving it to me."

"You never watch baseball," Shay said, and only when the words left her mouth did she realize there was probably a reason for that.

"I went to a game the day after she died," Callum said. "I have the scorecard. But that's the last one I'll go to."

Shay felt like she should have known about all this before now. But she wasn't into sports, never thought to ask about them.

"You know you're doing okay, right?" Shay asked.

"What?" came from her left.

She pushed up onto her hand so she could study his face. "You think you're failing on the Alphabet Man case, which makes you think you're failing at life. But that's not true."

"I think his victims might disagree," he said, almost meanly. Almost. But he had never been cruel to her once, not even when they fought.

"What do you think his answer would be?" Shay asked, because she knew it would throw him off.

"On something he loves?" Callum asked.

"Yeah."

"Killing people," he said, straight-faced.

"Come on," Shay said on a laugh. "Everyone loves something."

"Language," Callum said after a moment. "I don't understand how he uses it. But he loves it."

Beau had never excelled at English. She wasn't sure why she had that thought, but it popped into her head, fully formed.

"Do you ever start seeing killers in the people you love?" she asked.

He sat up at that. "What?"

"When you profile someone, do you start finding those characteristics in the people around you?"

"Sure, it's natural," Callum said, and Shay relaxed. That's what she'd thought. "Why? Who do you suspect?"

Shay coughed, hating that he was so perceptive. "No one."

"Come on," he said, and then half tackled her to the ground, his fingers finding her soft, ticklish spots. She laughed until she gasped and cried uncle.

"Sometimes, I think I could fit the profile," she admitted, a half-step admission.

"You're thinking about Max," he said, because she'd never been able to hide anything from him. Although, apparently, in this she could. Because she was no longer worried about her sister.

It was her other sibling who concerned her.

"No," she said quietly. "Not like you think. Not like Beau thinks. Not like Max thinks." She paused, trying to decide if she should confess to her past transgressions. "I did something bad once, though."

Callum made an inquiring sound.

"I found a box . . ." Shay waved that away. The details didn't matter. "Anyway, I freaked out. I visited her psychiatrist completely out of the blue and semi-forced the woman to deal with my panic attack about Max hurting someone."

"Oh, babe," Callum murmured.

"I'm not proud of it," Shay cried. "I thought Max might end up . . . I don't know. There are school shootings every day now, it seems."

"But she's never displayed anything like that," Callum reasoned. "Which is what I'm guessing the psychiatrist said as well."

"Yeah, you got it in one," Shay admitted. "I just get a little weird about Max, I can't help it. She's so cold sometimes that it makes me want to start researching sociopathy."

"She's not a sociopath," Callum said.

"How do you know?"

"Because she loves you," he said easily. "Very much so. In a way that's not self-serving at all. That girl would go to war for you."

I would kill for you," Max had said. Shay *had* believed her. But there was something different about hearing it from Callum's perspective.

"Did you know there's a warrior gene?" he asked.

Shay squinted over at him. "No, but that sounds far more romantic than it probably is."

Callum huffed out a laugh. "It is not romantic at all. The gene predisposes people to violence. Which, of course, during our medieval days would have meant the person was thriving. Hence, there's still people who have it. But it can lead to . . . well, serial murder, among other things."

"I would kill for you."

"I brought you here so you wouldn't have to think about serial killers," Shay said as lightly as she could. "And here you are, thinking about them."

Callum laughed. "That's not your fault. It's all I think about these days."

Shay straddled him, ending up in his lap, her knees on either side of his hips. "Are you so sure?"

"No," Callum said, and pulled her down into a kiss.

They didn't once mention a serial killer the rest of the day. Instead, they chatted about nothing. At one point, Callum chased Shay into the freezing-cold sea, and she dragged him in behind her. Ocean mist touched both their cheeks, and Shay couldn't help but think that it was all so different from Texas.

But water had a way of making it all seem like home.

A beach. Someone she loved. The sea-salt air in her lungs.

Callum had so few perfect days to give that when they came, Shay would hoard them to her chest, a jealous dragon.

"Do you think you have that warrior gene?" she asked sleepily as Callum drove them home, into the moonlight this time.

"I want to say something cool right now, like 'I think *you* have it,'" Callum said, with a half smile. "Because we associate warriors with being strong and amazing."

Shay laughed. "But we don't romanticize the warrior gene in this household."

He reached over, laced their fingers together. "Exactly right. I think you have the brave gene. The courageous one, the kind and fair and strong ones."

"Sap," she said, and he laughed, bringing her hand up to his mouth to press a kiss on the knuckles.

"Yeah," he said.

"I think you have all those, too," she said, because she wasn't sweet to him enough.

The quiet smile that tucked itself into the corners of his mouth reminded her to say nice things to him more often.

"I do have a warrior gene," she said. "Just to protect you, though."

"Hey, what did we talk about?" he asked, humor lacing his voice. He glanced over at her. She would never get tired of that look on his face.

Shay had always thought herself so hard to love. Hillary had never loved her; Beau and Max did, but that was a different kind of thing altogether. They'd gone through war—that kind of life solidified bonds without there needing to be any love involved.

Callum had chosen her, and continued to choose her every day. Even through the rough patches, he still looked at her like he'd burn the world down if he ever lost her.

He turned his attention back to the road, but the warmth of his gaze lingered.

"I have it, too," he murmured. "Just for you."

CHAPTER TWENTY-SIX

Raisa

Now

"Why did he use the Alberti Cipher?" Raisa asked. The prison had stuck them in an interrogation room and warned them that it might be up to an hour before they could pull Conrad to talk to them. There was a schedule to keep on execution day, after all.

"He never said." Kilkenny was sitting in one of the metal chairs, perfectly still, not fidgeting at all.

"It's just so simple." Raisa had her tablet out, and she was studying the letters again like a self-soothing exercise. With writing samples, she at least felt like she could regain a little control of the trajectory of the case. "What would you say Conrad prized in himself? Over everything else?"

"His intelligence," Kilkenny answered without missing a beat. Then corrected himself. "His supposed intelligence."

"Right. And he was goading you with it, taunting you—the tone is completely smug throughout," Raisa said. "His writing is extremely clean and grammatically accurate. He definitely saw himself as smart."

"But . . . ?"

"The Alberti Cipher is so simple," Raisa said again. "It's not complex; it doesn't take an above-average intelligence to understand it. A computer would have been able to decode it, given more than three days. There's nothing intellectually elegant about it. So why choose this particular one?"

Kilkenny hummed in thought. "I don't know. That always seemed to get pushed down on the list of importance."

Raisa nodded. She got it. Investigations were all about triage, and she wasn't about to parachute in later and criticize every mistake. But as a linguist, she couldn't help but be slightly appalled more focus hadn't been put on the code.

"You all had an expert who worked on deciphering each of them, right?" Raisa asked.

"Yes, he never could make much headway."

"No, I wouldn't imagine he could," Raisa said. The code was a simple one, but not when placed in a block like it had been. There was no way to cheat using short words and letters that often coupled up together. "Did he have any thoughts about the Alberti Cipher?"

"I don't remember in particular," Kilkenny admitted. "But I would think that means he didn't. Nothing groundbreaking at least."

Raisa nodded again, still staring at one of the letters from Conrad.

There was a crack in the foundation, she knew there was. And it was something she could exploit to bring the whole house down.

She just couldn't see it yet.

Years ago, she'd watched a movie about Alan Turing, the man who'd broken the Nazis' Enigma code—which had seemed impossible until it had been done. In one of the more cinematic moments, Turing was listening to two radio operators talk about how they recognized a particular enemy radio operator by the call signal he used—it was supposed to be random letters, but instead he used the name of his girlfriend. Turing realized that if they could isolate two or three words in a message they knew was coming every day, their primitive computer could use pattern recognition to decode the rest.

They realized the Nazis sent a weather report at 6:00 a.m. every morning and signed off *Heil Hitler.*

Raisa closed her eyes.

With both codes, a handful of letters of gibberish kicked off each message, but then, without fail, they started the same way.

With Conrad, it was *My dear Agent Kilkenny*—or some other overblown salutation.

With their impostor, it was *Dear Callum.*

It was one of the first things she'd noticed about the different idiolects.

She'd thought it was their impostor making a mistake—or not even trying to mimic Conrad's voice.

What if it served a different purpose, though?

Why me? Kilkenny had asked.

Why you? Conrad had taunted in one of those letters.

She stood and crossed to the door in three jerky strides. When the guard answered her knock, she asked, "Do you guys have a portable whiteboard I could borrow?"

The guard gave her a blank stare. "Um?"

"Shit," Raisa murmured, and swung back to Kilkenny. "This is why a linguist was never a waste of resources. Text me if Conrad's schedule frees up."

"Wait, what are you—" Kilkenny called after her, but the rest of the question was cut off by the door.

Raisa didn't slow, still clutching her tablet, where she had copies of both the encrypted and decrypted letters.

The guard helped her find the library, which had a room with a standing whiteboard. Raisa briefly considered pushing it back through the hallways to the interrogation room with Kilkenny, but the sheer absurdity of that image stopped her.

Instead, she grabbed a marker and pulled up one of Conrad's letters.

He hadn't wanted the investigation team to actually decrypt them before the victim was dumped. He wasn't stupid or sloppy. The whole shtick of including the name was just a power play from a sadistic asshole. But it could only be a power play if he came out on top every time.

Again, he was intelligent, or intelligent enough to try to think through any dumb mistakes that he could make. Using Kilkenny's name—even when throwing in some extraneous letters in there to fool the computer—was, in theory, a dumb mistake.

Somewhere in the first line, there was a double letter that would always equal k, and a double letter that would always equal n. Once those two pairs were pinpointed, they could figure out a handful of other important letters, certainly enough to at least partially decrypt the message.

If he'd really wanted to make sure his code was rock solid, he would have changed that up.

Which meant he'd used it for a purpose.

Raisa laughed in disbelief. It was so simple and so stupid and yet it had worked.

Why you? Conrad had taunted. Maybe it was partly because of Shay.

But it was partly because Callum Kilkenny had enough repeating letters to establish a fucking pattern, one that would show up in every single letter.

The only reason to take that risk, though, was to make sure the letter was decipherable to *someone*.

Raisa's butt hit one of the seats as the realization slammed into her like a blow.

Their two killers had been talking to each other.

Raisa breathed out a curse, let herself just stare for a minute, and then went to work.

The message to the impostor wouldn't have been an Alberti Cipher—it would have been hidden *beneath* that cipher.

She ran through the list of codes she knew. She discarded a few based on simplicity or complexity, and landed on the Vigenère cipher.

It was a close cousin to the Alberti, but it was more elegant and harder to crack. It also required a key word for it to work.

It checked enough boxes to be worth trying.

The first step required creating a table on the whiteboard full of Caesar ciphers. Those were notoriously some of the easier codes to crack—all they did was shift the alphabet down a letter instead of jumbling it. Where it got complicated was when you created a grid of them.

To do that, she wrote the alphabet across the top of the whiteboard and then vertically down the side as well. On the second horizontal line, she started the alphabet with the letter *B* and wrote out all the letters until they wrapped around to end with *A* getting paired with *Z*. With just those two lines, she had the simplest Caesar's cipher—here, each letter of the alphabet was shifted one spot.

KING became *L-J-O-H*.

She repeated the process all the way down her vertical line of the alphabet, each horizontal line shifting the alphabet one letter from the one above it.

Once she had her twenty-six lines, she had something to work off.

Then came the harder part—the key word.

If the two killers were communicating via publicly printed letters, it was safe to assume the key word would be in the message itself—something both of them could easily identify but would slip under the radar of the task force.

The name of the victim, of course, was an option—Raisa tried it both coded and uncoded.

Nothing but gibberish came up.

She chewed on the marker as she stared at the table she'd drawn.

The salutations. They were the only things about the messages that always remained the same. And in both, no matter how many letters they threw in front of the salutations as gibberish, they were still easy to find.

Which meant the easy letters to isolate for a key word would be the gibberish that came ahead of the salutations.

Sneaky bastards.

She picked a message at random, and wrote the five letters that preceded the salutation on the board next to her table of Caesar ciphers.

Raisa exhaled. The task was daunting. To manually crack a Vigenère cipher, she would have to write the five letters from the key word over each letter in the Alberti-encoded message.

When that was done, she had a message full of matching pairs: *R* and *D*, then *F* and *T*, and so on. That gave her two coordinates on her Caesar grid—where those two letters intersected in her twenty-six rows of alphabets was the letter it actually represented.

The process took her forty-five minutes to go through the shortest message, and she kept having to pull herself out of her near-fugue state to check her phone. No text came in from Kilkenny.

When she was done with the cipher, she stepped back from the whiteboard.

BETTER LUCK NEXT TIME

The knock on the door startled her into dropping the marker.

"Jesus," she breathed out as Pierce poked his head into the room.

He was about to say something but then caught sight of the board. "What's this?"

She didn't actually think Pierce was their impostor-and/or-vigilante. But it still made her pause, made her study him closely for panic or fear.

There was nothing on his face other than curiosity, though.

"I figured out a hidden message within Conrad's letters."

"Holy shit." He stepped fully into the room. He stared at her scrawled words, at the Caesar cipher table, at the crossed-out letters for a long time. "How did you figure this out?"

"Too long to explain," Raisa said, waving away the fact that she might have gotten the idea from a Benedict Cumberbatch movie. No one needed to know that part. "But I think our second killer and Conrad were talking to each other through these messages."

Pierce squinted at the board. "Can you figure out the other ones?"

"It would take a while," Raisa admitted, and waved at her work. "This took over an hour."

"Would a computer be able to do it, if it knew what to look for?" Pierce asked.

"Maybe," Raisa said. She wasn't the most technologically savvy but . . . she knew someone who was. Delaney had said she would continue to help, if possible. "I can send them to someone who probably has a program to run them through."

"They're approved?" Pierce asked.

Technically . . . "Yup."

"Let's do it," he said.

"Did you need me for something else?" she asked.

"We got an address for Max Baker," Pierce said. "It's about an hour away, and I'm going to drive out now. I know Kilkenny is waiting on Conrad, but I wanted to see if you wanted to ride along."

It would probably be a fruitful interview. Max was their missing component, the person who kept coming up time and again in their case.

Perhaps even playing vigilante—which given the hidden message Raisa had just cracked, seemed a more likely scenario than some of their other wild theories. She bet if she lined up the dates, she'd find this letter was close to the time one of the male victims had been killed.

But Raisa didn't shine in interviews. She knew where her strengths lay, and they were here, in this room, with a whiteboard and a bunch of letters.

She shook her head. "I'm going to keep working this angle."

"Okay, keep us all updated," Pierce said.

Raisa nodded, gnawing on the inside of her cheek as she debated asking. In any other situation, she wouldn't have pushed, but this was execution day. And if they were going to come up with anything to blindside Conrad with, they couldn't be squeamish.

"Did you not like Shay?" Raisa asked. It was mostly a shot in the dark. But for some reason when she pictured the Christmas party

Kilkenny mentioned, it wasn't Pierce hitting on Shay. It was him warning her off Kilkenny.

Pierce stopped, his back to her, the line of his shoulders tight. "Why would you ask that?"

Which sounded like a nonanswer, but really was one. Because if he'd liked her, he wouldn't have hesitated to say so.

"Just something else Kilkenny mentioned," Raisa said. "About a Christmas party."

She had expected that to ratchet up the tension in the room, but instead he relaxed. It was barely noticeable, but she could tell he'd been braced for something else. He shifted so that she could see his face once more.

"I remember that," he said. "It was nothing. It was our fourth year hunting Conrad, and I got a little weird with the women in my life. Started handing out Mace and enrolling them in defense classes. I probably came on a little strong, though."

"Yeah, I get that," Raisa said. But why had he been expecting a different question? Why had he been worried about it?

He stared at her, but she just sent him a smile.

The one he gave her in return was flat and forced. Then he turned and left.

She understood why Kilkenny had argued that Pierce wasn't their second killer. The reasoning was compelling enough that Raisa hadn't felt in danger just then.

Pierce was hiding something to do with Shay, though.

And Raisa hoped that if they figured it out, it wouldn't be the thing that made Kilkenny realize he could, in fact, be hurt again.

EXCERPT FROM *THE MAN BEHIND THE ALPHABET: AN*
UNAUTHORIZED BIOGRAPHY
By Delilah Marner

While much has been written about Nathaniel Conrad's terrifically
tragic and terrible childhood, as well as the years he spent as a hungry
predator terrorizing the Houston area, little has been discussed about
his teenage years.

After his monstrous father poisoned the rest of his poor family, little
Nate was sent to three different foster homes before landing with Carrie
and Michael Drysdale.

"They still can't bear to think about it to this day," says Linda Drysdale,
Nate's adoptive aunt. "I've told Carrie time and again that blood will
out. Nate's father was what he was. Are we really surprised the apple
didn't fall far from the tree?"

Linda is in the minority when it comes to those who knew Nate growing up.

"He was always very stable, considering," says Taryn Rust, Hillcrest
High's school psychologist. "I never once had to meet with him in a
professional capacity."

Rust explains that she formed a relationship with Nate because of his
interest in pursuing both social work and psychology.

"Nate had a little bit of a rough time of it right after everything with
his family," Rust says. "He wanted to make sure no other child went
through what he had to go through. For a while, he focused on mental

health training, but once he realized all he could accomplish as a social worker, he really devoted himself to making sure he had the right grades and accolades to get into the programs he wanted."

Linda Drysdale says she had some qualms about the idea of Nate working with troubled children. "Well, I was right, wasn't I? We see how that turned out."

But Martha Reinhard, the director of a nonprofit Nate volunteered with in high school, says he was a dream to work with. "All I can think was all that evil was hibernating because I didn't see a drop of it when he was here. He was particularly good with the children, having been through so much himself."

———

EXCERPT FROM A ONE-STAR REVIEW OF *THE MAN BEHIND THE ALPHABET*

> I think the biggest tragedy of Marner's mess, was that it could have almost been fascinating. Marner, unlike others, decided to focus much of the biography on Conrad's teenage years. Much like how Jesus was a baby and then a thirty-year-old prophet—with only snatches of his life shown in between—we often see Conrad portrayed as an eight-year-old and then a prolific serial killer as if his life got fast-forwarded to the inevitable conclusion.
>
> Marner completely misses the mark, but just think what could be done with a competent hand. If you extrapolate going off the information given from the nonprofit director and the school psychologist, you

can guess he was interested in abnormal psychology in children—perhaps sensing the darkness within himself even at an early age. Did he ever try to control his urges during those years? He must have. He didn't start killing until he got into his twenties. What did he do beyond researching what might be wrong with him? Did he ever confide in anyone about his fears? Was he afraid? Or was he a psychopath who reveled in the idea that he could take a life?

I don't want to see the moment he became a serial killer.

I want to see the moment he realized he could be one.

CHAPTER
TWENTY-SEVEN

Raisa

Now

Raisa tried to remember exactly what her old mentor had said about Pierce, but yesterday morning felt like a lifetime ago. It had been something about him using shady sources, she was pretty sure.

She tapped out a quick text to Matthew Nurse.

That tea you had on Pierce—was there anything more to it?

He responded quickly.

Like was he crooked?

Yeah.

The typing bubbles appeared, disappeared. Finally, a text came through.

I asked around about him as I was resurfacing that report that clears Kilkenny. Word on the street is that he's got a good moral compass, but he's an ends justify the means kind of dude . . . even with his eyes on the top spot, he still bends the rules. One person said they wouldn't put it past him to plant evidence, but only if he a hundred percent knew it was the guy.

Raisa exhaled. It wasn't anything he hadn't at least hinted at in their first conversation, but it was interesting to have it confirmed.

Zero rumors about him on the take?

Unanimously said he was a good dude with questionable tactics.

Raisa wasn't sure those two things could exist together, but she sent a thumbs-up emoji and a thanks.

Then she moved on to her next call.

Delaney picked up the phone once again on the first ring. "What do you need?"

It should have come off as abrupt, but instead Raisa could tell Delaney was just being succinctly helpful.

"Did you ever do any research into Xander Pierce?" Raisa asked.

"Hmm, no, not really," Delaney said, sounding regretful that she hadn't thought twenty steps ahead of Raisa. "Maybe the basics, but no deep dives."

"Okay," Raisa said. She couldn't expect Delaney to know everything, even if she wanted her to.

"You think he's your second killer?" Delaney didn't wait for an answer. "Vigilante."

"Right," Raisa said. She didn't want to give up too much, but was that really revealing anything?

"All those deaths I found, those people fit the profile of the Alphabet Man. So our second author might have been targeting people he thought was the serial killer," Delaney said, mostly talking to herself, it seemed. She certainly didn't need the logic confirmed. She was good at that. "Did something happen?"

He gave me a weird feeling, Raisa thought, but didn't say.

"I asked him about Shay and he got tense," she offered, even though that wasn't much better. "Not in a way I've seen before, either. He thought I figured something out that I didn't. It's probably nothing."

And with that, she remembered the real reason she'd called Delaney. She relayed everything that she'd found with the double code, and asked if Delaney could figure out a way to decrypt the rest faster.

"Of course. Send me what I need," she said.

Her phone buzzed in her hand, a message from Kilkenny.

Conrad here in less than ten.

"Gotta go," she told Delaney, and hung up without waiting for a response. Delaney would understand. Then she quickly fired off the email she'd already prepared with the codes and took off at a quick walk-trot through the hallways.

She beat Conrad by two minutes—enough time not to look out of breath when he came in but not enough to fill Kilkenny in on everything.

"A meeting with the feds," Conrad said, as he was locked to the table. "What a way to start my last day on Earth."

"You wanted me here," Kilkenny said softly.

"I did," Conrad agreed. "I wanted you to see my final show."

My final show. Something about the wording of that struck Raisa as strange. Perhaps it was the use of *my.* As if he were putting on his own execution.

"You don't care about Kilkenny, though," Raisa said, just hoping to throw him off enough to get some kind of reaction out of him. "Your letters weren't even meant for him."

Conrad's eyebrows rose. "Oh, you are a clever one. No one else figured that out. Not even your sister."

"You were talking to your . . . partner?" Raisa tried. She didn't think that would be how he would describe the relationship, but she thought she might get more out of him if she let him correct her.

He scoffed and looked away. "I take it all back. Not clever at all. No, that was not my partner. That was . . ."

Conrad broke off, shook his head once, and inhaled like he was gathering his own control.

"That was someone who thought they could stop me," he finally said.

"You didn't know who it was?" Raisa asked.

"I did and I still do," Conrad said, grinning. That dark space where his canine should be winked at her. "But, like I said before, I have no interest in doing your job for you, though."

"You say it was someone who thought they could stop you," Kilkenny said in that tone of voice she'd learned to pay attention to. Serious, thoughtful. Leading.

Conrad narrowed his eyes as if trying to decode the sentence. "That's what I said, yes. A-plus comprehension, Agent Kilkenny. You could have used a little bit more of that in the five years it took you to catch me."

"Who *thought*," Kilkenny repeated, completely ignoring Conrad's little gibe.

Again, Conrad missed a beat while searching for a trap. Finally, hesitantly, he said, "Yes."

"They didn't just *think* they could stop you," Kilkenny said, devastatingly calm. "They did."

Conrad's nostrils flared. "You're wrong, though that's not surprising given your track record. They had nothing to do with it. That was my own sloppy mistake."

That had to be a lie. The second author had deliberately used an old code, which was what had led to Conrad's eventual downfall. The motive for why they had done so might still be up for debate, but the fact that it had happened wasn't. At least in Raisa's mind. So why would Conrad—a noted perfectionist who liked to think himself superior to everyone in every room—not set the record straight there?

Kilkenny seemed surprised as well.

"You would rather say that, after five years of perfectly getting away with more than two dozen murders, you made an error instead of admitting that someone else turned you in?" Kilkenny asked, though it wasn't a question. It was, perhaps, a revelation.

"My final girl, the one that got away. She died five years ago, you know," Conrad said, back to being silky smooth. Like he'd regained the upper hand, but even Raisa, who felt a step behind, could see that he hadn't. "A car crash. How pedestrian."

He grinned again at his own wordplay, while Kilkenny tensed. Raisa fought off her own grimace. How terrible, to have just barely sidestepped a serial killer only to die a few years later from something so ordinary. Fate was a funny thing. If she were the type, she'd say it had corrected itself.

She wasn't that type.

"Why would you rather us think it's a mistake?" Kilkenny asked, a dog with a bone now, refusing to be put off by Conrad's tactics. "You want to set the record straight about Shay. Even though you could have died knowing, I would always wonder. Wouldn't that have been sweeter torture?"

"I don't care about you," Conrad finally said. "You are not interesting to me, and you've served your purpose. Isabel Parker had a price for her silence about my secrets, and that was that Ms. Tashibi drop her news at a particular time. Ms. Parker cares more about you than I ever did or will."

That was probably more of a lie than he would ever admit—Conrad had *just* admitted that he wanted Kilkenny to see his final show. There might some truth to it as well, though, and it did drive home the fact that the narratives built up around the case didn't seem much rooted in fact.

She tried to forget everything she'd thought before and look at the facts.

Better luck next time.

The cat and mouse game had never been between Kilkenny and Conrad. It had been between their two killers.

And if this *was* a game, their second author had effectively won. They'd made sure Conrad was caught. Him sitting in prison, so diminished, hours away from death, was a victory they could claim.

So why was Conrad—who'd presumably orchestrated an entire documentary to make sure his name was remembered long after he died, who'd figured out a way to gain control of the timing of the reveal of his biggest secret—letting the other person win?

The only answer was . . . that he wasn't.

If he wanted the person caught, all he had to do was give Kilkenny the name. He knew it, of course; that much was obvious. And he wasn't holding it back just because he didn't want to do their jobs for them.

He could win, or at least make sure it was a draw.

Both cat and mouse dead.

My final show.

He liked language, plays on words.

My final show. Like the documentary. Created by Kate Tashibi. She was a part of whatever he had planned.

"That was someone who thought they could stop me," Conrad had said. Who *thought.* Past tense.

Raisa stood, her chair dragging against linoleum with a terrible screech.

She pounded on the door, and the guard popped his head in.

"Where was Conrad before he was brought to us?" Raisa asked.

Kilkenny stood, too, now hovering at her shoulder, backing her up even though he didn't know what was going on.

"He was in the special visitation room," the guard said. "Inmates are allowed to receive guests there on execution day at any time."

"Please call and find out if Ms. Tashibi has an appointment with Nathaniel Conrad scheduled for tomorrow," Pierce had said.

"You don't have to make that poor woman go through all that work just to make your point. Okay, you're right. I have an appointment with Mr. Conrad in the afternoon."

Kate had wanted to make sure she got to Conrad first. Her appointment had been in the morning, and she hadn't wanted to risk them finding that out. So she'd admitted to a half lie to make it seem like she was telling the whole truth.

Whatever Kate and Conrad had planned together depended on Kate getting a head start on Raisa and Kilkenny.

"Who was he visiting?" Raisa asked, just so she could have it confirmed.

The guard held up a finger and pulled out his walkie-talkie.

"He met with Katherine Tashibi," he said after a quick consultation. "For twenty minutes before he came here."

Raisa pressed her lips together.

The only way to win was for the impostor to die sometime before Conrad.

CHAPTER TWENTY-EIGHT

Shay

January 2014
Two months before the kidnapping

Shay talked her way into Callum's next trip to Houston.

He didn't want her to come, but she needed to help iron out the Beau and Max situation. Even from Seattle, she could tell the two were on rocky ground. How could they not be? Max had thought Beau was a serial killer for years, and even if she hadn't confessed to that thought, Beau would still have been able to tell something was off.

As Shay had done all her life, she decided to simply go to Beau.

Except when she pulled into the neighborhood in her little, non-descript rental car, Beau was headed toward his own sedan at a light jog. He checked up and down the street—his eyes skating over her Honda—and then ducked into the driver's seat.

Shay hesitated, her foot coming off the pedal. She could beep, wave, and get his attention. If he had plans, he might invite her along. If it was work, then at least she'd know he was about to start a shift.

But she didn't do any of that.

Instead, she drove by him, without looking, so he wouldn't feel her eyes on him. She parked two streets over, where she had a view of the main street he'd turn onto, and she waited.

He took a left out of their neighborhood, and she scrambled to follow—not too close, not too far. It was a balance, one she'd never practiced before. She wasn't sure exactly how she'd explain this to him if he caught her tailing him.

Max thinks you're a serial killer, but I think we landed on the fact that you've only killed two people. Which is, you know, one short of most people's minimum threshold for the label.

They were also bad people who maybe deserved to die—does that factor into the ethical calculus of it all?

Shay shook her head at her own ridiculous life.

Beau drove for twenty minutes, until they were in the southeastern suburbs of the city. She had nearly lost him multiple times, but in each instance, luck swung in her favor. When he finally parked in front of a darkened ranch house, she took a right.

She left the rental—it was a sleek little thing that she doubted would look suspicious to anyone in the neighborhood—and then she took off toward the corner.

Shay got there just in time to see Beau jogging up to the front of the house. He didn't even pause at the door, just stepped inside and disappeared.

What had her argument to Max been? That Beau didn't have a house where he would have been able to keep the girls in a basement?

Her heartbeat kicked up, and she wondered if she'd just cornered a serial killer in his den.

She laughed at herself, even if she could hear the mania in it. This was Beau. Max had been wrong about him. Whatever he was doing in that house had no connection to the Alphabet Man.

There wasn't much cover on the street Beau had parked on, but she didn't need it. She had spent her childhood sneaking out of wherever she and Hillary had landed. And there were only a few chain-link fences between her and the house Beau had walked into like he owned it.

The rancher was flat to the ground, so when she got to it, she was able to peer in one of the back windows. All she saw was Beau's profile and arm. He was sitting at the kitchen table, staring at his phone.

She waited for him to do literally anything, but he didn't move for five minutes, ten.

Shay chewed on her lip as she debated. And then, without letting herself think too much about it, went to the back door, tried the knob, and stepped into the house.

Beau shot to his feet, his hand reaching for . . . something. A gun? Did he have another one?

Once he caught sight of her, relief crashed over his expression. Anger chased it almost as quickly.

"What the hell are you doing here?" he asked in a hissed whisper.

He didn't wait for an answer, just crossed the room, gripped the fleshy part of her arm, and started hauling her toward the backyard.

"Hey." Shay fought him, flailing so that it wouldn't be easy to drag her. "What the hell are *you* doing here is a better question."

"It really, really isn't," Beau said, and his anger had ramped up to fury. He wasn't shouting, but his voice shook with the emotion, desperate to control himself and nearly failing.

"You've gotten yourself into something, haven't you?" Shay guessed. "That explains the blood."

He faltered at that. "What blood?"

Shay seized the moment of surprise and wrenched herself free just shy of the doorway. "On your shirt. Max saw it. She knows you lied about helping out in a bar fight."

"Jesus Christ." He stared at the ceiling for a long moment before looking at her once more. "What does she think?"

"That you're the frickin' Alphabet Man," Shay said in that same hissed whisper, because maybe he was actually worried about people overhearing. Who that was, she couldn't begin to guess.

He shook his head. "What is with you two and that guy? First you think Max is a serial killer, now she thinks I am. You guys have gone off the deep end with that."

"I'm sorry . . . you're sitting in a dark, empty house alone, a place where you have no business walking in without even knocking, and you think we're strange for being paranoid?" Shay asked. "That doesn't even begin to cover what happened with Bi—"

"Shut up," Beau gritted out, and she got it. That particular information shouldn't be spoken out loud. It should go to the grave with all of them.

"Okay, but you know what I mean," Shay said. "You think it's really that wild to worry about you?"

"What would you have done if you'd walked in and I had a girl tied up?" Beau asked.

"This isn't funny," she said, shoving at his shoulder.

He held up his hands. "You're right, sorry. Just . . . what was the plan, Shay? Asking me to stop torturing my victims and tattooing them and leaving them in random fields all around the city?"

"I didn't have a plan," Shay admitted, and Beau rolled his eyes at the obvious statement. "I'm trying to help you, dumbass."

"I know." Beau sighed. "That's what I hate about this."

Before Shay could say anything else, the front door opened.

She met Beau's widening eyes, panic slipping into her own veins at his expression.

"Go," he mouthed.

But before she could get her feet to move, a silhouette emerged from the hallway, taking the shape of a person.

The man stepped into the room, and Shay inhaled sharply as she recognized the craggy cowboy face of Xander Pierce.

———

They all ended up at the FBI field office, the darkened house ruled too much of a liability to stay at with all three of them there.

"Okay, tell me what's going on," Shay demanded once Pierce had shepherded them into his office. "Isn't there a crime scene you should be supervising?"

"Yeah, I had to step away," Pierce said, tapping at his phone as if there were a flood of updates. "This was important, too." He checked his watch even though he'd probably seen the time on his phone. "I can't be gone much longer."

"So, did I interrupt a lovers' rendezvous?" Shay asked, so baffled at what this could be that she wouldn't be surprised if that hit the mark.

Beau flushed, and Pierce raised his brows at him before answering, "No."

He didn't sound offended, but there was a definite finality in his voice. So, they weren't covering up a tryst.

The blood. It had something to do with this—she was all of a sudden very sure of that.

"Look, when you started dating Callum, Pierce became interested in our family," Beau said.

Pierce had the good grace to look somewhat guilty, but his chin also tipped up in defiance. "I'm not just going to let him—"

"Slum it with a bartender?" Shay asked dryly, their conversation at the Christmas party all of a sudden making so much more sense. He hadn't been hitting on her; he'd been trying to drive a wedge between them. "Can't have that."

"No," Pierce said again, the guilt gone. "We had just stumbled onto a serial killer who Kilkenny profiled as being someone who would want to find an in on the investigation. Then he met you and the family you came with."

"People like us can't be trusted, huh?" Shay said, snide and mean with it. She knew she hadn't liked him.

"Shay, sheath the claws," Beau murmured. "He wasn't wrong."

"The more I dug, the more I found out about Hillary Baker."

"What? What does our mother have to do with this?" Shay asked, thrown for the first time. She had genuinely expected him to throw Max's past in their face, had been bracing for it so that she didn't accidentally reveal that Beau was the guilty party instead.

"She's into some bad stuff now," Beau filled in. "She keeps her head above the mess, but her boyfriend is shady, and we're pretty sure Hillary's hands aren't as clean as she wants law enforcement to believe."

Shay stared between the two of them. "Are you . . . Is this a sting? For Hillary?"

The idea was so far from what she'd been imagining that it took her a moment to rearrange her world. Beau wasn't the Alphabet Man, and for that matter, neither was Xander Pierce. She'd never really contemplated the latter, of course, but still, it was now a fact she knew.

"This has nothing to do with the serial killer?" she clarified.

Pierce's eyes went a little wide at that. "No?"

The contrast to his earlier certainty had her nearly laughing at the absurdity of this situation. "You recruited my brother to help figure out how much criminal activity our mother is involved in and you haven't told Callum any of this?"

That last part she was guessing, but from the twist of Pierce's mouth, she knew she'd hit the mark.

"Perfect, wow, just perfect," Shay said.

"You can't tell him," Beau cut in. "This is an ongoing investigation. You can't jeopardize it."

"Oh, you're law enforcement now?" Shay asked. She didn't know if she was doing a good job conveying how ridiculous she found that—given the two bodies in his wake—but she gave it the old government try. "You?"

"I want Hillary to stop hurting people," he said quietly. "She's lived her life like a wrecking ball. Every decision leaving casualties in its wake.

Everything she did to all of us? That was small potatoes. I'm tired of her not facing any consequences for her actions."

She had never realized before how much Beau was driven by this sense of fairness. You did bad things, you had to pay for them. And if no one else would take care of that, he was going to do it himself. Maybe he couldn't make himself kill Hillary—or maybe he thought he wouldn't be able to get away with it a third time—but she could see in his expression that was the kind of justice he wanted. For himself, for his family. For whoever was currently carrying the bruises from Hillary's actions.

"Okay," she said, with a sigh. "I won't tell anyone."

Pierce looked between them, nodded once, and then headed for the door. "You two can find your way out."

"Hey," she called out to stop him. "Is this why you warned me to stay away from Callum?"

For a second, she thought he might lie. But he studied her face and then met her eyes.

"No," he said. "I wanted you to stay away because I don't think you're good for him."

Shay absorbed the judgment and nodded. "That makes two of us."

"Asshole," Beau spit out, and took a threatening step toward him, but Shay grabbed his arm.

Pierce barely spared them another look before ducking out the door.

"Well," Shay said, staring at Pierce's desk. He must not keep anything of important in here if he had just left them alone. Still, she couldn't completely snuff out her urge to snoop.

"Shay," Beau chided when she rounded the desk, but the reprimand was perfunctory. He was as nosy as she was.

But her initial assessment had been correct. There was nothing to see on Pierce's desk, and opening drawers seemed a step too far.

"All right, let's go," Shay said, eager to get out of this place. She wasn't going to be able to tell Callum about this, and she was already itchy at the thought of lying to him like that.

They made their way to the parking lot.

"Hey," Beau said, nudging her shoulder, "I appreciate that you were going to confront me instead of siccing Callum on me. When you thought I was the Alphabet Man."

"It wasn't exactly a smart decision," Shay admitted.

Beau laughed. "I didn't call it smart."

And then he took off to his car without a backward glance. Shay watched him go and felt both stupid and fond about him.

She was just pulling out her own keys when she heard a familiar voice.

"Shay?"

CHAPTER TWENTY-NINE

Raisa

Now

Raisa and Kilkenny stepped into the hallway, leaving Conrad behind.

"Conrad told Kate the impostor's name," Raisa said. "He told her where to find the person."

"Maybe," Kilkenny hedged, like his instinct was to be the voice of reason, but the leaps in logic were too easy to make.

"You really think Conrad would go to his grave knowing the second author, the person who turned him in, was out there free to live out the rest of their life?" Raisa asked. "Does that fit with your profile of him?" She didn't wait for him to answer. "No. He plotted some way to make sure the impostor paid for what they did."

Kilkenny grimaced. "Yeah. But . . ."

"But what?"

"Is Kate really a killer? Because that's what we're getting at, right?" he asked. "Why would she do that for Conrad? It's not ambition driving her to do it. The series is already going to be successful."

"And that's a fairly unhinged way to gain fame," Raisa added.

"Right."

Raisa thought about Isabel. She'd used the podcaster persona as camouflage to get close to the investigation, but she'd also *been* a podcaster. She'd laid the groundwork with an entire earlier season so that she'd been legitimate. And she'd been good at it.

They kept thinking about this whole case backward, their preconceived views shifting everything out of focus.

"What if the documentary wasn't ever the point for Kate?" Raisa asked slowly. "What if her whole goal was to get close to Conrad?"

"Maybe. And what better way to entice him than with the idea of that kind of renewed infamy?" Kilkenny said. "But why?"

"To get the name of the impostor," Raisa said, bringing them full circle. "She promised him a documentary—a promise she was able to bring to the table because of her schooling. He gave up his secret before he died. That secret, that's what she cares about."

"But why?" Kilkenny repeated, a little helpless, a little confused.

"I don't know. But I think that's what we have to figure out." Raisa chewed her lip and stared at the now-closed door that hid Conrad away from them. "I don't think he's going to give us anything else. I think he was trying to delay us as much as possible so that we didn't interfere with his plans."

Kilkenny followed her gaze. His whole body went still, and she wondered what she was thinking. Would he go back in there for one more look at the man who had dominated his thoughts for fifteen years? Did he need that closure and hate himself for it?

This would probably be his last chance to talk to Conrad, to put any final questions to rest.

She wouldn't judge him no matter what he decided.

"You're right," Kilkenny said. "And I'm done listening to him talk. He's as irritating in person as he was in those goddamn letters."

Despite the tension thrumming through her, Raisa snorted out a laugh.

"He is unbelievably tedious," she agreed.

The corners of his mouth ticked up, and when he met her eyes, his expression softened slightly. As if letting her know he was grateful for her support. She nodded once and then cleared her throat.

"We have to find Kate before she gets herself killed," she said, because she was a professional, and even cocky documentarians who put themselves in danger still deserved to be saved from themselves.

"I think that means we need to figure out who the second killer is ourselves," Kilkenny said, grim again. That wasn't exactly an easy ask.

Raisa checked her phone and then realized she hadn't had time to fill Kilkenny in on the Vigenère code. She motioned for him to follow her back to the library as she explained everything as quickly as she could.

He didn't once look back at the interrogation room, and only mentioned Conrad when he stopped to let a guard know that they were done with him.

"I'll be surprised if we don't hear from Delaney soon," Raisa said when they got back to the room with the whiteboard.

There was something smug in Kilkenny's smile despite the chaos they'd been dropped into. She was pretty sure the psychologist in him thought it would be good for Raisa if she bonded with her newfound sister. The one *not* in jail.

"Speaking of your sisters, I can't figure out where Isabel fits," Kilkenny murmured, staring at the board like it held the answer. "It makes me wonder if figuring that out might lead us to our second killer."

"Conrad says they were pen pals," Raisa offered. "Maybe she got the ball rolling on all this?"

"But whatever scheme Conrad has going was launched more than three months ago," Kilkenny pointed out. "And she's only had reason to hate me for that long. If it's true that she resents me for saving her life."

Raisa shook her head, not because he was wrong but because she didn't know the right answer. "Maybe we're thinking too logically here? They're smart and they plan, but at the very least, Isabel doesn't think logically. Conrad probably doesn't, either. I mean, they both have such a warped worldview that they've justified killing into the double digits."

Kilkenny made an agreeing sound, but couldn't seem to tear his eyes from the board.

"They're so goddamn similar," Raisa said, and then paused as her words reverberated in the room. "They're so similar."

"You said that."

"No, they're so similar," Raisa said again, aware she wasn't making complete sense. "They're the same person, aren't they? Like, almost the same person."

"Close enough," Kilkenny said, finally turning toward her. "There's not much degree of separation in personality when you're already talking about serial killers."

"But even for a small sample size, they share a lot of quirks, right?" Raisa said. "Their origin stories are both rooted in a family-annihilation situation." She remembered what she'd asked Sasha, the journalist. "Was there ever any talk of Nathaniel being the one who poisoned his family rather than his father?"

"Once it came out he was a serial killer, sure," Kilkenny said. "I don't know how much faith to put in that, though. There never seemed to be any chatter at the time that he was the one who'd done it."

"There was never any talk that Isabel killed Alex and our parents, either," Raisa pointed out. "Though Nathaniel would have been a lot younger."

"Fits with poisoning," Kilkenny said. "Still, doubtful. But the possibility is there."

"Even if neither had been responsible, they both had these huge life-alerting tragedies in their history," Raisa continued. "Just like with Kate."

Kilkenny's brows furrowed. "Huh. There's coincidence and then there's—"

"This," Raisa agreed. "Twice is coincidence, three times is a pattern."

Kilkenny stilled, just like he had outside the interrogation room.

"What?" she asked.

He shook his head, the moment passing. "Nothing. Shay used to say that."

"Oh." Raisa chewed on her lip, not sure what to offer as comfort.

"Don't worry about it," he said.

"Okay." For lack of a better option, she pulled out her phone and texted Delaney.

Any chance you have Isabel's CPS file?

Do I have it (officially?) no of course not, was the immediate answer. Raisa rolled her eyes. Unofficially.

In your inbox.

Raisa refreshed her email, and saw not one but two unread emails. "Oh shit."

"What?" Kilkenny was at her back immediately, trying to read over her shoulder.

"I emailed the office where Conrad interviewed before his first kill, and they just responded," Raisa said, clicking into the email. It was short but pleasant. They told her they only had so much on record, and it was possible that Conrad had met with other people that day who weren't on the official list. "Do you recognize any of the names?"

She held the phone out to Kilkenny, who shook his head. "No."

Raisa deflated. For some reason, she'd thought Kate's tip about Conrad's job interview in Houston was going to lead to some kind of epiphany. Probably she'd just been screwing with Raisa.

The next email was Isabel's CPS file.

"Is this a waste of time?" she asked, even as she opened the preview for it on her phone. The file was from Washington State—so far away from Houston that she didn't know what she possibly thought she would find in there.

Kilkenny pursed his lips, which was a yes in Kilkenny-speak. But all he said was, "Not if you have a hunch."

This was probably confirmation bias speaking. She was so focused on Isabel, all she could see was causation where there was probably only chaos.

"No," Raisa said on a sigh, and then partly lied. "I don't have a hunch. And even if falling down Isabel's rabbit hole could eventually lead to our killer, I think we should focus on Kate. She'll get us there faster."

He nodded, even though he'd been the one to bring up Isabel. "You're right. I just don't see how we're going to figure it out."

She wasn't used to Kilkenny not knowing what to do next. She tried to clear her mind. The task was daunting, but they had been collecting a lot of threads over the past two days. One of them would lead them to their second killer. She had to believe that.

"We need to see the incident report," Raisa said. This was the knot, where Isabel's, Kate's, and Conrad's threads intertwined. "The carjacking for the Tashibi family."

"It would be a local request," Kilkenny said.

"Good thing we know the man in charge of the entire Houston field office," Raisa said, and Kilkenny smirked before pulling out his phone.

"Max isn't here," Pierce said when he picked up.

"We need an old report on a carjacking in Austin," Kilkenny said. "What's that department like? Do they share?"

"Yeah, text me the details. I have a guy over there who likes me," Pierce said, and hung up.

Kilkenny stared at his phone. "Is it strange that he went out to interview Max without having a local uniform swing by to see if she was there?"

"Yes," Raisa said, though she couldn't come up with anything beyond that. Kilkenny was typing out the information for the Tashibi case anyway, not seeming to need it confirmed.

Pierce didn't seem to be hiding anything in terms of the case, but he was hiding *something*. She was almost sure of it.

"You still trust him?" she asked Kilkenny, who grimaced.

"Yes," he said, echoing her simplicity for effect.

"Okay," she said.

"Just like that?" He'd asked her that less than forty-eight hours ago, but he still didn't seem to understand that whether she trusted Pierce didn't matter. She trusted Kilkenny.

"Just like that," she said.

They didn't have long to wait before Pierce came through on his promise to deliver the Tashibi carjacking report.

"What are we looking for?" Kilkenny asked, as he pulled it up on the computer that was already connected to the VPN.

"There was a sister," Raisa said. It always came back to sisters, didn't it?

"Hana Tashibi," Kilkenny read.

For you, H.

That had been the caption on the one personal photo Kate had posted to her social media page.

For you, Hana. At the time, it had read as a dedication or a tribute.

Now Raisa wondered if it was a promise.

Why would Kate Tashibi care about the person who sent the Alphabet Man to jail?

Raisa still didn't know the *why* of it all, but if they were looking for a reason for Kate to become a killer, why not listen to her own words?

She pulled up Google—people underestimated what you could find out just by doing a cursory search.

"There's a Hana Tashibi, of Austin, who died," Raisa said, feeling like everything was just about to click into place. It wasn't there yet, but they were close. "Five years ago."

"Long after the carjacking," Kilkenny said. "What of?"

"The obituary is sanitized," Raisa murmured, skimming it. "Which usually means suicide or drug overdose, but we probably shouldn't assume."

Kilkenny pulled out his phone and searched something. "No murder cases linked to that name."

"Were the girls split up?" Raisa asked. "To different foster families?"

"Yeah, looks like," Kilkenny said after a minute. "Kate ended up in Upstate New York, while Hana stayed in Austin. Both were adopted, which seems unusual for girls that old."

"It would have been nearly impossible to keep them together," Raisa said. Isabel had probably fought like hell to stay with Delaney, at least, but even *she* hadn't been able to get it done. And Kate and Hana had been much younger.

"If we're looking for some link to Conrad, Shay, or the second killer, I think Hana is our path in," Kilkenny said. "Since she's the one who stayed in Texas."

Stayed in Texas and died in Texas.

Hana Tashibi. Something about the name . . .

She squinted into the distance as she thought through all the materials she'd read in the past two days. It had been so much, but Raisa had always been good with details. And patterns. Just like Delaney.

It wasn't just the *For you, H.*

Raisa had seen something else that she'd dismissed at the time. But she must have filed it away because it itched at her brain now like a forgotten song lyric.

HT. Raisa had seen those initials somewhere.

"That name's not familiar, right?" she asked Kilkenny.

He shook his head. "What are you thinking?"

"I've seen 'HT' somewhere recently, and I can't remember where."

"It must be something that was connected to Kate," he said. "The external hard drive. It had a Word-doc file on it along with those videos, didn't it?"

"Oh shit. You're a goddamn genius," Raisa murmured, as she navigated to the folder where she'd uploaded everything Kate had turned over.

"I wouldn't go that far," Kilkenny responded, leaning over her shoulder.

Most of the files on the hard drive had been audio or video clips. But Kilkenny was right. There was a Word document in there, too. Raisa had skimmed over it before because the links had been to other media that had been put out about Conrad, and Raisa had assumed it was just a place to keep her research bibliography.

One of the links stood out among the rest, though. Next to it were two letters in parentheses: *HT*.

The link was to an individual reader's review of a self-published biography that—from what Raisa could gather—was more of a fangirl love letter to Conrad than a factual rendering of pretty much anything.

Why would Kate have included a random reader's thoughts on it, though? And why would she label it with her sister's initials?

She opened the review, read it three times through, and then shifted the computer so Kilkenny could see.

"Does anything jump out at you?"

His eyes swept across the screen, and then he shook his head. "What if . . . ?"

He navigated to the reader's profile page and came up with a whole list of reviews.

The one that came after the Conrad biography was titled *The Origin of a Serial Killer: Nature, Nurture, or Life-Altering Trauma?*

Raisa clicked into the reader's review of that book.

> Now this is what I've been searching for, the review started. An incredible deep dive, focusing in on that moment. That moment that someone becomes a monster.

EXCERPT FROM *THE ORIGIN OF A SERIAL KILLER*

There's no denying the world is fascinated by serial killers. But despite that, there's still so much we don't know about these monsters that have captured our attention.

Twin studies have shown that psychopathic traits are 60 percent inheritable. That means that nature (DNA, that is) is heavily weighted in whether someone could be diagnosed as a psychopath.

But not all serial killers are psychopaths and not all psychopaths are killers, let alone serial killers.

Does that mean nurture then comes into play, the person primed for violence but not necessarily destined for it?

That could be true in some cases. When children are abused, they sometimes are unable to create successful and productive coping mechanisms, which then leads to violent outbursts. As children, the tantrums can be written off, but the cycle is reinforced until adulthood, where the only way they can deal with anger, disappointment, and shame is to lash out and hurt someone else.

That all holds up until anyone looks at the backgrounds of some of the country's most famous serial killers. Ted Bundy, Jeffrey Dahmer, and Dennis Rader all had healthy childhoods with supportive family members and yet still they went on to kill.

A 2005 report from the FBI's National Center for the Analysis of Violent Crime emphasized that agents agree there is "no single identifiable cause of factor that leads to the development of a serial killer.

Rather there are a multitude of factors that contribute to their development. The most significant factor is the serial killer's personal decision in choosing to pursue their crimes."

The section "Causality and Serial Murder," however, ends with the bullet point that FBI agents agree more research is needed to identify the pathways of development that produce a serial killer.

Because even the best minds in the world still cannot pinpoint how a serial killer is created.

While the call for more research is admirable, the struggle is that the ethical constraints put into place—wisely—for everyone's protection tie the hands of the very scientists who could make forward progress with the field.

CHAPTER THIRTY

Raisa

Now

Nature, nurture, or life-altering trauma.

"All the kids," Raisa said softly. "All the kids we keep coming back to."

"The one thing that bound them together," Kilkenny said, easily following along. "Life-altering childhood trauma."

Raisa clicked into the description for the book itself. "Dr. Harold Pall is the author. Does that name ring any bells?"

Kilkenny shook his head and then made a face after he pulled up the message the social workers' office had sent over, the one that had the list of names of the people Conrad had met with on his interview day. "Not on here, either."

"It could be a pen name," Raisa said. "If they were trying to hide their identity, it would be easy to do. They didn't have to pass any peer reviews to publish this."

"But that doesn't help us now," Kilkenny pointed out, and Raisa sighed.

All their promising leads kept coming up blank, and Raisa was tired of it. Tired of it and also terrified for Kate, as abrasive as she might have been. Had she found their second killer yet? Was she still alive, or were they about to have yet another dead woman on their hands?

Her phone rang in her hand, and she nearly dropped it. A shaky laugh escaped as she answered. "What did you find?"

"I've got all the hidden messages," Delaney said. "That was genius-level work on your part, but my computer is an even match for you."

Raisa didn't want the praise. "What do they say?"

"I'm going to email you the list," Delaney said. "But there were some ones I found more interesting than others. Including in the letters that probably weren't written by Conrad."

"How do you know about those?" Raisa asked, immediately suspicious.

"I mean, how many times do I have to tell you I'm good with—"

"Logic and patterns, yeah, got it." Raisa huffed out a breath. "So what did you find?"

"The first one: 'You didn't even remember me,'" Delaney said, her voice changing, like she was reading off a list. "In the first impostor letter: 'You are my greatest success.'"

Raisa sucked in a breath.

"Those are the ones that are interesting, but I'll send the rest," Delaney said, sounding like she was going to hang up.

"Wait," Raisa said. "What did the last letter say? The one where the second killer gave away the next victim?"

"'The world needs to see what I've accomplished,'" Delaney said.

"Okay, thanks." Raisa's voice sounded distant to her own ears. She hung up and tossed the phone on the table before relaying the messages to Kilkenny.

"They take credit for him," Kilkenny said, summing up the messages with succinct precision. "Our second killer thinks they created the Alphabet Man."

Raisa thought about one of the lines from the *Origin* book.

Because even the best minds in the world still cannot pinpoint how a serial killer is created.

This wasn't a vigilante trying to rid the world of the Alphabet Man. This had been someone who'd tried to create a serial killer out of traumatized kids. And they'd succeeded.

The person had identified a child who had potential, and they'd nurtured that violence.

"They must have known him as a kid, right?" Raisa asked. "If they took credit for creating a serial killer, they must have known him long before he'd become one."

The first victim.

Conrad had been triggered into killing Sidney Stewart while driving home from interviewing for a social worker position. What if Kate's tip really had been right? What if the list the office had sent over hadn't been complete? All it would have taken was a glimpse of someone in the hallways or in passing. Someone, maybe, who'd worked on his case when he'd entered the system.

"You don't even remember me," Raisa murmured, then locked eyes with Kilkenny. "What if our second author had pretended not to know who Conrad was when they ran into each other again? When he was interviewing in Houston. What if that enraged Conrad?"

"That could have absolutely been his trigger," Kilkenny agreed. "And maybe even why he accepted the job in Houston. He became fixated on the person."

"Understandably so."

"Right," Kilkenny said, running a hand through his hair. "But I can't think of a single person who fits that bill. Not on his case from when he was young."

"What do you mean?"

"I mean, I've memorized the entirety of his DFPS file from when he was ten," Kilkenny said. "He didn't meet with anyone who would have been grooming him to become a serial killer."

"How do you know that?" Raisa asked.

"He had a social worker, a child advocate, and a police liaison," Kilkenny said. "We checked all of them once we finally caught Conrad. There's no way any of the three were involved in this."

Part of her instinctively wanted to fight back, to wave to the rest of the case and point out how much had slipped under the radar because they hadn't been looking for a second UNSUB.

"But there had to be other people who had access to him," Raisa said. She tried to think about everything she'd gone through. It had felt like she'd met so many people in such a short amount of time. Three seemed unfathomable to her.

She tapped back into Isabel's CPS file, opening it for real this time to see if she was remembering through the lens of a traumatized child.

Even just skimming the summary and table of contents, she could identify a handful of adults who would have interacted with Isabel. Doctors, nurses, psychiatrists, and a speech therapist, for some reason.

"Do you remember the social worker?" Raisa asked.

"Uh, Cathy or Cassie something," Kilkenny said, already pulling out his phone. It took a couple of minutes, but he eventually found her last name. "Carly. Carly Nolan. I have an old email from her with her cell phone."

Thank god for cloud storage.

He punched in the number and then put it on speaker.

"This is Carly Nolan," a woman answered. Sometimes it could be hard to tell on the phone, but Raisa guessed she was older, maybe even postretirement age.

Kilkenny introduced both of them, reminding Carly of the case and giving the broad strokes of what they were working on.

"Oh, I know what day it is," Carly said after Kilkenny finished. "I've had it marked on my calendar."

"To celebrate?" Raisa couldn't help but ask.

"No, dear," Carly said. "I went to church to pray for Nate. He was such a sweet boy. I don't know what happened to him."

And wasn't that the $64,000 question. "He said he had a rough time working his way through the system before he was placed with his adoptive family. Do you recall any reason that would be?"

"Oh, no," Carly said, clearly distraught. "No. It was my job to shepherd him through the process and protect him as much as possible. I don't know what could have happened that would have made him say that."

"It was a smooth process?" Raisa asked.

"Yes, surprisingly smooth, given his history," Carly said. "Usually children who go through such traumatic events need extensive help. But he was one of my easier cases."

Raisa didn't want to judge someone based on such little information. But she had only lost her adoptive parents in a car crash, and it had wrecked her to the point where she'd stopped talking for four years. Nathaniel barely escaped being poisoned by his father; likely saw the rest of his family die; and then was lost for several days—hungry, scared, and dehydrated. At ten years old.

In no world should Nathaniel Conrad have been one of Carly Nolan's "easiest" cases.

"Did he see a psychologist?" Raisa asked, because that seemed like the bare minimum.

"No," Carly continued, seeming unaware of Raisa's tone change. "The poor dear was shaken up, but not so bad that he needed all that."

Raisa inhaled sharply, and Kilkenny lightly tapped the table to get her attention. He shook his head and she exhaled, counting backward from one hundred. He was right—this wasn't the time or place to litigate what actions were taken after Conrad had become a ward of the state.

But she was starting to understand why he'd said it wasn't the best experience. At the very least, he'd been neglected, some fairly basic needs going unmet because he didn't make a fuss. That stank of an old-school mentality that had led plenty of children down the wrong path.

A good psychologist also would have noticed that Conrad might not be reacting quite as expected. They might have realized he had a personality disorder that could have been managed. One good psychologist could have saved nearly thirty lives.

Maybe.

"Although," Carly said, sounding like she'd just stumbled over a long-buried thought, "I did get an odd message one time about Nate."

"An odd message?" Kilkenny prompted.

"Yes, I think . . . I think it was from maybe a doctoral candidate doing research on traumatic life experiences in children," Carly said, her voice gaining confidence the longer she went on.

Raisa met Kilkenny's eyes. His were wide and alert, and they were both holding themselves incredibly still, as if any sound would spook Carly into forgetting whatever tidbit had surfaced.

"Yes, that's right. I remember thinking how inappropriate it was," Carly said. "I, of course, responded that I had no interest in letting them run experiments on a child who'd just been through what Nate had survived."

"Is there any way they could have circumvented you to contact Nate directly?" Raisa asked.

"No, no," Carly said. "Although . . ."

Raisa was beginning to both love and hate that word in Carly's mouth. "Yes?"

"Well, I, of course, wrote my follow-up reports," Carly said. "And by the second year, Nate's adoptive parents told me they had tried out a therapist for a few sessions. It didn't work out."

"That wasn't in the report," Kilkenny said, voice sharp.

"Well, it was only a few introductory sessions," Carly said, going defensive. This time it was Raisa who tapped lightly on the table and shook her head.

"So the psychiatrist who contacted you might have been the same one Nate saw while with his adoptive parents?" Raisa asked.

"No, it was a different name, I do remember that," Carly said. "Though to be honest, I don't remember either at the moment. I'm sure I could find them somewhere."

"Please look them up," Kilkenny said, and rattled off his email address. After a curt "Thanks," he hung up on Carly.

"Our guy doesn't want their name attached to the files," Raisa said.

"No," Kilkenny said. And then, slowly, his eyes dropped to Raisa's phone. "In Texas."

"What?"

"This is their hunting ground," Kilkenny said. "They can't have their name associated with any Department of Family Protective Services case in Texas. But what if they kept an eye out for cases across the country where they might intervene?"

The Parker family massacre had made national news. No one had thought Isabel was responsible, but if someone had been watching for stories about children and extreme violence, she fit the pattern.

"If they didn't want to be connected to Texas, they might have used a different name when they went out of state," Kilkenny continued slowly, like he was feeling out the idea himself as the words came out. "This was where they lived. This was where they wouldn't want to be found out."

"They might have used a name we'll recognize." Raisa finally caught up to his logic and scrambled for her phone. She pulled up Isabel's file, the one Delaney had sent over.

There, as an aside, was a note that Isabel had met with a psychiatric consultant, an expert in children who'd experienced some life-altering violent event.

She stared at the name on the file, then grabbed for the list from Conrad's interview in Houston. It wasn't the exact same, but it was close enough.

Her laugh was one of shocked disbelief.

They'd finally found their match.

CHAPTER THIRTY-ONE

Shay

January 2014
Two months before the kidnapping

The world was full of sliding-door moments—instances where one tiny decision completely altered your future. Forgetting milk could mean making a run to the grocery store, which could mean getting T-boned by that car that ran the red light just before you pulled into the parking lot.

Or you could decide to suck it up and drink your coffee black that morning.

Shay tried to piece together the moments that had led her to this one.

She remembered the bar that first night, when so many people had been talking about the dead girl and Callum had sat on his stool and secretly judged them all. She thought about the moment he'd almost left and she'd wooed him with her stupid story about that ridiculous stuffed cat.

She thought about the gun she'd hidden, the one that had taken a life and made Max suspicious of Beau, and Shay suspicious of Max.

She thought about Billy's funeral, where Kilkenny had wondered if there had been foul play involved.

She thought about Max's trip to Seattle, which had brought Shay to Houston now.

Thought about how, because of all that, Shay had followed Beau to an empty house, where Xander Pierce had walked in twenty minutes later.

If any one of those things hadn't happened, Shay wouldn't have been standing in the parking lot of the Houston FBI office watching Beau jog off toward his truck.

She wouldn't have almost dropped her keys when she heard a familiar voice call her name.

She wouldn't have turned, eager and with a big smile to greet a friend she hadn't seen in far too long.

She wouldn't have let her eyes slide back to the FBI building and wondered, for just one minute, what Dr. Tori Greene had been doing in there.

CHAPTER THIRTY-TWO

Raisa

Now

"Dr. Tori Greene," Raisa said out loud. It was there in black and white on the list of people Conrad had met with in Houston. And there in Isabel's file: "Dr. Victoria Langston."

"There's a chance it's two different people," Kilkenny said. She slid him a look, and he held his hands up in surrender. "It had to be said."

"Both psychiatrists working with children and teens who have faced life-altering trauma," Raisa drawled. Perhaps she could see the bones of that name shift better since her own—and Isabel's and Delaney's—had been altered in similar ways. Just enough to hide them in plain sight.

"Okay, let's say they're the same person," Kilkenny said. "And that she's our impostor. Why is Kate after her?"

Raisa thought of Isabel. Of Conrad. Of Shay's siblings. Of the male victims.

They all had the one thing in common.

For you, H.

"Her sister," Raisa said quietly. "Hana. She stayed in Texas. She was a kid who experienced life-altering trauma at a young age."

"And maybe Tori targeted her," Kilkenny said. "I don't know what that woman's methods were, but if she was trying to nurture a personality disorder in these kids . . . maybe she screwed with Hana's life enough to leave permanent damage."

"Enough that Kate would blame Tori for Hana's death?" Raisa asked.

Kilkenny lifted one shoulder. "Absolutely. It's true that we don't know exactly what creates a serial killer, but we have enough evidence that abuse contributes to it. I don't think she was exactly giving them hugs and praise to bring out their inner monster."

"Okay, well, then, maybe Hana and Kate reconnected," Raisa said, gaming it out. "Maybe Hana mentioned a Victoria Langston, but then died soon after. Kate couldn't find her and correctly assumed she was using a different name now."

"So she contacted the person she thought could help her," Kilkenny said. "Conrad."

"And she made a deal," Raisa said softly. "Kate films a documentary memorializing Conrad for all of history—or at least the next few years. Kate gets the name of the woman she views as responsible for her sister's death."

And Conrad would win the game.

"Shit," Kilkenny said, and then stood. "We need to find her now."

"How?" Raisa asked, but Kilkenny was already on his phone.

He pulled it away from his ear after a minute, frowning down at it. "Pierce isn't answering."

"He's driving," Raisa reminded him, but he shot her an incredulous look.

"When has that stopped him before?" Kilkenny tapped the screen and brought the phone back to his ear once more. Again, no answer.

Raisa stood now, too, energy thrumming beneath her skin. "Why did he drive all the way out to see Max?"

"I don't know. It made sense when he said it." Kilkenny was still staring at his screen as if willing it to ring. "He hasn't wanted to use resources other than himself for this case."

"Did he ask you to go?"

"No, he knew I was waiting for Conrad," Kilkenny said. "But I did tell him to check with you."

"He asked me," Raisa said, staring at the floor. "We haven't exactly been buddy-buddy, though. He probably just asked in case you texted me to make sure he did."

"But why would he . . . ?" Kilkenny trailed off. She couldn't guess what the end of that question was, and she bet that neither could he.

"Do you have his office number?" Raisa asked, and almost before she got the question out, Kilkenny was already tapping away at his screen.

"Hi, Betsy. Do you know where Pierce is?" A beat. "No, he said he was driving out to talk to Maxine Baker." Another pause. "You don't have that address? Or he wasn't given it yet? Okay, thank you."

Kilkenny looked at her. "She says the address for Max still hadn't come in last time she checked with him."

"Maybe he got it while he was here?" Raisa suggested.

"His secretary has access to his inbox," Kilkenny pointed out.

"Shit."

"Yeah," Kilkenny said on an exhale. "I don't get it."

Raisa shook her head. "I don't know. If we're right about Tori Greene, there's no reason for him to lie to us about anything. It's not as if he's the impostor and he's trying to cover his ass right now."

"Except maybe he *is* trying to cover his ass," Kilkenny said, and then strode to the door and left the room. Raisa stared at his retreating back for a moment before scrambling to follow.

With his long strides, he made it to the guards' room so far ahead of her that she missed his request. But in the next minute, security footage played on one of the screens.

Pierce.

They must have backed up to the morning, when Pierce had arrived. The guard managed to track him through the parking lot, into the building, through the check-in process. He then paused at a hallway intersection. Then he glanced up at the camera for a moment before turning toward the visitors' lounge area.

"He's looking for Kate," Raisa murmured.

"Maybe," Kilkenny said, his eyes locked on the screen.

There were a few people in the room, only one of whom looked up when Pierce walked in. He went straight to the coffee vending machine, and Raisa wondered if that was what he'd been searching for all along. But he shifted so that his body was angled toward the woman tucked in the back corner of the room.

He watched her for what felt like a significant amount of time but was probably only a minute and a half or so.

It was enough for her to feel his gaze.

She glanced up. Even from the terrible quality of the security footage, it was easy to tell she was gorgeous, with thick hair styled in a way to reveal a hip undercut. She had arresting features and a stubborn tilt to her jaw that made her seem intimidating despite her small frame.

Kilkenny had the guard freeze the picture, and she could tell from his expression.

"You know her?" Raisa asked anyway.

"Yes," Kilkenny breathed out, eyes locked on the woman, knuckles white where he gripped his elbows. "That's Max."

CHAPTER
THIRTY-THREE

Shay

January 2014
Two months before the kidnapping

The wine bar was dark and comforting, the low buzz of tipsy chatter and the clink of glasses familiar now. After Shay's freak-out with the serial-killer box, she and Tori had made it a point to meet up every month or so for drinks there. They were both hurting for friends in the area, and the gossip—even though neither knew the people involved—was always juicy and fun.

They'd lost touch when Shay had moved to Seattle, which happened more often than not when two women got busy and put a dozen states between them. Shay was used to relationships like that falling apart, but she'd mourned the loss.

She had been so happy when Tori suggested they hit up the wine bar that she'd mostly forgotten how strange it was that she'd run into her in the FBI parking lot.

Mostly, but not quite completely.

Tori beat her there, waving to get Shay's attention from a high-top in the back.

"I can't believe I ran into you," Shay said, kissing her cheek again in greeting before taking one of the stools. "What on earth were you doing at the FBI building?"

"What was *I* doing there?" Tori asked on an easy laugh. "What were you?"

"Oh, my husband works for the Bureau. I thought I mentioned that," Shay said, not bothering with the intricacies of explaining Kilkenny's fly-in, fly-out position. And she definitely wasn't going to go into whatever was going on with Beau and Pierce.

"Of course, that's right," Tori said, before turning toward the waiter and ordering for both of them, like she used to do every time. Back when Shay had been dating, that kind of behavior had pissed her off. But she liked when Tori did it.

Tori turned back to Shay, a grin tugging at the corners of her mouth. "Are you still enjoying your tall, dark, and handsome drink of water?"

Shay hadn't told Tori about the baby. There was no reason she would know that Shay wasn't living in that typical honeymoon bliss. And this wasn't the time to correct her, either. She forced a smile. "We're happy."

But she forgot she was talking to a psychiatrist. "Uh-oh. Want to talk about it?"

"No," Shay admitted, taking a too-big swallow of what was probably too-expensive wine to be gulping with such abandon. "Are you doing consultation work with the Bureau?"

"Mmm." Tori hummed the nonanswer. "So, what are you doing in town?"

"Oh my god, it's so stupid," Shay said, burying her face in her free hand. She debated if she should tell Tori anything, but she wanted to talk about it with someone who wasn't Callum or her teenage sister or even Beau and all his baggage. Just an abbreviated, sanitized version that left out the active investigation of whatever the hell Hillary was doing.

"Max decided she wanted to play detective," Shay said.

"Not another serial-killer box." Tori laughed. "It's my job, and I'm not even as fascinated by them as she is."

"What?" Shay asked.

"What, what?" Tori said, eyes still crinkled in amusement.

"I thought you worked exclusively with children who had violent histories," Shay said, her head going a little bit buzzy. They'd flown in that morning, and then everything with Beau had gone down. She should probably slow down on the wine. Instead, she finished her first glass.

"Yes, and they sometimes become serial killers," Tori said, some of the humor fading from her face. "You knew that."

Shay blinked and remembered a night almost identical to this one, perhaps even sitting at this exact table.

"To my knowledge, no one has ever really been able to pinpoint the moment in someone's life that sets them on an irreversible course."

"Right, yes, of course," Shay said, shaking her head to get rid of the whisper of *something* creeping along her skull. "Anyway, Max got it in her mind that—get this—Beau was the Alphabet Man."

"What?" Tori asked, again on that same burst of laughter. "Why would she think that?"

"She's sixteen," Shay said by way of explanation. "I came down to do some sibling relationship repair."

There was no need to fill Tori in on her own amateur sleuthing habits. The less said about that embarrassing hour when she'd also thought Beau really might be the Alphabet Man, the better.

"She must have found *something*," Tori prodded. Lightly, but there was an edge to her voice.

Shay frowned down at her now-full glass, glanced at Tori's empty one, and wondered if she'd switched them without Shay realizing it. Then she shrugged. It was something she'd done with plenty of people throughout the years when she could tell they needed it more than she. And she could call Callum to come pick her up. Or take a taxi.

"Oh, she had some maps and was talking about the hospital," Shay said. She squinted at Tori, remembering one particular visit with Billy. Tori had stuck her head in as a surprise hello. "You work there."

"What?" Tori asked.

"At the hospital," Shay said, her mouth operating faster than her mind.

"I don't work there," Tori said, that laugh of hers going completely brittle. "I have admitting privileges. And I'm called in every once in a while for a consultation . . ."

"Oh, right." That made sense, of course. It was the same with Nathaniel. "Is that what you were doing at the FBI building?"

Shay wasn't sure why she was so fixated on Tori being there, but she also wasn't sure why Tori hadn't answered yet. Even a pat *I'm helping with a case* would have been enough for Shay.

For some reason, she remembered what Pierce had just said when he'd explained why he'd felt the need to look into Shay's family.

"We had just stumbled onto a serial killer who Kilkenny profiled as being someone who would want to find an in on the investigation."

"What else made Max think Beau was the Alphabet Man?" Tori asked, dodging the question once more. Shay tried to remember why she cared about the answer and then forgot anyway.

"Something about a Dallas trip," Shay said, swirling the last remnants of her second glass. She should probably slow down, she realized. But then the waiter set another rosé by her elbow, and she smiled in thanks because she would never be rude to someone serving her drinks. It was the bartender in her. "Don't ask me, honestly. It didn't make any sense."

"Did she say anything else?" Tori asked softly, coaxing out the details.

"Just that it felt . . . familiar," Shay admitted, because that part had stuck with her the most.

"Familiar how?"

Shay shook her head. "She never really explained that part."

"Weird," Tori said, and Shay giggled.

"Yeah, that's Max for you," Shay said. "You really never thought she was going to grow up to become a serial killer?"

"No," Tori said with incredible sincerity. "I really didn't. She's not capable of killing."

"Huh, all that worrying for nothing," Shay said, still giggling. "Have any of your kids? The ones you see?"

"Shay," Tori said after a beat. "You know I can't tell you information about individual patients."

"That's a yes," Shay said, and stared down at her empty glass as she remembered exactly what they were talking about. "Oh, that's not good. What if one of those kids is *him*?"

Tori went still. "I think we should call you a cab, my friend."

Shay swallowed against the layer of sugar on her tongue, and all of a sudden, she wished the world had sharp edges instead of blurry ones. "Wouldn't that be funny?"

"Hmm," Tori hummed, already pulling out her phone. Somehow, they made their way outside, the process happening in that way it did when you were drunk. Blink, sitting down. Blink, opening the door to a taxi.

"Wouldn't that be funny?" she asked Tori again, though of course it wasn't. She didn't even remember what would be funny anyway.

"No," Tori said softly. She sounded sad. So sad. "I don't think it would be."

TEXT MESSAGES SENT FROM MAXINE BAKER TO BEAU SAMUELS

The morning of Nathaniel Conrad's execution

(6:43 a.m.) Conrad isn't lying . . . Tori Greene killed Shay . . . here's her address . . . if you need it for some reason

(6:44 a.m.) [address redacted]

(6:45 a.m.) I love you

CHAPTER THIRTY-FOUR

Raisa

Now

Kilkenny tapped the guard on the shoulder to get him to keep playing the footage after Pierce approached Max.

They talked for about three minutes, and then Max left the visitor lounge. The angle had been terrible, both of them tilted away from the camera so there was no chance of reading lips even if Raisa had been an expert. And, of course, she wasn't.

The guard helped them track her out to the parking lot, but then she disappeared behind a large media van and didn't emerge where they could see.

Kilkenny cursed and straightened. "She told him something."

If Max had been in the visitors' lounge, there was a tiny chance she was still on the grounds. She'd come to witness Conrad's execution—she wouldn't just leave.

Raisa glanced up at the rows and rows of monitors that showed too many views of the prison. Now, two hours after the run-in with Pierce, Max couldn't be seen on any of them.

"I'm going to go check the grounds outside," Raisa said. "Can you try to get Tori Greene's current address?"

"Yup," Kilkenny agreed, pulling out his phone. Raisa took off.

She checked with the security desk in front to confirm that Max hadn't come back into the prison.

After that, it didn't take long to find the van where Max had disappeared, and when she asked, the journalist pointed her in the direction of the far end of the parking lot.

Raisa jogged over, and started scanning the cars for signs of life.

And there Max was, sitting in the shade created by a beat-up Toyota, her back against one of the wheels, an unlit cigarette clamped between her lips as she furiously wrote in a battered leather notebook. Raisa exhaled and then dropped down across from her, leaning against a much nicer BMW. She hoped the alarms wouldn't sound.

"You're a fed," Max said, without looking up. She'd shown no signs of surprise at Raisa's sudden presence, either.

"Sort of," Raisa said, with a half smile that went to waste.

"There's no such thing as a sort-of fed," Max said, though there was some amusement in her voice.

"I'm a forensic linguist," Raisa explained, and that finally got Max to look at her. While she'd been objectively beautiful on that security footage, she was magnetic in person, her eyes a shockingly pale green in contrast to her dark hair, her brows thick and expressive. Raisa felt pinned against the warmed metal.

"Sick," Max decided, after a moment of studying her, sounding like the teenager she must have been when Shay was alive instead of the woman she was now. She went back to her journal.

Raisa decided to take the compliment. "You met with Xander Pierce this morning."

Max snorted. "Dickhead."

"Why's he a dickhead?" Raisa asked.

"You know the first thing I did in my session with Tori Greene?" Max asked, dropping the name of their second killer like it was nothing.

Like they hadn't just spent the last few days desperately hunting for that answer, without sleep, without stopping to eat. Raisa could only stare at her.

"She gave me a book of sudoku puzzles," Max continued, still scribbling away. "She didn't ask me any questions, she just handed that over along with a pencil."

"Okay," Raisa said, still reeling.

"Do you know why?" Max asked, but then didn't wait for Raisa to guess. "She said word-and-number puzzles are known to ease stress, anxiety, and depression. It was how she bonded with us assholes who didn't want to be there. I'm sad to say it made me think she was pretty cool." Max flicked a glance up at Raisa. "I looked it up. She wasn't bullshitting about the benefits of word puzzles, either. There are studies on it and everything."

"Word puzzles like figuring out an Alberti Cipher," Raisa said, and Max touched her nose before pointing at Raisa.

"Got it in one."

Raisa closed her eyes and pictured Nathaniel Conrad at ten years old, walking into an office with Dr. Tori Greene. Or Victoria Langston, at the time. Being asked if he liked puzzles. Would he like to try this simple cipher? Had she done it with all the children she met with? Had she done it with Isabel? The daughter of two math prodigies, a genius in her own right, would have scoffed at being given something so easy. But she would have remembered that moment.

It would have felt familiar if she'd seen the detail crop up in a serial-killer case.

"I just kept seeing all those articles about how the Alphabet Man used this stupid cipher," Max continued. "And all I kept thinking was, *Oh, that probably reduces his stress, anxiety, and depression.*"

She snorted in dark amusement. "I wasn't completely right. I thought she was the Alphabet Man. Wouldn't that have been amusing? We're such a fucking patriarchy we can't even conceive of women being killers despite the fact that one of the defining characteristics of the murders was no intercourse."

Raisa didn't want to interrupt her to point out that it *had* been a man who'd killed most of the victims.

"I know, I know," Max said, as if she heard the argument anyway. "But still. We shouldn't have assumed."

"No," Raisa said softly.

Max's lips twitched. "You're humoring me because you want me to tell you whatever I told Pierce."

"I want to know, but I'm not humoring you," Raisa corrected. "Bias in investigations leads to a lot of killers walking free."

"Hmm," Max agreed. "You know, I'm talking like I knew this whole time. I didn't. I didn't know until they caught Nathaniel. And we knew him, you know? Beau was friends with him. And so I thought, *Jeez, he was stalking Shay that whole time.* It made sense." She paused. "Like it fit perfectly that he would have killed her. So Beau and I shut the fuck up about knowing him, just in case that would throw something off with his trial, and we went on with our lives."

"What changed?"

"I went to visit Nathaniel," Max admitted. "I wanted to see him really there. Behind bars. On a long march to death."

"Did he tell you?" Raisa asked. "Did he tell you he didn't kill Shay?"

Max shook her head and swiped at her nose. "No. Not that first time. He asked about Tori, but it didn't register. Not really. Who would have thought there were two killers?"

"But you went back?"

"Two more times," Max admitted. "I could tell he wanted to confess something—he kept hinting at things. Like talking about Tori, how I should look into her research more. Talking about how he and I had things in common. Something about what he was saying must have, I don't know, clicked in my subconscious, because I went back."

Raisa couldn't imagine what that must have been like for Max when she'd believed Conrad had brutally murdered Shay. Conrad, who had spent time with their family, who'd likely been to their house.

"On the last visit, he said—" Max paused, heaved in a breath. "He said, 'You know I would never hurt Shay.'"

That wasn't exactly a confession, not from a serial killer who had maintained his innocence up until a few days ago. But Raisa could see how it might have stuck in Max's mind.

"I would have attacked him if the guard hadn't stepped in," Max continued, calm as anything. "I thought he was just being a dick, like, mocking me. It took a while for the rage to go away. But when it did, I don't know, it changed the way I heard the words. Then I kept thinking about the stuff he'd said about Tori."

"Did you go see him again?"

"No. But I started looking into Tori's research, just like he'd suggested." She huffed out a humorless laugh. "I was always good at digging. And I got obsessive about it. I found her marriage certificate."

"That's . . . advanced," Raisa said, surprised and impressed.

"Not really. It's public information," Max said with a careless shrug. "What was impressive was the name she put on there wasn't Langston. It was Carter. Victoria Carter."

That was probably what had stymied Kate if she'd made it that far.

"How did you get from Carter to Langston?" Raisa couldn't help but ask.

Max smirked a little, clearly proud of herself. "She didn't file a medical change under that name, so I figured it wasn't hers for very long. Turns out she got married in Vegas and then divorced three months later."

"And that led you to Victoria Langston," Raisa said.

"Yeah, it took, like, a year of searching, but I found her," Max said. "And there were enough photos of her from her grad school yearbook to confirm it was the same person."

"You were determined," Raisa said.

"Not much else to think about. And once I found her name, it was easy from there. She had all these grad school papers about the origin of serial killers. They included some real questionable ethics, about how we should go back to the early days of psychology, when you could just mess people up for the sake of knowledge." Max glanced up. "They're there. Online, digitized. Whatever. She must have done it herself. So fucking arrogant."

"Did you suspect her then?" Raisa asked.

"I mean, of being interested in serial killers? Sure," Max said, lifting one shoulder. "Of being a terrible psychiatrist, yeah, absolutely."

"So what made you realize she killed Shay?"

"Beau's phone," Max said, her lips twisting. "He gave it to me unlocked one day. Told me to send myself any pictures of Shay on there that I wanted. Those were the days of dumb-phones, but even shitty photos are better than nothing." She shrugged as if it weren't a big deal, even though it clearly had been. "He still had Shay's text messages saved, and I started reading through them."

She rolled her eyes. "Which is a violation of privacy, sure. But I found the final piece there. It was a while back, like two months before Shay's death. No one would have connected it to her disappearance. No one except for me, in that exact moment of time."

"What was it?"

"A text where Shay mentioned that she'd run into Tori," Max said. "She reminded Beau of how Tori had come to Billy's funeral, and just how nice that had been. They met up for wine, and Shay had gotten too drunk and nearly passed out in a cab on the way back to her hotel."

"What did Beau say to that?"

"He said he remembered, thought it was nice, too, and called Shay a lightweight in her old age," Max said. "And they both completely moved on from the topic."

"Two months," Raisa said softly.

"Tori was nothing if not obsessively careful," Max said. "She waited, and she was right. Two months was long enough. No one linked her to Shay's death."

"Except you," Raisa said.

"Fat lot of good that did."

"Why didn't you tell the police about your suspicions?" Raisa asked, even though she knew it might make Max shut down completely.

"Because I didn't have a good track record when it came to accusing people in my life. At one point I was convinced Beau was the Alphabet Man," Max said, still writing. It was impressive that she could do so while talking. "Shay pretty much laughed me out of her apartment when I laid out my theory. So. I didn't tell anyone."

"But all these years—"

"I didn't tell anyone right away," Max corrected. "I was gathering information. I thought Tori killed Shay because Shay was onto her. Which I still think was true. But I was pretty sure Tori killed other people, too."

At the very least, Marchand and Stahl. Probably some of the victims Delaney had found in her broader search.

"Could never confirm anything. But I must have talked to the wrong person," Max said. "About six months after my last visit with Conrad, Tori shows up at my place. She knew I hadn't gone to the cops, of course, knew I probably wouldn't. Killing me would have brought too much attention to her. She'd already decided I wasn't one of her pet monsters, and so her name was attached to my file. Which was something she was insanely careful about."

"Not careful enough, apparently," Raisa pointed out, and Max nodded.

"Anyway, she knew a secret of mine. She threatened to expose me if I didn't leave town and cut off all contact with anyone here," Max said. "I didn't have any actual proof she'd killed anyone, either. Not Shay, not anyone else."

"She knew that you killed your father?" Raisa guessed.

"She knew that I hadn't," Max said, meeting Raisa's eyes again. Each time Raisa was knocked back by the intensity of that strange color, the directness of her stare.

Raisa's mind made the quick leaps in logic. *Beau.*

The revelation must have shown on her face, because Max nodded once, quickly. "She wasn't bluffing. It would be a risk to kill me, a risk to expose Beau to prison time. But it was still better than me spewing my theories to Kilkenny. And I couldn't lose Beau. Not right after Shay."

"So you cut him out of your life," Raisa said. Everything she learned about him only added to his tragic narrative.

"Sucks," Max said, succinctly. "But life sucks. At least he's alive and not rotting away in prison."

She stopped writing and dropped the pen to the ground. Her eyes moved over the paper and Raisa sat quietly, afraid to make a move. Finally, she folded it up into perfectly neat thirds and stuffed it in an envelope.

When Max didn't do anything but stare at it in her lap, Raisa asked, "What did you tell Agent Pierce this morning?"

"Where to find Beau," Max said, her frown sliding into a satisfied smile.

"Where is he going to find Beau?" Raisa asked, gently.

"At an empty house," Max said.

"Why?"

"Because I told Beau that's where he would find Shay's real killer, and he wasn't about to let her walk free."

Raisa's heartbeat kicked up. She didn't want to think about why Pierce hadn't told them that was where he was actually headed. "Why is it empty?"

"Because I let Beau pull the trigger for me once before," Max said, still staring at the envelope. "And I wasn't going to let him do it again. Then I told Pierce where to find him, so there would be no doubt that he had an alibi."

Pierce was chasing after Beau, and Beau was chasing bad information. That left Kate Tashibi as a wild card. But Raisa had a feeling that point was moot.

"Kate Tashibi met with Conrad this morning," Raisa said. "We believe he told her where to find the woman responsible for her sister's death."

Max's chin jerked up at that, but she quickly hid her face once more. It had been long enough to get a glimpse of her expression, to confirm what Raisa had guessed.

Kate may have gotten a head start on Raisa and Kilkenny, but Max had gotten a head start on her. She would arrive too late to mete out the justice she so wanted.

That had already been done.

Raisa thought about the weight of her gun holstered beneath her blazer. Max was slight, but Raisa was small, too, as much as she didn't want to admit it. The woman might have hidden strength that could put her out on top. "Will she find Tori?"

"I'm sorry she lost her sister," Max said, her fingers tightening around the envelope. When she looked up, her eyes were completely dry, her mouth set in a determined line. There was not an ounce of guilt or regret there. "But I lost mine first."

CHAPTER THIRTY-FIVE

Shay

September 2009
Four and a half years before the kidnapping

Shay loved driving along the open road with the windows down, music blasting, the heat of summer baking skin that had been too cold all winter.

Max sang along beside her, body loose and relaxed after her session with Tori Greene. Her hand rode the wave of the wind. Joy filled the soft spaces of her face, the ones that hadn't sharpened with age yet. She was still just a kid, despite the fact that she'd lived too many years in her short life.

Shay pushed the thought away. They were headed to Galveston, and the world was theirs for the afternoon, a long stretch of endless possibility.

Any tension from the morning was gone, as was any memory of the gun and a junkyard and FBI agents too handsome and adorable for their own good.

They found a cheap store for Max to get a bikini, and Shay, without regret, parted with the fifteen dollars. She dug out her own suit, half-buried beneath a twelve-pack of Diet Coke and a tote that she always tried to remember to bring into the grocery store with her but inevitably forgot.

The sand and water beckoned, and the two of them made do with one towel. Salt stung Shay's eyes as she dived under the waves that could barely be called waves, with Max beside her doing the same.

They played like children for a half hour, Max brushing Shay's ankle with her foot, making her shriek and flail enough that the lifeguard stood up in his stand.

Max collapsed into the water with unbridled laughter that Shay hadn't heard in the entire time Max had been living with her and Beau.

When their fingers puckered into raisins, they lay out beneath the sun, Shay graciously allowing Max to take over the towel.

Sand stuck to all the wet bits of her, and Shay knew she'd be finding granules in uncomfortable places for days to come. But for now it just made her feel like she was a teenager again—no responsibilities, no job, no bills, no kid to feed. Max was her friend today, not a dependent who caused her to constantly worry.

She dozed, and when she came back to reality, Max was sitting up, staring at the ocean. But she had done so in a way that kept the sun off Shay's face. Her heart and belly squeezed at the tiny gesture of love and kindness.

Because they didn't say nice things to each other in moments like these, Shay instead shoved her gently, the surprise of it tipping Max over into the sand.

"Hey," Max barked, and Shay seized the moment to take off toward the water again, hot and sea-salt-sticky and loving the way Max scrambled up behind her, laughing and wild.

They dived into the ocean once more, swimming out past a sandbar to where they couldn't touch and the threat of something actually scary brushing against their legs kept them both well behaved.

"I wish you could always have this," Shay said. Wasn't that the dream? For someone you loved to have a joyful and stress-free life? To have days at the beach that didn't feel as glorious as this one because they weren't rare? Just another happy day in a life full of them.

Instead, what Max got was Shay and Beau trying to cobble together a bit of normalcy, but mostly running around like two chickens with their heads cut off.

The only alternative, though, was the foster system, and Shay couldn't imagine Max faring better there. Not at twelve.

"I like what I have," Max said, chin tipped up like it always was when she got stubborn about something. Her eyes were closed, the sun kissing her face. "I like our little family."

Shay ducked beneath the water to hide her sudden rush of tears. When she reemerged, Max was smirking.

"Fucked up as it is," she added, looking so pleased with herself for the curse word and the little jab.

Before Max could brace for it, Shay reached out with both hands and pushed down on her shoulders. Unprepared, she went easily, and Shay kicked off toward the beach to avoid the inevitable retaliation.

Max was still cawing like a gull when she emerged from the sea, hair and eyes wild. Shay cackled and slipped her jean shorts on.

"Come on, you owe me ice cream."

Shay had to blink away emotion when Max pulled a crumpled ten-dollar bill from her pocket even after Shay tried to pay—"A deal is a deal"—and accepted her cone so she had something to do with her hands.

They walked the pier and licked at the ice cream dripping down over their fingers and hands and forearms.

When they got to the end, they leaned against the railing, looking out at the endless stretch of ocean that lay before them just like the endless stretch of road had hours earlier.

"Hey," Shay said, bumping her shoulder into Max's before placing a sloppy kiss on top of her sea-salt hair. "I like what I have, too."

CHAPTER THIRTY-SIX

Raisa

Max held out the envelope.

Raisa was so surprised by the gesture that she took it without thinking about evidence gloves or bags or proper procedure.

"Can you make sure that gets delivered to Conrad?" Max asked.

The paper felt heavy in Raisa's hands. She couldn't promise that, not after that near confession. Max was already standing, though, wiping at the seat of her jeans.

When Raisa looked up, Max shrugged.

"I don't actually care all that much if he knows peace before he dies," Max said. "Make whatever decision you have to."

And then she turned and walked away, sliding behind the wheel of a car that wasn't the one she'd been leaning against. The trained agent in Raisa made note of the license plate along with the make and model, but Max seemed smart enough to know Raisa would do that.

She'd probably ditch the thing once she got to the city limits.

Raisa knew she should be calling Kilkenny, knew she should be rousing the guards, even to simply detain Max until they located Victoria Greene or Langston or whatever she was calling herself these days. Maybe she was still alive. Maybe these minutes mattered.

Instead, all Raisa could think about was Max's fierce stare when she'd said, *"I'm sorry she lost her sister. But I lost mine first."*

Raisa now knew better than most the complexity of what that meant.

For three months, Raisa had been living in some flight-fight-or-freeze panic triggered by the memory of Isabel. The idea that Isabel's fingerprints had been all over her life had thrown her completely, and here they were again. This time, though, her connection to Isabel had helped Raisa solve a murder that would bring Kilkenny a kind of closure he'd never had.

For ten years, he'd blamed himself for Shay's death, for dragging her into the crosshairs of a serial killer. And yet it had never been his fault.

Maybe he wouldn't ever be able to get rid of the guilt completely—hating yourself became addictive. It insulated you from the pain of moving forward. But now that she knew more about him, she realized the perfection that had seemed so intrinsically part of his nature was actually him trying so hard and so constantly to not make another mistake that he probably hadn't breathed freely in a decade. He wore his tailored suits like armor and delivered his careful word choices like any slip might be the difference between life and death.

Was it strange that they might have Isabel to thank for that—in part, at least? Had they both completely misread her expression in court that day? She had said she wanted to screw with Kilkenny's life, but Isabel, above all else, was a liar.

Maybe she really had wanted to pay him back—in the literal sense—for saving her life.

Raisa felt her world tip back into place, a click that rearranged her spine and her mind. Just a little bit.

She pushed herself off the hot concrete and headed for the prison's lobby. At the front desk, she asked for a pen and paper and found a quiet place to work on the letter Max had handed her.

The message was coded—with the Alberti Cipher, which she didn't bother to decrypt. Instead, she went through her process with the more complicated one. She needed a key word for the Vigenère code, but she barely had to think about it.

Conrad wouldn't have to, either.

It was *Shay*.

Of course it was *Shay*.

The process was still tedious, but now that Raisa had shaken off the cobwebs, it went faster.

When she got to the end, she was proven right.

Those wasted minutes hadn't mattered.

DECODED MESSAGE FROM MAXINE BAKER TO NATHANIEL CONRAD ON EXECUTION DAY

She thought I didn't have the temperament to kill. Isn't it sweet that the last lesson she learned was just how wrong she was?

CHAPTER THIRTY-SEVEN

Raisa

Now

When the clock ticked over to midnight, Raisa clinked her beer bottle against Kilkenny's.

It wasn't in celebration but rather in acknowledgment.

Kilkenny was here, in the sand, on a small stretch of beach in Galveston, rather than in a cramped execution-viewing room watching the death of the serial killer who had consumed five years of his life, and then another ten after he was caught.

Raisa would never say something cheesy in this moment, but she was proud of him.

They went back to staring out at the ocean in silence as the minutes passed by.

Kilkenny's phone buzzed.

He closed his eyes before checking it and then exhaled when he did.

"It's done," he said.

"How do you feel?"

"I don't know," he admitted. He was wearing sweatpants and a sweatshirt, which felt akin to seeing him in his underwear. His hair was mussed by the breeze coming off the ocean, and he even had the makings of a five-o'clock shadow. Was this a Kilkenny who had slayed his demons and come out the other side realizing perfection wasn't the answer to being a human?

Or was she romanticizing the exhaustion of a man who'd just spent the last seventy-two hours the way he had?

She liked to think it was at the very least a combination of both.

He ran his thumb over his wedding ring, a habit she hoped wouldn't disappear but would take on new meaning. Before, when he did it, he was reminding himself of all the ways he could fail if he made the wrong choice. Maybe now it would just be him remembering Shay the way she was when he loved her. Not the way she'd looked in crime scene photographs.

Especially now that he knew, with certainty, that her killer was dead.

They'd found Victoria Langston, a.k.a. Tori Greene, in her parked car near an abandoned Little League baseball field. It looked like she'd eaten her own gun, though Pierce had made sure Max's letter was submitted into evidence. Was it enough to issue an arrest warrant? Probably not. Especially if the scene was as clean as Raisa suspected it was.

Max had been planning that kill for ten years. She might get away with it.

Raisa shouldn't think it, but she secretly hoped she would.

They had found a treasure trove—along with Kate Tashibi—at Tori Greene's apartment. Kate had fumbled with a story about interviewing the psychiatrist about her work with violent children. She hadn't hidden the gun tucked in the back of her jeans well, but it was Texas. No one was going to jail over carrying a gun.

And anyway, no one paid attention to her for very long. In Tori's office, local agents had uncovered boxes and boxes of "research" into children who'd gone through violent experiences during crucial stages in their development. Raisa had no interest in whatever manifesto Tori had penned beyond what she could learn about her idiolect for teaching purposes.

The long and the short of it was that Tori had found ways to worm her way into the lives of these children in hopes of identifying the ones who could prove her thesis correct. She especially targeted children she thought might have been responsible for the violent episode in their youth.

The two male victims were examples of that. Stahl and Marchand—one who'd killed his mother's boyfriend in self-defense and the other whose mother had died in a suspicious house fire. Tori had posited that the latter had been set on purpose. Both boys had shown potential, and so she'd stayed in their lives for long enough to leave an impression.

Why she killed them wasn't yet clear—they would probably find an explanation in the records she so meticulously kept. But for now, Pierce thought it was because they'd blackmailed her once the Alphabet Man started making headlines. Like Max, they'd known enough to connect the dots back to Tori.

Kilkenny had a different theory, one that made more sense to Raisa.

He suggested she'd become so attached to her thesis about childhood trauma and serial killers that when one of her prime examples failed to deliver the results she'd expected—read: they'd become healthy and well-adjusted adults—she lost her ability to cope. So she'd gotten rid of the data point.

That would explain the other deaths Delaney had turned up as well.

And it would make sense as to why she'd turned Conrad in instead of killing him. He was her greatest success. She wanted him to go through the justice system, to be found guilty and be killed for being exactly what he was. Everyone would know Nathaniel Conrad had become a serial killer.

They hadn't uncovered much about Shay yet, but Pierce had filled in a crucial piece of the puzzle.

Apparently, frustrated that they weren't getting anywhere with the case, he'd sought the help of a specialist without going through the proper channels. Dr. Tori Greene was well known and well respected throughout Houston for her work with childhood trauma and serial killers. Throughout the years, Pierce had been sent her name but hadn't wanted to step on Kilkenny's toes.

He'd invited Tori for coffee and to the headquarters a few times. They'd all been casual meetings, none that had materialized in any insightful conversations about the case, and so, to avoid any drama with Kilkenny, Pierce had logged the meetings as general instead of related to a specific investigation—so Kilkenny had never seen her name on any case files related to the Alphabet Man.

There had been a strange confluence of events that had led Shay to the FBI offices the same day Tori had a meeting scheduled with Pierce. She'd never shown up for it, and now, with hindsight, they were all left wondering if that was because she'd run into Shay in the parking lot.

That also hadn't been the only thing Pierce had been keeping from them.

He'd been hiding the fact that he and Beau had some kind of friendship or relationship that had sent him personally chasing after the man to stop him from confronting Tori instead of bringing the full weight of the FBI down on him. Because Max had simply sent Beau to an empty house, nothing was ever going to come of it. Pierce hadn't known that, though.

All Raisa cared about now was Kilkenny. The cards would fall as they may with the rest of them. Kate would get an explosive ending for her documentary. Beau would probably get off for his fifteen-year-old murders, because all the evidence had likely been lost and Max wasn't exactly going to testify against him. Pierce might live with some guilt, but would, in the end, likely cover up enough of his mistakes to keep climbing up that ladder of success at the Bureau. Conrad was dead. Tori was dead.

Raisa no longer felt like she was going to lose a few hours to panic if she was reminded of sisters and all they could do to each other.

And Max? She was a survivor. That had been clear from meeting her only once in a hot parking lot, where she'd managed to find shade, and also the only spot that couldn't be picked up on the security cameras.

Raisa wasn't too worried about what would happen to her. After she had translated the more complex code from Max's letter, she'd taken a picture of it. In the hours of waiting for Conrad's death, in waiting for news from Tori's house, in driving down to Galveston because Shay had always talked about how much fun she'd had there, Raisa had managed to decode the simple message written in the Alberti Cipher.

Once she had, she knew it had been written to Kilkenny.

She didn't care about happiness. She cared about family. You were her family.

When she'd showed him, he'd stared at the screen for a long time, and she could tell he wished that he had the physical paper it had been written on.

Now he touched his ring again as he watched the ebb and flow of the ocean at his feet.

"What are you thinking?" Raisa asked quietly.

"Everyone believes that my biggest regret is dragging Shay into the serial-killer case," he said, like he'd just been waiting for the right question. "And of course that was. But something I hadn't been able to talk about was how unhappy she was. Our tragedy flattened us into a perfect couple, and I allowed that to happen. It wasn't their business, and it felt like I was protecting Shay that way."

She didn't care about happiness. That was hard to say about anyone and make it believable. Everyone wanted to be happy. But desire and value were two different things. Raisa could believe that Shay cared more about being with someone who loved her than having a perfect life full of sunshine days.

And now maybe Kilkenny could believe that, too.

"Happy days are overrated," Raisa said, a little sardonically. But that was okay—that was the mood tonight. "I like a good storm."

He huffed in agreement, and she thought about the storm that had been her last three months. Right now, sitting here, she was almost— almost—glad everything had happened with Isabel. She deserved to be behind bars, where she couldn't hurt anyone else, but maybe it didn't have to mean *nothing* that Raisa was related to her. Maybe it could be a benefit instead of the thing that brought Raisa's whole world down.

Because she looked at Isabel and saw what she was capable of being.

And then she looked in the mirror and saw what she was.

Every day became a choice, and Isabel became a reminder.

Someone didn't have to bring happiness into your life to be a good thing for it overall.

"Family, huh?" Kilkenny said.

"Can't live with them," Raisa said, toasting the ocean, toasting life, toasting her sisters and sisters everywhere.

Kilkenny lifted his own bottle and said so quietly she almost missed it, "Can't live without them."

ACKNOWLEDGMENTS

This was my second foray into the wild and wonderful world of forensic linguistics, and I'd be remiss if I didn't acknowledge the real-life experts whose work helped make this story as authentic as possible. Those include, but are not limited to, Robert Leonard, Jim Fitzgerald, Malcolm Coulthard, Alison Johnson, David Wright, Alison May, and Rui Sousa-Silva, among others. You all are rock stars. Thank you.

A huge amount of thanks goes to Megha Parekh and Charlotte Herscher, my phenomenal editors, and the rest of the Thomas & Mercer team who have made this book sparkle and shine and find its way into the hands of readers.

And as ever, I need to thank Abby Saul, who goes above and beyond on every project.

I want to send many hugs to the mystery-writing community, who are as fun and supportive and wonderful a group of people as can be. And, of course, to my Team Larkers—I wouldn't want to muddle through all this with anyone else.

Lastly, thank you to my dear readers. I would not be here without you.

ABOUT THE AUTHOR

Photo © 2019

Brianna Labuskes is the *Wall Street Journal, Washington Post,* and Amazon Charts bestselling author of *The Lies You Wrote* in the Raisa Susanto series; *See It End, What Can't Be Seen,* and *A Familiar Sight* in the Dr. Gretchen White series; as well as *Her Final Words, Black Rock Bay, Girls of Glass,* and *It Ends with Her.* She grew up in Pennsylvania; lived in Washington, DC, for many years; and now calls Asheville, NC, home. She enjoys traveling, hiking, and spending time with her pup. Visit her at www.briannalabuskes.com.